Deadly

Trevor Womack

Chaotic Books

DM 7.i (2021)

ISBN: 9798622478314

Deadly Money is a work of fiction. Any resemblance to any person or organisation is entirely coincidental and unintentional.

Consulting Editor: Patricia Womack

The trade in illegal drugs is huge. Estimates vary, but global values are believed to be in the billions of dollars, with the majority of the trades never being intercepted. Comparatively little of the cash generated by this activity is ever recovered.

Contents

Prologue

1 - Charnley
2 - Stella and Gus
3 - Questions
4 - Missing Millions
5 - Discretion
6 - Star City
7 - The Phone Call
8 - The Deal
9 - Hamish
10 - Plan B
11 - Naples
12 - Finger Food
13 - Gunter Roth
14 - Options
15 - Amsterdam
16 - Champagne
17 - The Smiths
18 - Paris
19 - The Fire
20 - Dealing
21 - The Drug Business
22 - The Makarov
23 - Stirring the Pot
24 - The Statement
25 - A Surprise Visit
Epilogue

Before You Go

Prologue

Lie still. Just stars. Light from somewhere. Glinting off the bottles. Crates. Nothing else. The cellar?

So hard to breathe. Can't move. Fucking pain again. Can't call out. Mother of God. The thudding noise. Did I imagine it?

A fall. It was a fall. Makes my head swim. That loud thud?

In the morning, they'll come down to restock. Find me.

The money! Oh my God, the money! Harry's got it safe. God help me if he hasn't. Giuseppe! Phone Giuseppe.

Someone did this. Opened the trap. Surely not Gus? Bastard.

Can't feel much. Just pain. And cold. Freezing, cold stone floor.

Exhausted. Sort it all out in the morning. Get Hamie on to it. Sooner than I'd thought to get the boy involved. Twenty-three. At his age, I'd ... Not quite ready yet, is he?

Radio. Faint.

Gus grilling roadkill. Hedgehog. Squirrel or two. Up there in the apartment. Disgusting.

Phone vibrating. Twice now. Can't reach. Giuseppe? Oh my God, the money!

Doc, first thing. Get fixed up. Painkillers. Get Hamie on the case. He'll need to learn fast. Find out which motherfucking bastard did this.

That last smoke. That last whisky, standing in the yard's quiet just before turning in. Bliss.

For years now, he realised, he'd lived each day just for that.

1

Charnley

He drank way too much. He realised that. He'd be a fool not to. Sometimes he tried hard to cut down. But each year, he drank a little more heavily.

I've become a cliché. Man my age and occupation. So what? Who does it hurt?

Not that he had to drink. He was sure he wasn't any kind of alky. He liked drinking. Correction - he loved it. Simple as that. Bingeing. That was the truth of it. The anticipation. The bite. The hit to his throat. The warmth in his belly. The slow, warm build-up to the pleasant burn it gave you.

And the sudden oblivion. The complete blotting out of all the shit. All the worry, remorse, guilt, and regret. And right before that happened, you got those few moments of almost religious ecstasy. Priceless.

And up here on the Point? What else? A stroll along the beach. A lonely meal in one of the handful of restaurants dotted around the village centre. Or a walk to the store to buy groceries and a bottle or two. That was about the extent of it.

But give the Point its due, there was a fair selection of sporting activities, clubs and leisure groups that he could involve himself with if he chose. But he didn't choose. He wasn't a joiner, preferred to keep himself very much to himself. It was easy enough to manage a conversation across a bar counter and, on a purely social level, that was usually about as far as he let things get. It was all he needed. Just to keep going.

3

Ever since Paris. He would always blame himself for that. He should have been more careful. They both should. But Wendy had trusted him to take care of her. And he hadn't.

He'd considered finding himself another woman. But what he found instead was that he didn't want the commitment. On the few occasions he'd tried to form a lasting relationship, it simply hadn't worked out. So he'd given up on the idea.

No more than I deserve. If I'd not been pissed out of my mind, she'd still be here.

It was a nice enough box, sitting there on the sideboard. Good quality. Glossy cardboard. At some stage, he'd need to get a proper casket and inter her ashes somewhere suitable. Which would be where, exactly? So there was that.

And, in any case, it would seem too final. Too soon. Too soon? How easy it was to overlook the fact that well over two decades had passed since he'd lost his wife.

He carried the empty whisky bottle out to the recycling bin and shivered. Spring should have been just around the corner, but it wasn't looking that way on this particular morning. The cold easterly made him feel his age, his lack of condition. He glanced up and down the road at the lines of nineteen-sixties semis marshalled bleakly in the dawning, grey light.

"You all right?"

Oh, God. Tooth, next door.

"Fine. Yourself?" He could do without Alan Tooth right now. Best try to be pleasant.

"Haven't seen much of you lately. Wondered if you'd gone away. Or died."

Cheeky bastard, Tooth. Twenty years older than me, at least.

"Going for a run on the beach later, if the weather holds. Fancy it?"

"Busy, really. Work. You know? Like some of us still have to?"

"Right."

"Lot to do."

He hurried back inside and turned up the heating. Mustn't let old Tooth get to him. He knew what he was thinking. What they all probably thought by now. Sod 'em.

Then he noticed the coffee-stained bank statement lying on the kitchen table and felt vaguely threatened by his obvious shortage of funds. And he hadn't even opened the post from CareSafe, the care home where Wendy's mum, Beatrice, sat and waited out her accelerating dementia. Where he hardly ever visited her and where she no longer recognised him when he did. They'd never been close, but he was sure he owed it to Wendy, somehow, to see to the wellbeing of his mother-in-law in her declining years. Just as she would have wanted to do herself if she'd still been here.

It was expensive, and it was getting harder to manage the financial side of things. But as care homes went, it was a good one, and he knew he should try his best to keep her there. Rather than the low-cost old folks' barracks, she'd most likely end up in if he didn't.

There was no way to borrow more against the house. He'd lose the place soon if he wasn't careful, and if it came to that, he'd have bugger all, nothing left to show for all his time on the planet.

Fucking bank. As if they cared.

Then he remembered the new job and the fees that would come with it to ease matters a little. And if he could just hang on until the spring, things might pick up.

Coffee now. Short, strong and black, like always. The first of the morning. Always the best.

The job had come in the day before. From a man he'd never met. The one he thought of as the 'Voice'. Corny for sure. But then he didn't regard himself as being particularly sophisticated.

"Jack Charnley," he'd said when he got the call. He didn't add the usual 'Private Investigation Services'. The Voice didn't need to hear that part again.

"Got. something for you. That Blue Warehouse business in town. You heard about all that?"

Beyond noting the broad Lancashire accent, he knew nothing about the man on the other end of the phone. Still, he'd done a few jobs for the guy in the past.

"I read about it in the local paper. Some stuff online. Bits and pieces."

Drug dealer? Weren't they all into drugs now? The big-time gangsters. Or people smuggling? A lot of that these days. Whatever. Not really his business, was it?

"I want you to ask some questions, you know, discreetly. Find out what you can about what's been going on down there. Okay?"

He didn't like the idea that he sometimes worked for criminals, but what alternative did he have? The tone that came across with the phone call suggested, subtly enough, that turning down the job wouldn't be an option.

"Such as what? In particular?"

"Nothing in particular. And I don't want you drawing attention to yourself. Right? Be discreet."

"My middle name. Discretion."

"Just ask around, casual like, and see what people are saying about the bomb thing. Beard's death. All that. And see what you can find out about those missing Whites. And Hamish Beard. The son. Find that one and you get a bonus."

"You're lucky. I'm between jobs at the minute. I can get right on it."

"Keep me posted."

The Voice rang off

He needed the money. And while it was hard to feel enthusiastic about the kind of work he did, it did pay the bills. Some of them, anyhow. Everybody needed money, right? But his work didn't pay all that well. And these days, for some reason, it was hard to come by.

Back when he'd first set himself up as a private investigator in town, he'd had the stupid idea that it would, if nothing else, be interesting.

It hadn't turned out that way. People cheating on their partners. Systematic petty theft, usually from warehouses near the docks. Missing persons, usually people who really didn't want you to find them. That was the level of most of it. It had become boring pretty quickly.

This new thing, though. That could be different. And the Voice paid better than most. It had been all over the media. All about the explosion at that place in the Baltic Quarter. And there'd been that young girl's overdose. Sad that. Lily White. He remembered her name because it was unusual. Her dad had disappeared first. And her brother, Lawrence, had vanished too. At least, no one seemed to know where either of them was.

It was the missing dad, Percy, who linked the White family to the Blue Warehouse nightclub. He'd worked for the boss there, Claude Beard. And the boss himself had died not so long ago. In a fall of some kind. Sometime before Christmas. So there were a couple of deaths and at least two missing persons. Three, if it turned out that Hamish Beard had now vanished as the Voice seemed to have it. And, of course, there was the explosion that had cost Claude's younger brother, Gus Beard, his legs. And all linked, directly or otherwise, to the nightclub.

He sat with his morning coffee and began to brood his way into the job.

*

In the early evening, he went into town and spent an hour or so propping up the bar in the Blue Warehouse. Trying to make a pint of hugely overpriced beer last as long as possible. At least he was unlikely to get himself pissed in here. Not at these prices. The place wasn't busy. A largely empty sea of tables and chairs in chrome and smoked glass, with upholstery in ivory-toned leather.

The bargirl made time to chat. He bought her a drink. She got herself a cola from the chiller.

"Quiet, isn't it?" He had often found a brief statement of the blindingly obvious to be a good way to begin these probing conversations without arousing suspicion.

"Early yet," said the girl, sipping her cola. "It'll warm up later. Usually does."

"From what I read, though, things got pretty noisy around here not too long ago. Some kind of explosion? There was something in the papers about it. Yeah?"

"Oh, yes. There was for sure. I was working here at the time. It made a terrible mess. Put the boss's husband in hospital. Lost his legs."

"Poor bugger." He adopted a pained expression, pursing his lips.

"The place was closed for days. What with the police

8

all over it and all. And the repairs. It was a mess all right."

"So, how's he doing, the one who lost his legs? Is he okay?"

"Gus? He's gone. He left. Kevin and Stella took him and all his stuff over to that new apartment block down by the docks. The Turret. A while ago."

"Kevin?"

"Works for Gus. His carer now, I suppose."

"Right. So who runs all this these days?"

"Oh, just Stella. Always was her, really. Her place, I think."

"I suppose her son's helping out? What's his name? Hamish?"

"Haven't seen him in ages," said the girl, as she walked over to take the order from two new arrivals making themselves comfortable in an alcove.

She seemed talkative, so he waited until she'd finished dealing with the new customers and got himself another beer. He told her to keep the change, and she dropped the money into a beer glass by the till. Fifty pence. The only cash in there. He guessed it would be a lot fuller by the end of her shift.

"So where's he gone, this Hamish? Seems a strange time to clear off and leave Stella to deal with everything on her own."

"Well, he always seemed a bit strange to me. Supposed to be pretty smart, actually. So they say. Didn't show it, though."

"How so?"

"Well, he dropped out of uni. Drank too much. I don't know. Aimless, that's all. All he was doing before he left was odd jobs around the nightclub."

"Really?"

"Yeah, just filling in around the place. Didn't even get behind the bar. You felt sorry for him. You know how some people are."

"Something of a waste of space, then," he said.

A bit like my good self.

"Don't think I've seen you in here before, have I?" asked the girl, suddenly suspicious. "You a reporter or something?"

"Something like that."

"Well, I'd best not say any more. If there's anything else you want to ask, you should speak to Stella. She'll be down later. She always is. Only she told us not to talk to anyone asking too many questions. No offence."

"None taken," he said, smiling. "I can come back and see the boss some other time, maybe.

"Nice talking to you," he called, over his shoulder, as he left.

*

The next morning, he gave the matter some more thought.

Nothing useful had shown up in the media. The police had played down suggestions of some sort of gang war and had gone quiet on the subject. Did that mean anything? Most likely, it meant they had no idea what was going on.

He pulled out the stopper from a fresh bottle of single malt and let the soft, peaty smell tease its way into his nostrils. Would he drink today? He considered the question carefully while he poured himself a double.

He sat for a while, nursing his whisky, thinking about nothing much, and then grabbed his laptop and typed 'Blue Warehouse Nightclub Baltic Liverpool' into the search bar. Nothing new online.

Taking one view, it might be that the death of Claude Beard, the owner's husband, was a simple accident. A fall on a dark night. Down into a cellar.

Likewise, the disappearance of his associate, Percy White, the death of Percy's daughter, Lily, and Lawrence's disappearance, too, could all be attributed to non-criminal causes. The Beards' son, Hamish, also seemed to have gone off the radar. Although Hamish appeared to be the sort of aimless oddball who might well be anywhere, doing anything. Nonetheless, he remained unaccounted for, as far as he could glean from the news reports online.

But the big giveaway was the attempted murder of Claude's brother, Gus, who had been seriously damaged one winter morning by an ancient hand grenade wired to explode beneath his bed. That was something it was impossible to attribute to a non-criminal cause. It added a new flavour to the whole situation and changed everything.

He thought back to the few random conversations he'd overheard in various bars and drinking dens at the time. He remembered that, apart from the Blue Warehouse, the Beards had also had connections with a scattering of other businesses and establishments around town. But that didn't help much, the precise nature of those connections being far from clear.

He made himself a coffee, and the fog generated by the previous night's whisky gradually began to dissipate. He took a big gulp. It was hot, almost scalding his tongue. So much the better.

Soon the clarity afforded by the mixture of coffee and the first scotch of the new day kicked in. Obviously, the Beards and their associates had been involved in something much more dangerous than simply running a nightclub and maintaining an interest in a few bouncers and late-night massage parlours.

That something must have been the same thing that the Voice had a stake in. Whatever had happened to the Beards and their friends had also adversely affected his client in some way. Not exactly rocket science.

Well, it would be another job. That was all. Nothing

would really change. His life would trudge on as before. From this job to the next one and then the next. Until the money finally ran out, and the bank got the house. Better not think too much about that.

That afternoon he drove up through the gloom to the care home.

"Here to see Beat," he said into the device that guarded the door. "It's Jack."

They buzzed him inside, and he padded along the thickly carpeted corridor to Beat's room. She had stopped using the communal lounge a while back and no longer stared out of her window much. She simply sat and waited for the next happening, usually a carer to guide her to the lavatory, or the shower, or the dining area. This afternoon the next happening was Jack.

Time was he'd have taken her out for a walk, weather permitting. But not now. She'd grown too feeble for that.

A smile. Give her that, at least.

"Hello there, Ma. How's things?" He sat down, facing her.

"Everything okay?"

"Who are you?"

"It's me. Jack."

"Are you my husband?"

His visits grew shorter as they grew rarer. This afternoon he gave up after twenty minutes. It was depressing. When he got back out to his car, the light had faded. It was completely dark by the time he let himself into his empty semi.

2

Stella and Gus

Gus had woken up screaming and covered in sweat. It was the sudden force of the thing all over again. Not the noise, deafening as it had been at the time. It was the irresistible force that was so terrifying. Lifting him off the bed. Flinging him at the wall behind. Upside down. Face first.

That fucking cat of Stella's had done it. Jumping up onto the mattress like that when all he'd been doing was lying there, trying to have a well-earned rest. The little fucker had got what it deserved, though. Out through the window with all the glass. In bits. Won't do that again.

"No one in their right mind would ever call you a good patient, Gus." Stella sighed.

"Really?"

"Really. That morning we rushed you into the emergency room. Me in tears. You with your legs shredded. You were quiet enough then."

"Didn't want to make a fuss," he said, wanting to sound stoical. He hadn't been stoical. He'd been in shock.

"You couldn't have made a fuss if you'd tried. You were all but comatose. They'd pumped all that stuff into you for the pain. You'd lost pints of blood."

The medical team working on him that day had been able to save Gus's life, but not his legs. That day he hadn't even been looking for any trouble. He was simply relaxing in his room, planning out his next round of small-time illegality, when something had exploded beneath his bed. An event like that can make big inroads into a person's sense of optimism and natural good humour. Not that Gus had ever enjoyed a great amount of the latter.

"You've tried your best to help me feel better, Stells. I know that."

True. She'd tried hard to accommodate his needs. To take care of him in their apartment above the nightclub. Forensics had done their work and gone. But Gus's room was still being repaired and refurbed when he came back from the hospital. So she'd given him Claude's old bedroom, next to her own. Except for her two remaining cats, Stella slept alone.

Even viewing everything through the distorting lens of his enormous sense of self-centred entitlement, she felt that Gus must have been aware that his new situation had made things difficult for her. Despite Kevin being there to provide support all the way through from breakfast to bedtime.

He had a constant need for attention. For help with his toileting, his thirst, his medication, and his laptop. And then there was the endless ranting about how he was going to find out who the fuck had done this to him and make them fucking well pay.

He made an effort to control the ranting, but she could see he found that difficult. That he found the ranting therapeutic.

"Just for now, Gus," she'd tried to suggest, "you should maybe leave all that to the police. Concentrate on getting well. I can carry on running the place myself. Like always."

She straightened the bedsheets lying across his lap. "And Kevin can help you with anything you need to deal with during the day. We'll manage."

Stella had convinced herself that whoever had gone out of their way to harm her husband would probably be satisfied with the damage they'd already done. They wouldn't feel the need to try again. At least, she had to hope that they wouldn't.

*

Kevin was Gus's longtime minder, enforcer, and general-purpose factotum. He was a big man and strong enough to heave Gus from his bed and into his wheelchair without so much as a grunt.

Kevin had been more accustomed to the kind of human contact that involved breathing heavily into someone's face while making thinly veiled threats. Or breaking a person's fingers, one by one, in order to solicit compliance with one of Gus's more questionable schemes. So no one was more surprised than Gus when he took so easily to his new role as his personal carer.

Gus had long been used to discussing things with Kevin. Using him as a sounding board for his ideas. And Gus had things on his mind.

He pressed pause on the zombie film he'd been watching. "One important point about the explosion, Kev, is the fact that it was an old hand grenade that did it. From as far back as World War Two. According to the cops."

"Yeah," said Kevin. "Right."

"They said someone had got hold of this piece of kit and wired it up behind my headboard. My own movements were supposed to pull the pin and explode it."

"Right," said Kevin, who'd grown tired of going over all this days ago. "So?"

"So what does that tell us? That the scumbag arsehole who did this to me wasn't a pro. Get that? And it was someone who had no way of getting his miserable, motherfucking hands on anything better to do the job with."

"Good thing too," said Kevin, thumbing through the sports pages in the morning paper.

"Like the cops said, if the grenade had actually done its job and gone off when it was meant to, it would've blown your fucking head clean off."

"So it would."

"Would've sent it flying across the bedroom and smacked it into the door."

He chuckled. He had always had a talent for seeing the funny side of things. It was one of his more positive characteristics.

"They think it must have been the poor condition the grenade was in that stopped it exploding just when it was supposed to."

Gus winced at the thought. "And if it hadn't dropped onto the floor and got itself pushed about a bit by the cats or the hoover or whatever, that's most likely exactly what would've happened to me when it did manage to explode. I'd have been decapitated."

"Lucky that."

"Not really, Kev. Not actually so fucking lucky. Lucky would have been having the bastard explode when I wasn't there. Or not explode at all. Or even better, explode when the bastard, lowlife cunt who put it there was messing with it."

"True," said Kevin agreeably. "Want me to get you your camomile tea now? Only I could do to nip out to the betting shop at some point."

"No," snapped Gus. "I don't want you to get me my camomile fucking tea! Why the fuck would I want camomile fucking tea? Think you're being funny? You can get me a whisky! And it's after lunch, so you can make it a big one."

*

16

The Blue Warehouse, along with almost everything in it, was in Stella's name, and she'd been left in sole charge after the night-time fall into the beer cellar which had caused the death of her first husband, Claude. She had come to terms very quickly then with the way her life had changed. She had married Claude's brother, Gus.

And since the blast which had incapacitated Gus, she had been forced to take stock once again.

Unlike his brother, Gus had never shown much interest in the nightclub. To him, it was simply a convenient front. A place where his small but violent gang could hang out in peace.

They were known locally as the 'Firm'. Claude had always thought the tag was unoriginal and said so. But Gus liked it. Day to day, he'd been the one who'd run the gang. It had been his end of the business.

Stella enjoyed the nightclub. Sitting elegantly on her barstool perch in the evenings, she felt like a queen. And it made money. Her pension pot was growing, comfortingly.

The whole enterprise had been created from a disused warehouse by Claude many years before. But it was her domain. She and the nightclub had matured together. It was no longer the sort of place which appealed to the young 'clubbers around town' set. The clientele now was older, more settled. She liked that. It was where she felt in control and respected. Stella didn't feel that she needed anything more.

And at this point, with Gus disabled the way he was, she was beginning to think that he might well have become surplus to requirements. She had been fond of him. That was true. And she'd been attracted to him. But that had only worked when he'd been the powerful gang leader he used to be, able to ensure her protection from predators.

But, since the explosion, she'd begun to wonder whether the predators had been largely of Gus's own making. Just as they probably had been in Claude's time. Maybe they had been interested only in the Firm's illicit activities. Maybe, now that all that seemed to have gone, she could be left to run the Warehouse in peace, like any other normal nightclub. It was an appealing idea. The more she considered it, the clearer it became that from this point on, Gus was only going to be an inconvenience. He needed to be sidelined somehow. Put out to grass.

Lucky for them both that he still had Kevin, the only member of the Firm who had remained loyal to Gus after the blast.

"Me and Gus and the boys had quite a few things going, you know, Stells."

The place was closed, and they were standing in the empty bar discussing business, well out of Gus's hearing.

"Like?"

Kevin turned away to face the mirrored wall where the various bottles of shorts were lined up along a glass shelf. He studied his reflection as he straightened his tie.

"There were lots of things. The security consultancy and the bouncers, for starters. They were good earners."

"People are scared of Gus, Kevin. That's obvious. Or they were. And I hear stuff. Stories. It wasn't just nightclub doormen you two were into, was it?"

"There were a few... different things. Best not to get into too much detail. You know? It's complicated."

Stella knew what 'complicated' meant. It meant 'illegal'. Better not push it. It was none of her concern in any case.

So he didn't tell her about the waste dumping operation. Or the money-laundering facility for small-time criminals who might find themselves in possession of a sudden pile of illicit cash. Or the 'protection' afforded to vulnerable enterprises like brothels and unlicensed gambling dens, and so on. He was a considerate soul and kept that kind of disturbing information to himself.

Legally or otherwise, the Firm had provided employment for a select group of individuals whose activities had once been robustly managed and directed by the Beard brothers, Claude and Gus. Claude had been very much upper management, more director level. Gus had been more hands-on. But Claude's fatal fall had left Gus Beard as sole proprietor.

"But now there's no one running things and no one paying the wages. It's all gone," said Kevin, turning back to face Stella.

"The guys have pissed off elsewhere. And some of our more lucrative activities have been taken over by the Davidsons. Gus isn't even aware of that yet, because I haven't told him."

"Taken over how, exactly?"

"God knows how, but Junior Davidson seems to know all about us. All about our contacts and our operations. And with all that info it was easy for him to step in after Gus was blasted. His boys just showed a bit of muscle and took over whatever they wanted."

"So the Davidson mob has grabbed all Gus's best lines, and the rest is simply... gone. Is that what you're telling me?"

"You got it, Stella. Like I said. It's all gone."

She knew that Gus would find this intolerable once he found out. And that would make Gus intolerable in his turn. Not that he wasn't becoming fairly difficult to tolerate already.

"Isn't there anything you could do to take back control? Before he finds out?"

"How? Once the money went, our boys went with it. Their loyalty was the sort that had to be paid for up front."

Kevin turned around and leaned on the bar top, facing Stella. He took care to keep the sleeves of his designer jacket clear of the previous night's spills and drips, now congealing stickily as they waited for the cleaners' next shift to begin. He looked her straight in the eye.

"I'm on my own. And I've got my hands full taking the Boss to the loo and fetching his whisky from the supermarket. There is no way back."

"Hasn't he asked about how things are going?"

"Almost every morning since it happened. I just say everything's fine and not to sweat it. Don't know what else to say."

"Don't tell him any of this until you think he's recovered enough to be able to cope with it. I can't imagine how he'll take it."

"I'll try, but I can't keep him in the dark for much longer, Stells. He's going to want to see the books soon. He's bound to."

*

A couple of days later, after a meditative sip from his whisky glass, Gus had continued with his line of thought.

"So whatever we have here, we aren't dealing with a pro, for sure. It isn't that somebody with the necessary contacts had sent an even half-decent hitman to get me out of the way. What we have here is some arsehole chancer with a grudge."

"Could be, Boss. Makes sense."

"Probably some guy acting alone, on his own behalf. And it's going to be someone who wouldn't find it too difficult to get up to this apartment and into my bedroom. Someone who could bypass all our so called fucking security, for whatever fucking use that was. Yes?"

Kevin just grunted. It didn't matter what he said, anyway.

Gus paused for a moment while he reached over to grab his whisky bottle from the cabinet beside his bed. He poured himself another large one.

"And if it was some amateur loner, then it isn't likely it was an attempt to gain some business advantage. A guy like that wouldn't be in a position to take over any of our operations. Must've been someone looking for revenge. Kind of grudge, maybe."

"Could be," said Kevin. He was busy tidying the assortment of medication, surgical dressings, whisky bottles, glasses and other paraphernalia occupying the top of Gus's dressing table.

"Could be that. There are a lot of people out there who hate you. That's for sure."

"Hate me?" Gus sounded surprised. "Really? There are lots of people who actually hate me?"

"Oh, sure," said Kevin encouragingly. "Loads of people hate you. You're most likely right about it being a grudge thing. Some lone chancer. Like you said. It's not like we're at war with any of the competition at the minute, is it?"

"Well, okay then," said Gus, trying hard not to feel too affronted by Kevin's remarks.

"We should try to narrow this down a bit. Work out who would be our prime suspects. The cops won't have a clue where to start. Thank Christ. Don't want them sticking their noses into our business."

He dipped his finger into the whisky in his glass and then sucked on it meditatively.

"We'll just act dumb, like we're good at. Keep the cops out of it. We can deal with this ourselves."

Kevin was silent for a noticeably long moment.

"Any reason we can't?"

"Well, no," began Kevin, looking concerned, "but there's something you don't know about. Stella said not to bother you with it until you were well enough to cope."

"Something? Like what?"

"It's just that once you'd been blown across your bedroom like you were and put out of action... well... everything kind of, you know, collapsed."

"What collapsed? What the fuck are you talking about? Our business?"

"Yeah." He was standing by Gus's bedside and looking him full in the face now.

"The Davidsons took over some of the better lines. The waste management. And one or two other things. Others took what was left."

"What?" shrieked Gus from the nest of pillows on his bed, spraying spittle and single malt in all directions.

"And you sat back and let all this happen? You let the fucking Davidsons take over the best bits of our fucking cash flow?"

"And I was supposed to stop them how, exactly? I was on my own. The guys just left. They'd gone."

"Gone where?" asked Gus.

"Various places," said Kevin with a shrug. "When the money stopped coming in, which it did the day you got blasted, there was no way to pay the wages. I didn't have access to any proper funding, did I? So they all pissed off. Pronto. One or two of them even seem to be working for the Davidsons now."

"Why didn't anyone tell me all this at the time?" wailed Gus, grief-stricken at the news. "I could have done something about it. I thought you were taking care of everything. Letting things tick over until I got back up and running."

"With respect, Gus, you were in no fit state to do anything. And while I don't want to sound repetitive about this, I was on my own and busy looking after you. And I don't want to sound like I'm being picky either, but you still aren't fit to do much."

He stepped closer to the bed as Gus sank back onto his pillows, his face expressionless now.

"You need to understand that I'm only still here, myself, out of loyalty to you. We've been together almost from the start. And where would I go? I'm too well known as your enforcer for anyone else to trust me. I've hurt too many people."

"Good God, Kevin," growled Gus. He was staring hard at Kevin through narrowed eyes. "I can't get my head around all this. I really can't."

"We're going to have to work out a way forward on our own, Gus. You and me. I'm assuming you have enough stashed somewhere to keep us in funds for the foreseeable?"

"Yes," said Gus, looking suddenly ten years older. "I still have the necessary. You needn't worry about that. Fuck it!"

"Yeah," said Kevin. "Fuck it!"

*

Having lost his legs, his gang and his income stream, Gus felt that he had reached rock bottom. He was wrong.

"What do you mean I can't stay here?" he demanded when Stella put her suggestion to him. "We're married, aren't we? This is our nightclub, isn't it? Our place."

"I'm sorry, Gus, dear."

She was finding this surprisingly simple.

"I appreciate how hard this must be for you, but it's better we get this straight. I own this set-up. Not you."

She sat on the edge of the bed and stroked Gus's hair.

"And I don't want you running any more of your dodgy goings-on from here. And I know what you're

23

like. That's exactly what you'll do. Just as soon as you and Kevin can come up with something. But those days are over."

"I don't believe I'm hearing this," said Gus. "What are you saying?"

"I'm saying there's no role for you here now, Gus." She had to steel herself to say the next thing.

"I want you to move out. I've talked to Kevin. He'll go with you."

"Move out? Where to?"

"I've been looking at a few places, and I've found the perfect accommodation for you. It's a modern apartment, high up. Wonderful views over the river. It's in that new block they're calling the Turret. You can see clear across to Birkenhead."

"What?" said Gus. "You've already found me somewhere? That's just so fucking good of you."

"Wait until you see it. I think you'll be impressed."

"I don't believe I'm hearing this," said Gus again. "From my own wife, even. Where's the loyalty?"

Stella pressed on. "It's a nice, modern, well-maintained block. You'll know the one. Lots of plate glass. Concierge. Artwork on the walls. On-site parking."

She looked hopefully at Gus. Gus stared right back in silence. His eyes dark with despair.

"It has a beautifully designed kitchen, and think how much you love to do your experimental cooking. All those lovely roadkill things you do.

"It's perfect. I'm sure you'll love it. Big enough for you and Kevin both. So he can be on hand twenty-four seven."

No response. Time for the coup de grâce.

"Kevin's taking some of your stuff over to your new place right now. When he gets back, we'll get you over there. You'll see for yourself what a great idea this is."

3

Questions

The Albert Dock was heaving with flocks of tourists making the best of the first sunny Saturday of the approaching spring. Threading his way down through the crowds from the underground station at Moorfields, Jack walked an easy distance south along the river and came to the Turret. He followed a group of young, foreign-looking women, most probably, he thought, students from wealthy families abroad, and went in through the main entrance. Instead of his usual ancient blue suit, he was wearing a baseball cap and sunglasses, with jeans and trainers. He wanted to look the part.

The concierge glanced up as he approached the desk.

"Special delivery," he said, brandishing the package he'd brought. "For a Mr Beard."

"Just leave it with me," said the concierge, looking back down at the pile of paper he was dealing with. "I'll make sure it gets delivered."

"Can't. Sorry. Needs to sign for it. Personally. Can you call up? See if he's in?"

"Forty-eight A." The concierge didn't bother to take his eyes off his paperwork a second time. "You can go up."

Jack walked out of sight of the front desk and spent five minutes locating Gus's apartment before heading back out again. He'd got what he had come in for, the number and position of Gus Beard's place, facing the dock and the river.

The fine weather made it a simple decision for him to park himself on a bench opposite to the building's frontage. For a few hours on each of the next three days, he watched the Turret's main entrance. And he used the telephoto lens on his camera to spy on the windows of forty-eight A.

On the first afternoon, there'd been a good many happy snappers from the cruise liner berthed nearby. And there were always others using cameras, so he wasn't too worried he'd be spotted. Even so, he used his lens sparingly to avoid drawing attention to himself. But apart from occasional glimpses of a man he took to be Kevin moving about, he saw nothing much to arouse his interest. Except that he did get a clear view of Kevin and Gus as Kevin pushed his boss, in his wheelchair, out of the front door and along to a neighbouring bar each lunchtime.

By the third day, he was bringing scraps of bread to feed the gulls, and he realised that, on the whole, his surveillance operation was a fruitless waste of time.

He spoke to the concierge again. He was a young man who seemed to take his job very seriously.

"Hi."

He'd taken care to choose a quiet period at the desk. Without the baseball cap and sunglasses, he knew there was little chance he'd be recognised as the person who'd called in to deliver a package three days before.

"How's it going?"

"Can I help you?"

"I hope so," he said, leaning against the desktop. "You seem busy, so I'll get straight to the point."

"Which is?"

"Which is that I'd be very interested in any information you can give me about a couple of your residents."

"We don't give out details like that. Sorry. The management doesn't allow it. And I wouldn't do it in any case. Why would I? And just who are you, anyway?"

"I'm a journalist," he lied. "That's all."

Being able to lie easily was useful in his line of business.

"I work for one of the national dailies, wanting to investigate the activities of the Beard family and the goings on at the Blue Warehouse. I imagine you heard all about that."

"Heard about it, yes. But no more than anyone else. If you want to know about the Beards, why don't you speak to Mr Beard himself. If he'll talk to you, that is."

"Not ready to. Not just yet. The Beards have been keeping schtum, so I'm doing a bit of digging. Looking for background."

"Like?"

"I'm not expecting you to tell me anything damaging. Maybe a little info about any visitors they might have, that kind of thing. I can pay you well for whatever you want to tell me. No one need know. What do you say?"

The concierge looked thoughtful for a few seconds before replying.

"How much?"

*

In the event, the concierge hadn't been able to tell him very much of interest. And it was mainly negative. Beyond a brief, weekly visit from Mrs Beard, Gus seemed to get no visitors, aside from the medical types who called in periodically to check on him. And, apart from the occasional pizza or crate of groceries, he got no deliveries to speak of. He never went any farther than the bar at the end of the block, always with his minder, Kevin. And that was it.

He dug around some more. He spoke to some of his old drinking buddies, retired coppers, carefully befriended and cultivated over long years. And to one or two acquaintances from the other side of the fence. His efforts yielded little that was helpful.

When the time came, he phoned in his report apologetically enough. But what, after all, could he say about nothing?

He'd been expecting sharp words in return for his lack of useful information, but his contact seemed unsurprised as if Jack was confirming what he already suspected.

"Okay. Just keep your eyes and ears open. Find out what you can about the three who are missing. Hamish Beard especially. And stay in touch. Your money will be in your account as usual."

And the Voice had hung up.

Sitting in the lounge of his semi for the next two days, living on coffee and the ready meals he kept stashed in his freezer, he tried to work out the best way forward. He made a few phone calls and sent some texts and gradually discovered that the word on the street was that nobody out there knew anything either.

Until a single, flimsy thread showed itself through the fog of his investigation, and one of his contacts mentioned that at least two of the men who had been working for the Beards now seemed to be employed by a certain Junior Davidson at his limo hire in town.

He'd heard about the Davidsons occasionally, down the years. Most of the people operating at street level had. They had been known as small-time criminals in the past, but lately, since Freddy Davidson had retired, his grandson Junior was believed to have stayed on the right side of the line. Maybe he had. Or maybe Junior Davidson was playing things more cleverly than the old guard had done.

It could be there was nothing in it. But still...

He made some more calls, more focused this time. And, that evening, got the train into town to visit some of the drinking dens where the Davidson mob had sometimes hung out. He didn't find out much more. Just that Freddy Davidson seemed to be living in someplace called La Oliva, in the Canaries, these days, and that Junior was running things his way.

Word was that Junior was doing well and seemed, lately, to be growing his business activities. Maybe even filling in a few of the gaps left by the collapse of Gus Beard's Firm. But he found out nothing more than that. Nothing immediately helpful.

He went back to the Blue Warehouse. It was later in the evening than his last visit. There was a different girl behind the bar, and there were a few more customers dotted around the lounge. Another woman, much older than the girl, was perched elegantly on a barstool, looking like she owned the place.

What's that she's wearing? A cocktail dress, I suppose you'd call it. Black nylons. Hair all done up. High heels. Glamorous. Classy.

"Who's the glamour puss at the end of the bar there?" he asked as he bought his second drink, taking care to tell the girl to keep the change. He was just making small talk. He already knew who the woman was. He'd recognised her at once.

"Oh, she's the owner. Stella. Likes to keep an eye on things down here most evenings."

He strolled casually over to stand close to where Stella was sitting and began to study a row of framed photographs on the wall behind her. The wall led along the side of the bar to the stairwell and the kitchen. Most of the shots were of visiting celebrities, footballers and the like, and two or three posed groups of what could have been staff parties. Some of the faces he recognised from the reports he'd seen online. One of the groups included Hamish Beard. Hamish was holding a small dog.

"Interested in photos?" Suddenly Stella was standing next to him. "I don't think I've seen you in here before, have I, Jack?"

"So you do still recognise me, then? I thought I might have aged too much for that. It's been a while. How long has it been exactly?"

"Couldn't tell you, Jack. Years and years and years. Way before all this. Way back to before you went off to invade Berlin."

"You've hardly changed, Stella," he said. A lie, of course, but she did still look good enough for the lie to be almost believable, with a little goodwill and soft lighting. "Gorgeous as ever. And even more sophisticated."

"Well, you have. You look a bit more lived in than you did when we had that summer kicking around together."

From her tone, it was evident that Stella Beard hadn't spent the intervening years pining for Jack Charnley. But then, she didn't sound unfriendly either.

"I was sorry to hear about Wendy."

"Yeah, well. Stuff happens. Right? Like with Claude dying like that. And then with what happened to Gus. Must've been a shock."

"Your first time in here then, is it?"

"Almost. Came for half an hour the other night. That's all. I don't get out much these days. Just at a loose end this evening."

"You were living up on the Point, I remember, years ago. You still there?"

"Still there. Still in my semi. No reason to move."

"And you came all the way down here for a glass of beer? It's a distance."

"I suppose. But then I was reading all this stuff in the paper about how the Baltic has become the cool place to be, right now. So I thought I'd check it out. Keep up to speed with how the city's going."

"Well, that's true enough. The area wasn't much more than a collection of disused old warehouses and such when Claude bought this one. No more than an empty shell back then."

It was strange to be talking to Stella again, after all this time. After all that had happened. Better not to think about how he felt. 'Kicking around together', she had called it. It had been more than that. For him, at least. He turned back to look at the photographs.

"I can see you're in this group yourself, and it might be I've seen the guy next to you somewhere before. The guy there with the dog. Looks familiar."

Stella's face tightened. "That's my stepson, Hamish."

"Oh," he said, trying to sound surprised. "Of course. I recognise him now. Must have seen him in the paper or online, maybe. He's okay, I hope?"

"He went to New York, on business for my husband, sometime before Christmas. No one's seen him since. I don't know where he is."

"I'm sorry," he said. "Didn't mean to pry. Must be very worrying for you."

"Don't upset yourself," she said. "It isn't a problem. People often ask if we've heard anything. Or they used to. Not so much now."

"Still. Difficult for you." He noticed that Stella had drained her glass. "Get you a refill?"

Loner that he was, part of his stock in trade was an ability to get people to talk. And getting people to talk about themselves and their problems was usually easy. He spent what turned into a pleasant enough hour chatting to Stella. She seemed entirely unsuspecting of any ulterior motive he might have.

Before taking his leave and heading off to get the train home, he gave her his number and told her she could call him if she needed help locating her stepson.

"Finding missing people is sometimes the way I make my living these days."

"I'll keep the number, just in case," she said. "But Gus seems pretty sure that Hamish is wandering around New York, doing his thing."

31

"Maybe not your average kind of guy, then?"

"Far from it. Hamish has always been like that. He doesn't always stay in touch. And to be honest, from past experience, he could be anywhere by now. He'll turn up when he runs out of cash or gets lonely. Always has. He's wandered off somewhere, trying to find himself a life. That's all."

A half-hour train ride, with a ten-minute walk at the end of it, got him back to his darkened semi. It was time to reflect. He sifted through the conversation he'd had with Stella Beard. Two facts stood out. First, there was the fact of her marriage to Gus Beard, her brother-in-law. That hadn't been too long after Claude Beard's death. Why so quick to remarry? Was there anything in that? No reason to think so, he decided. People had all sorts of reasons for getting married, after all. He'd daydreamed of marrying Stella himself once, all those stretched-out years ago.

Then there was the dog. Hamish, it seemed, was very attached to the little Yorkshire Terrier. Stella had told him that he had entrusted the dog's care while he was away to someone called Harry Love. Love had worked for Claude and then for Gus after Claude's death.

It was possible that Harry or the dog could provide a helpful link to the missing Hamish. It would seem odd, he knew, if he showed too much interest in Harry Love's whereabouts without good reason, so he'd feigned an interest in the man's dog-minding capabilities. It was the best he could think of at short notice.

"Is he anywhere around here? Only, one of my neighbours has a pooch he needs someone to take care of. Going in for an op and he doesn't want to put her into kennels."

"You won't find Harry around the Warehouse these days," she'd told him.

"He's moved on?"

"I think he's driving now. For the Davidsons."

"He took the dog?"

"He took good care of the dog. It's called Keith. Keith and Harry always got on well. Keith didn't go with him, though, when he went. He put Keith into some boarding kennels. So I doubt if he'd be much use to your friend."

"Didn't he want to leave him here? With you?"

"I'm more of a cat person myself. Don't really want a dog around the place. All that dog walking business. And my oldest cat, Winston, he never took to Keith. They just don't like each other."

"There can't be that many boarding kennels around here, being practically in the city centre as you are," he'd said. "Must've had to drive the little bugger out of town somewhere, I imagine."

"No. There's a place only ten minutes walk from here. Keith often got left there."

*

In the bright sunlight of the following morning, the Baltic Kennels looked just a shade on the sunny side of ramshackle. High metal-link fencing surrounded a gently sloping patch of clearance, covered with chipped bark and gravel. A few rough, wooden buildings, one of which housed the reception and office, stood grouped between long-abandoned warehouses.

Two teenaged girls were coming and going with bowls of dog food, attending to the dogs barking for their breakfasts in some of the sheds.

A middle-aged woman, wearing a scruffy fleece jacket and a ponytail, staffed the office. She was typing hard into a laptop but looked up and smiled as he entered.

"Help you?"

"Hope so," he returned the smile. "I'm trying to trace a dog that's gone missing."

"No dogs go missing from here," said the woman, her smile disappearing.

"Oh, don't get me wrong. I'm not suggesting they do. I'm just hoping you can help me. That's all."

He fished a business card out of his wallet and showed it to the woman. The card gave his name, Jack Charnley, and his occupation, Private Enquiry Agent.

"It's a Yorkshire Terrier, name of Keith. The owner has become a missing person, and the family is anxious to find him. Which is why I'm involved. I'm hoping that the dog might be a useful line of enquiry."

From outside came the sound of those residents still waiting for their breakfasts, barking more loudly than ever.

"The family thought it was being looked after by someone they've lost contact with. Chap named Harry something. A friend of the guy I'm looking for. Anyway, they asked me to look into it."

Leaning back in her chair, the woman stared up at Jack, now standing by her battered old desk. She flicked her ponytail and pursed her lips, nodding.

"It seems this Harry left the dog here at the request of the owner. So I'm hoping you can tell me if Keith's still here."

"You must mean Keith Beard, then. We don't tend to get very many Yorkies of that name. He's stayed with us a time or two."

"That would be the one," he said, smiling again. "Have you still got him? Must've run up quite a bill."

"Well, he would've if he'd stayed. He went a while ago. I remember him leaving. Isn't every day we're asked to deliver a dog to the airport."

"So he took a flight?"

"Seems so. This Harry you're talking about. I suppose it must've been him. He told us that someone from the airport would take charge of Keith when he got there. We had his permission to let the animal go. Harry paid his bill in cash and left us all the paperwork for the flight."

"Which airport? John Lennon?"

"That's right. He had to be signed onto a flight out to someplace in the Canaries."

In a cafe not far from the kennels, Jack sat and thought things through over a double espresso. His second double that day. Excessive. Too many coffees could easily mean more whisky later. To help him sleep.

A kind of win-win then, when you think about it.

The cafe was a typical Baltic enterprise. Walls covered with varnished chipboard and tables made from what appeared to be old railway sleepers.

Supposed to be cool, yeah? Cheap, anyway. Still okay to say 'cool' is it? Something else now. Sick? 'Place looks sick'? Doesn't sound right.

The people using the place were an assortment of students and hippy types, with the odd ageing eccentric thrown in for good measure. He was surprised to see the hippies. Hadn't they died out years ago? Come to think of it, they seemed too well-heeled for hippies.

Probably just a fashion thing. Sick, right?

It was too early in the year for tourists to be wandering out this far. And too cold. The place looked rough and ready for sure, but it had atmosphere. And the coffee was good.

The dog, he reasoned, was hardly likely to be wanted enough to warrant the cost of shipping out to the Canaries by anyone other than Hamish. This Harry

Love character, who had been left in charge of Keith, was now, according to Stella Beard, employed by the Davidsons. Freddy Davidson, he'd been told, was living in the Canary Islands in semi-retirement. Where was it? Someone had said the name of the place. He pulled out his notebook and checked. La Oliva, that was it.

Things were beginning to look up. His phone rang. It was the care home.

"Charnley."

"Mr. Charnley, it's Tina. I'm a manager at CareSafe."

The tone of voice. Practised, professional, caring. He knew at once.

"Something happened to Beat?"

"I'm so sorry, Mr. Charnley. Beatrice is no longer with us. We found her in her room half an hour ago. She was a lovely person. We'll all miss her. I'm so very sorry."

"Oh."

He felt the weight fall somewhere deep inside his chest. Grey. Like lead. Why hadn't he expected this? Of course, he'd expected it. Another chapter. Another end. Never a beginning. The grief of losing Wendy came back all at once.

"Oh."

What was he supposed to say? He couldn't find the words.

"Would you like us to make some arrangements with the undertaker? We usually use McKinleys Rest Rooms, but if there's someone else you'd prefer?"

He recovered himself.

"Thank you. That would be helpful. McKinleys is fine."

"You'll want to see to her things. No rush. Anytime this week will be okay. McKinleys will contact you."

4

Missing Millions

Once Gus and Kevin had taken up residence at the Turret, Stella began to feel a new chapter of her existence opening up right in front of her. Independence. Freedom. Her own boss, her own nightclub, and no man to worry about twenty-four seven. A weekly visit to check on Gus would be a trip out. She could fit in some shopping.

She got a call from someone she had never met. The caller wanted to discuss an important money issue to do with her dead husband, Claude.

This was not a welcome development. Now that she'd decided to be her own woman and that she'd be better off, after all, without some man controlling events, Claude's doings were threatening to seep back into her life and complicate things again.

"It's a matter that's been hanging fire since your husband passed away. My principals let it ride for a while. To allow everything to settle. But they feel it's time now to resolve things."

"I don't know anything about what Claude was up to. Nothing. I don't think I can help you."

But he was insistent. He was polite, but his smooth manner struggled to hide a sense of implied threat she couldn't quite get a handle on.

"I need to talk to your present husband too. Claude's brother, Gus. One of you, at least, might know something useful without even realising it."

It was obvious that the man, who declined to give his name, was not going to let the matter drop. In the end, she agreed to arrange a meeting at the Turret so that

Gus could be there. Better to get the issue dealt with. Then she could forget about it and get on with her life.

He was a small, dapper man with a thin moustache and highly polished patent leather shoes. He sat on a chair in Gus's bedroom and explained politely to Stella, Gus and Kevin that the people he worked for were very much aware of the Beards' new circumstances. They offered their sympathy for the position they now found themselves in.

"But the thing is," he went on, "that as the surviving senior members of the Beard Firm you have a duty to your clients."

"I'm not a member of any Firm," said Stella. "I run the nightclub. That's it. Talk to Gus."

"And I don't have any clients," said Gus. "They've all gone. The Firm's gone. There's only me and Kevin left."

"Not quite. There are important clients, the people I have the honour to represent, who have unfinished business dealings with your family. They want to progress all this as soon as possible."

He smiled.

"What dealings?" asked Gus, looking puzzled.

The man let his head hang forward a touch and sighed. A small sigh which went nicely with his slightly furrowed brow. A little performance to make them aware that, while he was trying his best to give the pair an opportunity to explain themselves, his patience was being tested.

"Very important business dealings," he said. He raised his head again and looked Gus straight in the eye. He'd stopped smiling. "Involving sizeable sums of money. Money which belongs to my principals and which is now missing."

"What money?" asked Stella. "Claude never spoke to me about his shady, backroom dealings."

"I'm referring to money entrusted to the care of your departed husband. He was to arrange, as he had sometimes done in the past, for its transportation to a more convenient offshore location." He glanced at the stumps of Gus's missing legs, resting on his wheelchair.

"My clients, whilst appreciating your current difficulties, wish me to make it clear that they hold you responsible for the speedy return of these balances."

Gus looked stunned. Stella said nothing and shook her head in bafflement. Her hair, which she was wearing loose, fell across her face.

"If you don't mind, Boss," Kevin interjected, "I'd like to ask our friend here just who are these clients he's talking about?"

"I can't tell you that," said the man. "But here," he held out a piece of paper to Gus, "is a list of the missing amounts."

Gus made no move to take the paper. Stella stiffened on the chair she had dragged into Gus's bedroom from the dining area and folded her arms.

Kevin reached out and took it.

"Jesus!" he said. "You can't be serious. When did we ever see this kind of cash? There's some mistake. Or you're simply trying it on."

"I can assure you," said the man in the patent leather shoes, "that neither of those is the case. The situation is as described."

"There is no fucking money," said Gus. "I'm down to my last few thou'. It's the London thing, isn't it? Claude handled all that side of things. Moving cash offshore. All that stuff."

He picked up his whisky glass from the bedside table. It was empty. He put it down again.

"I worked off the street mainly, around town. Small amounts. A few thousand here and there. Nothing big."

"Well," said the man, getting to his feet, "I'll leave you to think the matter through. I'll be back in a day or so with a colleague who might be able to help you remember things more clearly."

"But there is no money. What do you expect me to do?"

"Find it."

"How? Find it how?"

"Well," said the man again, brushing imaginary specks of dust from his jacket sleeve, "I've really no idea. But if you take my advice, you'll get hold of it somehow. And quickly. If you don't... oh, dear."

"Oh, dear? What does that mean? What the fuck are you saying?" asked Gus, perplexed. This was all wrong. He was the one who demanded money from people. This was all the wrong way around.

"I'll leave that to your imagination, shall I? Thank you for your time. I'll let myself out."

"But hold on," said Gus. "How much? You haven't told us how much we're looking for."

"Three million," he said as he opened the door to go. "Sterling. But the equivalent in euros or US dollars would be acceptable. Your friend has the details."

For a full minute after the man had left, Gus and Kevin sat staring blankly into space. Stella sat with her head in her hands, sobbing quietly.

"Fuck," said Gus at length.

"You can say that again," said Kevin.

"Fuck," said Gus.

Stella decided that the quiet sobbing wasn't doing much to help. She sniffed and dabbed at her eyes with a tissue she'd pulled from the kitchen roll on Gus's bedside cabinet. Someone had to get a grip on all this.

"Did you bring Claude's old laptop over here when you moved in?" she asked, looking at Kevin. "He kept tabs on everything he did on that thing. It's the only place I can think to look. Failing that, we'll have big problems even finding somewhere to start."

"Yeah, I brought the laptop along in case Gus needed it. It's in my room," said Kevin, getting up. "I can fetch it right now. But how can we be sure that guy was genuine? I mean, any chancer could waltz in here and demand three million, couldn't they? He didn't offer any proof. He wouldn't even give us his name."

"That's true," said Gus. "But Claude was moving serious amounts of cash for some very serious people. He told me as much. And he kept all the details to himself. Kept me out of it. Obviously these guys are desperately hoping that one of us knows what's happened to their missing dosh."

"He would have committed none of this to paper," said Stella. "I'm sure about that. He did everything on his machine."

It took less than twenty seconds for Kevin to fetch the computer from his room. He handed it to Gus.

"Not that I don't trust you or anything, Kev," said Gus. "But what were you doing with my dead brother's laptop, anyway? Have you been poking around in it?"

"Don't have the password, do I?" said Kevin. "No way I could do anything. I put the thing in my room because it had to go somewhere. Like I said, in case you needed it."

He'd been trying to get into the laptop ever since the explosion had hospitalised his boss, without success. He'd checked, but the password wasn't listed on the card full of passwords and door codes and other such information that Gus kept in his wallet. No doubt Claude would have warned him to keep it entirely to himself, for emergencies only.

"We'll have to pray there's something useful in here," said Gus. "It's our only hope."

"To be clear," said Kevin as Gus opened up the machine. "What we're talking about here is 'your only hope' and definitely not 'our only hope', as you put it. I'm just an employee in this situation, right? This is on you, Gus. Sorry."

"Well, that's rich," said Gus. "Need I remind you who's paid your wages all these years. Not to mention whose luxury apartment you're living in. Try to remember how well I've looked after you."

"And maybe you should remember, Boss, who it was stuck by you after you got blasted and everyone else pissed off. Rapido. And who it is looking after you right now, day in day out, when even your own wife doesn't want the job."

There was an embarrassed silence. Stella looked away.

"Sorry, Stella. No offence."

"There's no time to take offence," said Stella. "Let's just try to focus."

Kevin stood by the bedside and watched while Gus typed 'warehouse1' into Claude's computer. The machine came to life.

"Glad to see you've kept it up at least," said Gus. "Even though you haven't been messing with it. Now let's see what we can find."

There wasn't much on the laptop apart from a lot of poorly disguised notes about the operations the Firm had been running on the street, a few copied emails and draft business letters. And two sets of accounts. The first was a copy of the official accounts kept for Claude's accountant for the purpose of satisfying the Inland Revenue. The second set, hidden amongst a collection of miscellaneous images and disguised as image files with a file extension of 'jpeg', was the set Claude had used to keep track of his illicit activities.

"Bingo," said Gus. "Looks like we're onto something here."

"You never looked in here before?" asked Stella. She crouched by the bed next to Kevin and peered at the screen. "After Claude died? I would've thought that would've been one of the first things you might have done."

"Of course I did," said Gus. "I just didn't look hard enough. I had other priorities, to deal with back then. I never found all this hidden stuff."

He grunted and pounded away at the keyboard, opening the jpegs directly from the text editor. He worked rapidly, his podgy fingers surprisingly accurate on the keys.

"I'd forgotten how he used to disguise some of his important stuff as photo albums. And I never suspected anything about missing millions, did I?"

Some of the files would not open as text files, but many did. These were mainly the files that Claude had used as his lowest level of accounts. Amongst these, Gus uncovered lists of transactions involving what appeared to be codes or abbreviations against dates and amounts. The amounts were sizeable. Against all the older transactions and most of the later ones was the letter 'c.' It didn't take much effort to guess that 'c' probably meant 'completed'.

If that was the case, then it left three of the recent transactions uncompleted. Each of the three was for one million pounds. The start date and amount of each transaction matched the items on the list the man had given to Kevin before he left.

"So there's our three mill," said Gus when they paused for coffee. "Right there. Easy peasy."

"Looks that way," said Stella. "But is this going to help? You can see when the money came in to Claude and how it seems to move along. But it's all a bit mysterious, isn't it? How do we know what all this means in reality? Either of you have any ideas?"

Stella's question was answered, eloquently enough, by silence.

"And it's quite a while since the cash left Claude's customers and got to wherever it is now. Wherever that is. The surprising thing is that no one's come looking before. Right?"

"There's been a lot of activity around the Warehouse since Claude's fall," said Kevin. "Percy's death, disappearances, the blast. Lily, too. We've had cops all

43

over everything for ages. Must've scared off the money men. Whoever they are."

"Could've," said Gus. "And maybe three million isn't such an enormous deal for them. Who knows?"

"Well, it's a big enough deal for them to have come looking for it now, isn't it?" said Stella. "We've got to get this sorted."

They looked more closely at the last six items in each of the three uncompleted transactions.

... Smt £1m Harry G K BV1
... Smt £1m Harry G K BV2
... Smt £1m Harry (G K Cay1)

There were dates against the items in each transaction, and each transaction was dated a week apart.

"Not too difficult to figure out, is it?" said Stella.

"No?" asked Gus. He sounded bemused.

"Not really. Looks like the guy who brought in the cash is 'Smt'. Smith? One million pounds is one million pounds. Harry could be the Harry Love, who worked for Claude. G must be some other guy or firm along the chain. K is probably code for some outfit or company or bank or whatever that takes the money over from there. Let's say Harry gets the cash over to G, who moves it through some bent bank arrangement and gets it into an account of some sort."

"Possibly a shell company or something like that," said Kevin. "You must have read about that sort of thing?"

"Think I've heard of shell companies," said Gus. "Probably."

"They're companies that don't actually do anything," said Kevin. "They're only used to hide transactions and identities. From there it gets transferred into some offshore account. In the first two cases here that would

44

look like the British Virgin Islands and, in the last case, the Caymans. How about that?"

"Didn't know you were such a financial wiz, Kev. I thought you were just a fucking pretty face."

"I keep my eyes and ears open. That's all. I read stuff."

"And the brackets around that last bit?" asked Gus. "What about them?"

"Dunno. I'm a smart guy and I read, but I'm not psychic."

"So what next?" asked Stella. "Where does all this get us?"

"We need to find Harry," said Gus.

"Last I heard," said Stella, "he was driving for the Davidsons."

5

Discretion

Keep it discreet, the Voice had said. So trying to talk to Gus and his man, Kevin, was out. But the dog was a godsend. The dog connected Harry to the missing Hamish, and Harry was peripheral enough to count as discreet.

His next move was to visit Junior Davidson, Freddy's grandson, in his office above Jimmy's Limo Hire. Jimmy's name was still there, even if Jimmy, Freddy's son, was long gone.

Junior sat back in the chair behind his desk and stared across at him. He was short and well-muscled with blond hair, closely cropped. He had studs in his ears and something that looked like a gremlin, sporting an enormous erection, tattooed onto his left shoulder. The sleeve of his T-shirt covered the tattoo, but Junior made sure that Jack got a clear view of the obscenity by the way he scratched at his shoulder as they spoke.

Junior's muscular physique suggested long hours spent in the gym supplemented, perhaps, with more than a little hormone therapy. Jack judged his age to be somewhere in his early twenties.

Junior glanced briefly at the business card his visitor handed him across the desk.

"Private investigator? Really?" He flicked the card aside. It landed, face down, on the desktop.

"Never expected to see one of you twats in here," he said by way of a greeting. "So what do you want?"

"I come in peace," he said, doing his best to ignore the rudeness. Ignoring bad manners was part and parcel of his working day. These days he hardly noticed.

"It's just some loose ends I'm trying to tie up for a credit agency I work for."

"Always happy to help the Money," said Junior sarcastically. "So what's come loose, exactly?"

"Harry Love. He was working for you, last we heard. I want to ask him what he aims to do about some debts he was busy running up before he disappeared so abruptly. Nothing huge, but enough to make folk anxious. Some people are like that. They fret."

"Well, you're out of luck," said Junior with a smirk. "The fucker's long gone."

"To where?"

"Dunno. Might be anywhere by now. Said something about London. Could've gone to see the Queen, d'you think? Haven't seen anything of him since."

"London? Any idea where in London? I understand it's a pretty big place."

"So I hear. Is it so important?"

"Not so's you'd notice," said Jack. "Like I said, a few loose ends."

"Don't see why I should help you out. But since Harry's pissed off and left me short of a driver, I'm not inclined to watch his back either."

"Seems reasonable. Anything you can tell me? Who knows when I might be able to return the favour?"

Junior stared in silence at Jack for a while, as if he was wondering whether he should bother to talk to him at all.

"He lived with his gran," he said.

"Where exactly?"

"Can't say exactly. St. Bride's, near Catherine Street. Don't have the number. So you owe me. Right?"

"I'm grateful for your help. Keep the card. Any time you need a PI..."

"Okay," said Junior, shrugging his shoulders and getting to his feet. "Time's up. Things to do now."

His next call was to the small terraced house where Harry's grandmother lived. It hadn't been hard to find.

It was a neat-looking house. Brick fronted and Georgian with stone lintels and sash windows. The door was opened by a neat-looking old lady.

"Mrs Love?"

"Yes," said the old lady nervously, taking care to keep her foot behind the barely opened door.

"So sorry to trouble you," he said, smiling broadly and trying hard to appear at his most likeable.

"My name's Jack. I know your grandson, Harry. We both worked for Claude Beard before his accident and I still work for Claude's brother, Gus. Perhaps Harry mentioned my name?"

"I don't believe so. What is it you want?"

"Well, it's a business matter, Mrs Love. I need to talk to Harry about it. Urgently."

"I'm sorry, Jack, but that's not possible. Like I told the other man, Harry is away on one of his trips. It's been a very long one already, and I don't know when he's coming home. You should phone him."

"Which other man would that be? Did he give his name?"

"He said his name was Kevin, I think."

Gus's man?

"I seem to have lost Harry's number. Could you give it to me, perhaps?"

"I've already given it to Kevin."

"I'm afraid I don't know Kevin personally. Do you think you could let me have it as well?"

She seemed to consider this request carefully before coming to a decision.

48

"I do have Harry's number, Jack. As I told Kevin. But you see, I don't use the telephone myself. I find it worrying. Harry wrote it down for me in case of emergency. Of course, even then someone else would have to use it. I'll get it for you."

So saying, she closed the door firmly in his face.

When it re-opened a few inches, as before, Mrs Love held out a sheet of paper through the gap. "You can copy the number from this if you want. I'll need it back, mind."

"Thank you," he said, taking the paper. "I appreciate your being so helpful."

He took out his phone and copied the number into it, and then he looked more closely at the paper. It was a sheet of notepaper with a business letterhead showing two addresses, one in London, the other in Naples.

He photographed the letterhead, thanked Mrs Love for her help and went straight back to his semi. Once there, he waited patiently for his ancient laptop to stagger into operation. It seemed as though it would make it. Then the screen froze.

Please. Not now. I'll take you to the repair shop right after I get this month's bills paid. Please, little buddy. You know I love you.

Nothing.

Start up, you little bastard!

Nothing.

He tried the number he'd been given. The call went straight to voicemail. He left a message asking Harry to phone back. He didn't expect a response, but it had to be worth a try.

The laptop was still struggling, so he dug out his tablet instead. He didn't enjoy using the tablet for searching online. His fingers were too big and clumsy for the on-screen keyboard. It would take him much longer.

His luck changed. The laptop came to life and let him log in. He'd lied to it about the repair. He was going to buy a new one just as soon as he had cash to spare. He went online and checked out the outfit described in the letterhead.

The business in question, Giuseppe De Lorca - Financial Services, was situated in a high-rise complex on the waterfront in downtown Naples. Giuseppe also had an office in London, at an address in Euston.

Next, he tracked down the place he'd been told Freddy Davidson had retired to. The only La Oliva that came up in the Canaries was on Fuerteventura. That must be it.

So, he reasoned, Keith, the dog, linked Hamish Beard to Harry Love. Harry had gone to work for Junior Davidson. Freddy Davidson now lived in the Canaries. Keith had been flown out to the Canaries.

In the absence of anything more solid, he persuaded himself that there was a fair chance that Fuerteventura could be where Hamish Beard was hiding out. Percy and Lawrence, too, if he got lucky.

But what about this finance guy, Giuseppe, in Euston? And Naples, even? Things were beginning to open up. He needed to think.

The following morning he drove out to McKinleys funeral parlour in Southport. It was located conveniently close to CareSafe, the care home. He was shown into the Chapel of Rest and left alone with Beatrice. They'd done a good job. Beatrice looked better than she had the last time he'd seen her alive. Amazing what a skilled make-up artist could achieve with a corpse.

Not knowing what else to do, he stood and looked at his mother-in-law's body for a few minutes.

"So long, Beat. Hope it's all good where you are," he murmured under his breath, feeling foolish. It was all he could think of to say.

On his way out, he called into the office and spoke to a sombre looking individual sitting behind a desk. He answered the questions the man put to him. A cremation, yes. Locally, yes. There'd only be him, so he'd use his own car to follow the hearse. No special arrangements. The usual standard vicar-speak would do. He left the choice of music to the man.

The man got him to sign a form and said there was no need to make any payment upfront. They would be happy to bill him after the event.

After the funeral home, he called at CareSafe and collected a few of his mother-in-law's personal possessions from her room. There wasn't much, clothes mainly, but he wanted the photo album and her few pieces of jewellery and any paperwork which might prove useful. Before leaving, he spoke to Tina, the manager.

"I've got everything I want to take," he said, waving a plastic carrier bag in her direction. "What do we do about the rest of it?"

"Her clothes?"

"More or less. Just clothes."

"We can deal with that for you, if you like. Would you mind some of it going to some of the other ladies here?"

"I'm sure she'd have wanted that."

Tina handed him an envelope.

"There's never an ideal time to mention money when someone dies. It's our final account. There's no rush."

Back in the semi, sitting at his kitchen table, he opened the envelope and put the bill on top of the one for the previous month, still unpaid. He looked at the undertaker's leaflet. On the reverse was a schedule of charges. He did a quick mental calculation. Life could be expensive, he thought, but even death had its costs. And right now, he was broke.

He took the carrier bag of Beat's few possessions upstairs and put them in the box-room. Wendy's things had been in there ever since she'd died. A few bits and pieces in a spare room. All it came down to in the end. And him, of course. He wouldn't forget them. But after he was gone? Nothing. And who was going to remember Jack Charnley? Maybe the barman at the Railway? Or he might glimmer briefly in a corner of Stella Beard's memory? He'd be forgotten soon enough.

He didn't feel much these days. But now, a sudden, unexpected sadness threatened to overwhelm him.

Is there any point? Escapes me if there is. This is it, Charnley. Maybe time to check out?

But there was Beat's funeral to deal with first. If he didn't go, then who?

He phoned the Voice.

"Yeah?" It was the same low, even tone as before. The same broad accent.

"I've got two leads to chase up. One on the Hamish Beard character. Reasonably strong. I'd need to go to the Canaries and spend a bit of time out there to check it out."

"And the other?"

"A guy called Harry Love. Worked for the Beards, but not now. Went off to work for the Davidsons."

"You speak to him?"

"Spoke to Junior Davidson. He has a limo hire thing here in town. Harry's gone. London, probably. Or Naples. There's some money guy involved. Giuseppe. And I have an address. Two, in fact. Want me to follow up on the Giuseppe end of things?"

There was a pause. Jack felt he could all but hear the mental cogs turning at the other end of the connection.

"A money guy?"

"Giuseppe De Lorca. Financial Services. Don't know what exactly. I have a photo of his letterhead, that's all."

Another pause.

"Don't go near the money. Leave that and this Giuseppe to us. Focus on Hamish. Copy me the letterhead ASAP, then forget all about it."

"So, what about the Canaries lead?"

"Yes," said the Voice. No hesitation now. "Go over there. We'll cover your costs. Anything else?"

"I need some cash."

"You'll be paid when the job's done, like always. We're not a fucking charity."

"I need money up front. I've got unexpected expenses. You can sort that, can't you?"

"For fuck's sake, Charnley. How much?"

"Five grand."

"You cheeky cunt!"

"It's what I need."

He managed to sound resolute. Easy when there's no other option. Five thousand plus the four he had remaining on his credit card would keep him afloat until he got his next proper payout.

There was a brief silence before the Voice relented.

"In your bank in an hour. This is a one-off, so don't ask again. Anything else?"

"No, that's it. Thanks."

"Keep in touch," ordered the Voice and rang off abruptly.

*

He hadn't visited the Canary Islands before. He had never been one for beach holidays. Sand and sun weren't exactly his thing. More accurately, holidays had never really been his thing. At least, not since Wendy. The idea of spending time in a resort actively, or even passively, 'enjoying' himself was alien to him. He suspected that if he ever tried to take a beach holiday, it would only end in his finding some backstreet bar and drinking the tides and nights away. Better to stay home and save the expense.

But this was different. This would be a trip with a purpose. A trip with a point to it. Most likely, he would need to dig into the reality of the place.

He called the undertaker and pleaded for an urgent move on Beat's funeral.

"I have to go abroad on business. Email me your invoice and I'll put your cheque in the post tonight."

Thirty minutes later, he had the invoice. Thirty minutes after that the undertaker was on the phone with an offer of a slot for the following afternoon at the local crematorium and a request for a bank transfer instead of a cheque.

Easy to get things done when you've got cash in the bank. Maybe you can find a way through this, after all, Jacky boy.

And there was no reason to wait. He was lucky and managed to get a flight from John Lennon for the day after next. He packed a bag with the kind of clothes he imagined tourists might wear over there. Enough to see him comfortably through a week or two. Lucky again that he'd done the laundry the day before. As it was, his bag took all his clean stuff. If he ran out, he could buy more. He was on expenses, wasn't he?

His passport, kept current for such rare eventualities as this, he seemed to have lost track of. He came across it, hiding in the bottom of his sock drawer. Another stroke of luck. A good omen.

Beat's funeral took less than half an hour. He was the only mourner apart from Tina, who'd come along to represent the care home.

"She'd been with us a long time, after all. Lovely lady."

The priest went through some standard texts. There were no hymns. Nothing in the service resonated with him. Before leaving, he shook the priest's hand and thanked him.

Driving back to his semi, through the winter gloom of the late afternoon, he felt a strange mix of emotions. Sadness, for sure, but a kind of liberation too. And something akin to optimism. He found it confusing, and later, before bed, he looked to the whisky for enlightenment.

The enlightenment failed to appear, but at least he slept.

The following morning he was up early, glad to find his bag ready packed, his paperwork in order, his boarding pass printed. En route to the airport, he stopped off briefly in the village centre and used his credit card to buy euros.

You can be an efficient little bastard when you try. Maybe there's hope for you yet.

On the flight out, he tried to read the copy of the Daily Mail he had picked up in the departure lounge. He read the first page before giving up. He couldn't get interested in the news.

After a while, he got as comfortable as he could in the cramped conditions and closed his eyes. He wanted to sleep but, for no reason he could think of, found himself reflecting on the course his life had taken. A sad catalogue of time squandered and wasted opportunities. No proper focus. Apart from Wendy.

There were reasons for his lack of focus. He hadn't exactly had what anyone might call a normal upbringing. He had no idea who his parents were. He had spent the entirety of his childhood and early adolescence in various foster homes. Some good. Some not so good. And then out on his own at sixteen. A succession of dead-end jobs.

At eighteen, there'd been that summer with Stella before she'd dumped him for someone much more upmarket. What was he supposed to do? As soon as he could, he'd joined the Army.

And that had worked out well, had it not? Not really. That was when the drinking had begun in earnest. He hadn't discovered the interest and excitement he'd hoped for in army life. Mostly, he'd been in Berlin, working in the stores. Then he'd spent some more time packing up the Army's bits and pieces as the Brits pulled out more and more of their personnel.

He'd liked Berlin well enough but soon got bored and found the wrong people to drink with. And then his drinking had become a problem, and he and the Army had parted company.

The British Army, understandably, didn't like its soldiers to be drunk for much of the time. Not while on duty, for sure.

He'd learned from that experience, though. He'd got his boozing under some sort of control. Enough to allow him, after a further succession of hopeless jobs, to get taken on by a private investigations bureau. And, eventually, to set up on his own.

At first, he'd hoped that his new occupation would be interesting. Exciting, even. But his work as a PI proved to be equally boring to standing guard on a compound in Berlin. By that time, though, he had learned to accept a degree of boredom as an inevitable part of life. Of his life, at least.

When he found Wendy, things had suddenly looked up. They'd got married and bought the house out at the Point. The semi he still occupied.

But then he'd lost her, and the light and fun had gone out of everything. After that, he'd settled for simply getting through as best he could. A process of managed decline.

Sod it, he thought, realising that his mood was verging on self-pity. Overthinking things again. He flagged down the girl pushing the drinks trolley and got himself a couple of whiskies.

6

Star City

Jack had looked through the guidebook he had bought and read that Puerto del Rosario, otherwise discouragingly known as the 'Goat Port', was Fuerteventura's capital. But that was okay. He had nothing against goats. He decided that Rosario, warm and sunlit as it would surely be, would be a good base from which to begin his investigations.

From the moment he stepped off the plane, he felt energised by the light and colour of his surroundings. And by the sudden heat. The contrast with the cold, damp greyness of the place he had left was extreme.

Asking the taxi driver, in heroically experimental Spanish, to choose a hotel saw him checking into a modern-looking building overlooking the beach. His sixth-floor room had an ocean view.

As soon as he'd showered and changed into clothes more suited to the climate, he found a table in the bar and ordered a beer. It was ice cold and tasted like nectar. Between gulps, he studied a map of the island he'd picked out from the rack of tourist information in the hotel lobby. It showed that La Oliva was in a hilly area inland, around fifteen miles to the northwest. He decided he'd take a look out there in the morning and passed the rest of the time familiarising himself with his new neighbourhood. It was quiet and unpretentious. Nothing like the tourist resort he'd been half dreading. He liked the place.

The following day he took a bus out to La Oliva itself and spent a pleasant hour or so exploring. It was a small town with the usual elderly church standing in the plaza. It boasted an arts centre and a fort-like building, La Casa de Los Coloneles, the Colonels' House, which his guidebook told him had once housed the island's rulers.

Beyond these, there was a collection of largely unremarkable houses and a pavement cafe.

Within half an hour, he felt he'd seen all he needed. He got a taxi at the local rank. In a place this size, the taxi drivers would know the location of everyone worth knowing about.

"Señor Davidson," he said as he settled himself into the rear seat. "Por favor."

The driver said nothing in reply but started the engine and drove off along the main road through the settlement. After a few hundred yards, they turned right, onto a track going uphill. It was a winding route, climbing the side of what appeared to be a long-extinct volcano. Eventually, they came to a halt outside the gates of a large old finca. He got out and paid the driver. Once the taxi had driven out of sight, he walked up and down the path running by the house to get whatever view he could of the property.

He considered his options. He could settle for having found Davidson's location, walk back down the hill, and get himself back to the Goat Port. Or he could stroll up to the front door and knock and explain to Davidson that he was looking for Hamish Beard without being able to tell him exactly why. That would surely be a mistake.

There was no sign of anyone at the finca and no vehicle parked anywhere in view. Maybe there would be no one at home right now.

He considered the possibility of there being some huge and dangerous guard dog lurking somewhere in the grounds.

So you could get a dog bite or two. So what? Risk it. You haven't come all this way for nothing.

As he was opening the gate, a woman came from around the back of the finca. She was carrying a yard brush, busy with her outdoor cleaning round. She looked startled to see him standing there.

"Ah," he said, equally surprised. "Buenos dias, Señora. Señor Davidson? Is he at home?"

"Not here," replied the woman. "Sorry. Out. Arrecife. Best to phone."

Not good, Jack. Not really. Probably alerted Davidson now, possibly the Hamish boy too, for no real gain.

"Okay," he said. "I'll do that then. Adios." At which he turned away and strode off, back down to the village.

So he'd located Davidson's residence and learned that he wasn't alone. There was the woman he'd seen. Most likely the housekeeper from the look of her. It was a start.

But while there'd been no evidence of a guard dog, there'd been no obvious sign of the Yorkie, Keith, either. That could mean that Hamish Beard wasn't with Davidson after all.

The housekeeper had mentioned Arrecife. Wherever that was, maybe it would be worth a look.

Just as he left the junction, where the track met the road into the village, he saw a car turn off and start up the track toward the finca. There were other buildings on the way up there. But very few. And not many of those had even looked habitable. So there was a reasonable chance that the car, a Mercedes, could be Davidson's.

He'd got a glimpse of a driver, and there had been a man, the right age for Davidson, sitting in the back. He made a note of the number.

His phone rang. It was Stella Beard.

"Hi, Stella," he said, sounding as surprised as he felt. "Are you wanting to make use of my missing persons expertise after all?"

"It's not that, Jack. Hamish is still out of touch. But something else has happened." She sounded worried.

"Like?"

"Some man came to visit me and Gus a few days ago and told us that there's money gone adrift from some business Claude was into."

"What kind of business?"

"Something dodgy. I really don't know what. Moving money around is a part of it. There's a lot of it involved."

"How much? Thousands?"

"Millions. They claim to be missing three million that Claude had been handling for them. Gus claims he doesn't know anything about it."

Three million? Jesus.

"And does he, do you think? Know nothing about it? Three million is a hell of a lot of cash. Drug money maybe?"

"I've absolutely no idea. But these people looking for it are dangerous. The man came back today with another man and gave Gus a meat slicer as a present." Stella's voice was shaking.

"A present?"

"They used it to slice off one of his fingers. Said they'd be back to remove a few more if he didn't find the missing cash pronto."

"Good God. Did Gus manage to cough up the dosh?"

"He still says he knows nothing. We'd been going through some accounts with Kevin to try to sort it, but now Kevin's disappeared. I've no idea where he is."

Kevin again? Whose side would Kevin be on?

"Any use involving the police? This is all sounding like desperate stuff."

"I doubt it. This is going to be dodgy money, and these are very dodgy people. Dangerous. Obviously. And Gus isn't exactly Mr Clean."

"Take your point, Stell. Maybe best to deal with this in-house if possible. Tricky either way."

"I'm moving Gus back here until we get this sorted. He's had the wound treated, but we couldn't find the finger. The swines must have taken it. Gus told the surgeon he'd had an accident making his dinner and lost it down the waste disposal."

"The thing is, Stella, I'm away right now. On a case. I'm not even in the UK. Can't say when I'll be home."

"Oh," said Stella. She seemed disappointed. "But that's not the worst of it. The same two men have just been here, making what sounded like threats about the cash. Then they searched the office."

"You expecting them back?"

"I'm not sure. It seems possible. Sorry to dump this on you, but I don't know who else to talk to. Gus is useless, and he's frightened. I can't trust anyone around here, and Hamish is still missing. What do I do?"

"You could close up the Warehouse and hide out somewhere?"

"I'm not leaving this place. The Blue Warehouse is my life."

He could have pointed out that staying put to guard her territory might well cost her the life she was trying to protect. But he didn't. Stella would probably have considered any advice of that kind unhelpful. He couldn't think of much else to offer, so he made the best suggestion he could come up with.

"You could buy yourself some time if you use Gus's contacts to hire some muscle. See if you can persuade Gus to get himself back together for long enough to do that. I wouldn't try to do it yourself. That might just make things worse unless you really know what you're doing."

"Sounds expensive."

"It'll cost. But as I said, it could buy you some time to work out a way through this mess. If you want to stay put, I can't see you have any other options."

*

The same day, back at the Goat Port, Jack hired himself a car. A small, grey, anonymous-looking hatchback. Much like the one he had at home.

He looked up Arrecife. It was the capital of Lanzarote. So it wasn't even on the same island. If he ever needed to get there, he'd have to take a ferry or a flight. Later, after a few cautious whiskies in the hotel bar, he got an early night.

The following morning saw him parked in the shade, some way down the road from the finca track, at La Oliva. Watching and waiting. Something he was well used to.

He thought about the situation back in the Baltic and how Stella and Gus might be handling things. It was worrying for sure, but there was little he could do to help. Not that protecting the Blue Warehouse was any of his business.

At least he was beginning to get some idea of what this was all about. It was probable that he was searching for Hamish on behalf of the same people who were putting pressure on Gus and Stella. Drug dealers, probably. Looking for their missing cash.

Should he have told Stella that he felt he was close to discovering where Hamish was? He couldn't see any advantage in that. Not for her or for himself. Better to say nothing for now. Information could be valuable, but not if you gave it away for free.

The road was quiet. He was parked well beyond the end of the village, and no one had walked out that far in all the time he had been there. He sat there all day, sipping, occasionally, from a large bottle of water and munching on the supplies he'd got from the mini-market near the hotel that morning. He made a couple of quick trips back, using the footpath, to the little cafe. A double espresso each time to keep him sharp. And a visit to the loo. He could go for long periods without relieving the pressure on his bladder, but there were limits.

He watched the shadows lengthen on the dusty pathway. At around four in the afternoon, an enormous ginger cat came sauntering along the path and lay down in a patch of sunlight. It yawned and stretched. Then it curled up and closed its eyes. Apart from the cat, he saw nothing of interest.

Okay. So wait.

He did the same the next day with no result. Discouraging, true, but he had no other leads.

On the third day, just as he was thinking of heading back to the hotel in Rosario, the Mercedes pulled off the track, onto the road ahead and drove off.

He followed what he hoped was Davidson's car at a careful distance.

The drive took him through the north of the island, through volcanic hills, scrubland, carefully tended farms, smallholdings and small settlements. The road he was following would end at a town on the coast called Corralejo. There was a ferry link there, northwards across a narrow patch of Atlantic Ocean, to Lanzarote.

Corralejo itself was a place of contrasts. On the approach, he saw a surprising number of half-completed and apparently abandoned developments scattered about the area in bare, unfinished concrete blocks. An enduring monument, he imagined, to the last financial crash.

And then the long stretch of road going down into the town reminded him of a warmer and more cheerful version of Blackpool's Golden Mile in high summer. With its endless shops selling tourist junk and beach toys. Other areas had neat developments of brightly painted villas. Some with large sale boards, in English, aimed at tourists and expats looking for a sunnier existence.

He found the drive relaxing. But when the Mercedes he was following joined the line of vehicles waiting for the ferry at the dockside, he became worried. He couldn't be sure if there would be room on board for his hatchback. And he didn't know if he'd be able to get his car off the ferry in time to track his target at the other end. He parked up and boarded on foot.

He knew, from his guidebook and map, that Lanzarote was just a short stretch of ocean away.

After a boat ride of less than twenty-five minutes, they docked at Playa Blanca. He made sure to be among the first to disembark.

He would have liked to try to get eyes on his quarry on the boat but couldn't risk making himself too obvious in the confined space. So he'd stood in the prow, looking out for flying fish. He'd never seen a flying fish before. By the time they'd docked, he'd seen three.

He got himself a taxi and was waiting as the cars rolled out of the harbour and off up the road. The driver spoke English well and had no difficulty with his request to follow the Mercedes.

It was a trouble-free drive of around thirty minutes until the Mercedes glided to a stop on the beachfront, across from the towering Gran Hotel in Arrecife. The only high-rise on the island.

He'd kept an eye on the meter and was ready with a handful of euros, more than covering the fare. He got the taxi to pull up a short distance behind what he had to hope really was Davidson's car.

He was already strolling towards the Merc as its passenger climbed out, carrying a plastic shopping bag, and strode up to the door of a small apartment block. Judging by the man's age and by photographs he'd seen on his Facebook page, the man he was now following was indeed Freddy Davidson.

It never failed to amaze him just how much personal information people were happy to spread around the Internet. More fool them, in his view. But it usually made his job a great deal easier than it would otherwise have been.

Freddy looked on the young side for someone who was Junior's grandad. Nice haircut, a colourful shirt, chinos and a pair of quality casual shoes. He had a decent tan to go with the outfit. Why wouldn't he? Living out here as he did. Not paunchy either. Good muscle tone. The man took care of himself.

Jack was dressed in jeans and a T-shirt, topped off with his baseball cap and sunglasses. With his British pallor, he looked much like any other tourist as he walked slowly past his target, standing at the door of the apartment block.

Davidson was pressing the topmost button on the bank of push buttons by the entrance. He was being buzzed inside as Jack sauntered across the road and up to a low wall by the beach. He sat on the wall, his cap pulled down to shield his eyes from the glare, and studied the building. Like several other similar buildings in the vicinity, it had a rooftop apartment with an open terrace. He guessed that was where Davidson was right now. He walked back over the road and read the name on the card by the buzzer. 'Sra. Fran. Rimmer'.

Usual thing, then. How long to sit here on this wall and watch the doorway? They can get eyes on me from the terrace. Too hot out here.

So here, he reflected, was a man who seemed to live alone, apart, perhaps, from his driver and housekeeper, visiting a woman's apartment late on Friday afternoon. Davidson had been carrying a bag of groceries and a bottle of wine. So his guess had to be that Davidson was here to see his girlfriend or his woman, whichever term proved to be the most appropriate. In Jack's wide experience of these affairs, he would most likely be staying one night, at least. Maybe two.

The Merc had already pulled away, turned around higher up the road, and driven off, back the way it had come.

The sun was too strong to sit for long out in the open, so he found himself a shady spot by the Gran. From there, he could keep tabs on things for a while. But checking out the notices in the lobby window, he saw that the hotel had a cafe, Star City, on the seventeenth floor.

He took the lift to the seventeenth and found the cafe. It had extensive views of the town and beach on three sides, and he got a table by the window, overlooking Señora Rimmer's apartment. The place was busy. Couples mainly. The whole thing overlaid with the clattering of cutlery on china and cheerful holiday conversations.

He ordered coffee and a pastry and pulled his compact camera out of his small backpack. The zoom lens made it a simple matter to examine the location he was interested in. No one would suspect he was snooping. Anyone seeing him, sitting there with his camera, would see just another tourist framing his holiday snaps.

The apartment he was watching opened out onto a terrace overlooking the street and beachfront. And there was his quarry, the man he had watched climb out of the Mercedes, stretched out on a sun-lounger next to a woman on an identical lounger. Both were wearing shorts and T-shirts. The man was propped in a semi-sitting position and seemed to be talking, moving his hands. The woman, presumably Fran Rimmer, lay still, her hands by her sides. She, as far as he could tell from his vantage point high up in the Gran, could well be ten to fifteen years younger than Davidson, who he estimated to be somewhere in his mid-sixties.

Nearby, on a flat cushion in a shaded corner, lay a small dog, a terrier. He clicked off a few shots as his coffee and cake arrived.

He sat at his table in the cafe window, viewing the rooftop scene as he enjoyed his snack. The view was sunlit, colourful and relaxing. Like he imagined being on holiday might be once you got the hang of it. He struggled to remember how long it had been since he'd had a real holiday. Too long. He'd lost the habit years ago.

The couple he studied so intently were sharing a bottle of wine. And why shouldn't they? Perhaps he should have a glass of something himself?

He registered the familiar ache in his throat as he signalled the waiter. He had been reasonably well behaved, so far, on this trip and managed to limit his drinking to a few whiskies in the bar before bed. True, he'd also gone through a bottle in his room. But in the daytime, he'd been good. And why not skip the whisky for once and try some wine? He examined the wine list for a whole thirty seconds before admitting to himself that he had no idea what he was looking at. Wine was a foreign country.

He ordered a speculative half-bottle of something white and dry. The waiter brought it to his table in an ice-bucket and poured him a glass. He liked the taste. Maybe he should drink the stuff more often. Didn't they say it was never too late to learn? He was thirsty, and he drank up quickly before ordering another half-bottle. Red this time, for the contrast.

Before he'd got through the red, Davidson and the woman had disappeared inside. Probably they were getting ready to eat or sleeping off the drink they'd shared. Whatever the reason for the couple's disappearance, once he'd finished the second half-bottle, there was nothing to be gained by staying put any longer. The wine was beginning to make its presence felt, and he couldn't risk drinking any more.

Since he felt sure that Davidson would be at the Rimmer place for a night or so, it would make sense for him to stick around too.

Back on the ground floor, he tried to book himself a room in the Gran, but there were none available. The man at the reception desk pointed him down the beachfront. There were a couple more places down there worth a try, the man said.

He took a stroll by the beach and quickly found another hotel, the Lancelot. Full also. He strolled on, consulting his guidebook as he went. He learned that the beach was known as Playa Reducto and that he was walking down the Avenida Fred Olsen. Towards the far end of the Reducto, the shore curved out toward a small promontory on which he could make out a kind of park with palm trees. But before he reached it, he came upon the Hotel Diamante. And there, thanks to a last-minute cancellation, he got a room for the night.

He'd had the foresight to put a change or two of socks and underwear into his backpack, along with his shaving gear and toothbrush, for such an eventuality as this. It was his usual practice when out spying away from home.

His room had a balcony and, like the one back in Rosario, a view of the beach. So he opened the doors, stretched out on the bed, and listened to the waves lapping gently onto the sand as the tide came in.

He woke sometime later, feeling hungry. He made his way down to the dining room and ate his fill from the buffet as he worked diligently through another half-bottle of red. It was as well that he'd had the short walk down the Fred Olsen and that hour or so of sleep. Best not become too inebriated while on duty. There'd been enough of that problem down the years.

He dismissed the idea of going back to keep watch on the apartment at this point. More useful to get a full night's rest and start fresh and early tomorrow.

At the desk, he booked the room for a further two nights. It would make a good base for the Arrecife end of his enquiries. Even better, the Voice was paying his expenses, and he liked it here.

He searched out the bar at the front of the hotel and decided to chance another glass or so of wine to help him sleep. He seemed to be developing a taste for the stuff.

He got himself a table with a view of the street and tuned into the sound of the conversations in Spanish between the drinkers, who looked more like locals than tourists, sitting nearby. He understood nothing of what they were saying.

He sat for a long time, drinking steadily through the wine brought to him by the barman and watching the evening play out in the warm darkness beyond the windowpane. People were walking, jogging and cycling along the broad pavement under the palms. The scene lit at intervals by the streetlights. He found it so agreeable, sitting there with a view of the avenida, that he decided on one last drink. But, getting to his feet to place his order, he was suddenly unsteady and had to make a grab at the window sill.

Abandoning all hope of more alcohol, he had to pay close attention to his movements as he weaved his way out of the bar. Thank God he was booked in here. Walking back along the beachfront would have proved next to impossible.

"Ciao," said the barman, as he left.

Ciao? Wasn't that Italian? He half-turned and grunted something in reply, staggering a little as he resumed his unsteady progress toward the lift.

Not good. Blame the wine. Not used to it.

But he'd been here before, via other routes. Regrettably often.

Stay focused. Careful with the stagger. Make it back to the room.

The following morning he woke to discover his clothes carefully folded and placed neatly on a chair by his bed. The sun streamed in through the open balcony doors, and the sound of small waves came drifting up softly from the shore. He had no memory of the previous evening after he'd left the bar. That, he had to admit, was a bad sign.

He had never been able to understand how, when he got so drunk as he had last night, he invariably woke to find everything in order. Back home in the semi, he would always find the lights and appliances switched off, the doors locked and his clothes, as they were now, folded neatly by the bed.

He was okay. A little muzzy, perhaps. But that was only to be expected. He had long thought that he'd been blessed with the kind of genetic disposition that enabled his liver to process alcohol better than the average drunk.

Later, sipping a coffee and munching on an omelette-filled bocadillo in the dining room, he reflected on the events of the previous day. Things were progressing well. Finding Davidson's weekend haunt had been a significant step forward. And the presence of the dog, which he was now convinced must be Keith Beard, indicated a likely connection between Señora Rimmer's apartment and the missing Hamish. True, the dog could be a simple coincidence, but his instincts told him otherwise. He trusted his instincts.

But, so far, no sign of Hamish himself.

His phone rang. The Voice.

"Hi."

"You haven't phoned. Any progress?"

"Sorry. Been busy on the case. Some progress. Yes, some for sure. Nothing about Percy or Lawrence yet, but I think the lead is working out in terms of Hamish Beard. I have eyes on a particular location here in Lanzarote since yesterday. I assume I'm still good for the expenses? I'm spending money. I've had to book into a second hotel for a few nights."

"You're okay for the time being. Keep on it. But phone me. Stay in touch. I don't want to have to phone you again for an update."

"Will do. Thanks for the cash advance. It came through pretty quick. Appreciate it."

No response. The Voice rang off.

He finished his breakfast and decided to walk back up the Fred Olsen to take another look at what he now had tagged as the 'Fran Place'. He strolled by the ocean side of the avenida, looking across at the beach as he went. A warm and gentle breeze brought ocean smells his way. And the smell of burgers and sun-cream.

The usual collection of sunbathers and swimmers were enjoying the winter sun. He felt excluded. He had long been a misfit who envied these people their relaxed lifestyles and their easy ability to enjoy themselves. Once upon a lifetime ago, he'd been able to live that way. Losing Wendy had put an end to that.

He'd grown tired of spying on others for a living. And he wasn't young anymore. One day he might be lucky enough to find that he'd survived to old age. Would that be lucky? It wasn't even all that far off when he thought about it.

Truth was, he'd never thought much about the prospect of old age. But he didn't want to get there and find nothing much to look back on other than bereavement and a few decades of wasted time. Sad to think that might well be the way things were going.

Walking towards, and then past, the Fran Place, he saw no signs of life up on the terrace. He went straight on to the Gran and took the lift up to Star City.

From there, over an espresso, he checked out what he could see of Fran's place. There was no one in view. Not even the terrier. The doors onto the terrace were closed.

Had they gone out to walk the dog? Unless the animal had a cast-iron bladder, he guessed it would need to be walked two or three times a day.

Then he spotted them coming along the pavement by the beach, the little terrier trotting beside them on its lead. He used his camera zoom to examine them more closely. Davidson had two carrier bags, out of one of which poked a large baguette. The pair seemed easy in each other's company. Unhurried. Taking their time.

Shortly after going into the apartment block, they appeared on the terrace. The woman, Fran, carrying a dish of water for the dog. Davidson carrying coffee cups.

He took a minute to study the woman. Good looking. Not the glamorous type. Simply dressed. Nothing garish. Not like some of the fashion statements he'd seen strolling about over here. Took all sorts, he supposed.

Now what? He could hardly sit here all day. It was busy, and others would be needing the table soon. And, although he always enjoyed the stuff, there was a limit to how much espresso he felt he could safely drink.

He decided to spend some time exploring the area on foot to get some background to the situation. You never knew when a little background detail might come in useful.

Down at ground level, he set off to trudge around a few of the back streets before the day became too hot and the effects of last night's wine caught up with him.

His walk revealed an eclectic conglomeration of old, new, and decaying buildings. A number of the more modern structures were empty. Some of the more recent developments seemed never to have progressed further than the breeze-block stage. They reminded him of the approach to Corralejo.

Many of the smaller streets, some filled with crowds of happy tourists, shopping and snacking, crossed each other at strange angles, making it easy to get lost.

After an hour or so of aimless trudging, he headed back to the Gran, intending to look again at Fran's terrace from Star City. It was hot now, and his head wasn't as clear as it should be. He was beginning to regret the previous night's excess.

His phone rang. Tooth.

"Yes?" He was trying not to sound irritated.

"It's Alan. Where are you?"

"I'm off the coast of Morocco. On an island. What's the prob?"

"There seems to be a cat trapped in your garden shed."

Fucking amazing!

"And you think that because...?"

"I can hear it meowing."

"Are you wearing your hearing aid?"

"No. I never wear it when I'm gardening. Why?"

"I'm wondering how you can hear a cat in my shed, all the way from your place. You're pretty deaf."

"I was in your garden, not mine."

"Because?"

"Just keeping tabs on things, while you're away."

"Very kind of you, but there's really no need. I have absolutely nothing worth stealing. If anyone breaks in, they'll most likely leave a donation and go."

"There's always the fire risk. You know. That sort of thing. Maybe you left the oven on."

"I didn't. I only ever use the microwave. It's all fine."

"So what about the cat?"

"What cat?"

"The one trapped in your shed. It's locked. Can I break in?"

"It's not locked. The door sticks if the wind blows it closed sometimes. I probably left it open and the cat's found it's way in. I haven't time for this right now. I'm working."

"Leave it to me, Jack. I'll sort it. Enjoy your holiday."

"I'm working. I told you."

He terminated the call.

On reaching the hotel entrance, he glanced back and saw Davidson leaving the apartment building. He looked up to see Fran looking down from her terrace, onto the pavement, staring down at the doorway with a kitchen towel in her hand, as if daring herself to drop it onto her man as he left.

Fran stood watching Davidson as he turned right and walked off, following the footpath. Jack kept his head down, hoping she wouldn't notice him as he strode purposefully across the road. His faster pace would mark him out from the other pedestrians, but he didn't want to lose track of his quarry. Once in position a few yards behind, he slowed his step to match.

He noticed Davidson pull out his phone and begin speaking into it, turning as he walked to glance back over his shoulder. He guessed that Fran had seen him and was warning him that he could have someone on his tail.

What does she think? A mugger? After his wallet?

But he knew she couldn't be sure he was tailing Freddy. He carried on.

Davidson put his phone away and turned off into Calle Mexico, where he went into a cafe. Jack moved into a shop doorway and watched the place, as reflected in the window of an abandoned ferretería, a hardware emporium, across the street. He saw Davidson pivot to get a view of the street. He felt certain he would have seen nothing.

After a few minutes, he sauntered past the cafe before striding quickly back to stand in front of the window. He pretended to be interested in the menu hanging there. Davidson stood inside, talking to a man standing by one of the tables, holding a tray. Suddenly Davidson looked across and stared him full in the face. He turned away. Too late. Davidson had seen him.

As he left the cafe and set off back down the street. Jack followed.

He was reluctant to push his luck. These things had a protocol of their own. If he got too close, it was possible that Davidson would choose to turn around and challenge him. If he left a reasonable distance, it would allow his quarry to take his time about deciding what to do and still hold on to his self-respect. The man might challenge him in any case, but that would be up to him. Jack was just doing his thing.

He'd been sloppy, he realised, allowing first the woman and then Davidson to spot him so easily. Too late to worry about that now. He reminded himself it could sometimes be helpful to let people know they were under observation. It could make them edgy enough to make mistakes.

He saw Davidson go back into Fran's block. Then he walked over to the hotel and leaned on the wall. He could see the edge of the terrace across the avenida. Fran came to stand there, overlooking the street, pointing over in his direction. Then Davidson came over to join her, to take a look.

Davidson would realise, of course, that his tail would be likely to be the same man who had been asking about him at his finca. The housekeeper would have told him about that. So now he'd be sure that someone was on his case. He just wouldn't know who or why. But he would want to. Jack headed off back down toward the Diamante. He'd leave the next move to Freddy.

*

He had to have a break. He wasn't feeling at his best, and the heat tired him. Served him right, he supposed. He needed to cut down on the drink. Especially in this heat. How could it possibly be so hot this early in the year?

He plodded down the oceanfront toward his hotel. Halfway there, he turned as if gazing along the length of the beach to take in the view. Fifty yards or so behind him, he saw an older couple walking a terrier. He walked slowly on to the Diamante, and once inside, as he was stepping into the lift, he glanced back at the entrance. Davidson and the Fran woman stood outside with the dog, watching him.

He knew that Davidson would be thinking hard, trying to work out what exactly was going on. However much he might have tried to keep a low profile, he must surely have made one or two enemies during his career. He must now be wondering just which of those enemies was stalking him.

And what did Hamish Beard and Davidson have to do with the missing millions that Gus Beard's tormentors were searching for? Had either of them got their hands on the millions somehow? The Voice had told him to stay away from the money and to find Hamish. So, on the face of it, that was unlikely.

From the brief enquiries he'd made back in Liverpool, he had learned that Davidson had, in the past, been suspected of involvement in counterfeiting, amongst much else. Not to mention some difficult business with the Beards and an episode involving some gentlemen from Glasgow around the time his son, Jimmy, had mysteriously disappeared.

All this was rumour. Nothing clear cut or actionable. But still, it all helped to paint a picture.

He couldn't guess what the Fran woman knew about Davidson's past, but he suspected that Freddy wouldn't have told her a great deal about anything beyond the limo hire business his grandson used as a front. Why complicate a presumably pleasant relationship with unnecessary and challenging details. He might need to tell her a bit more now, though.

*

As the daylight began to fade, he decided to forgo lying on the bed in favour of sitting on his balcony. He watched the strollers, the joggers, the cyclists and the hand-holding couples progressing up and down the walkway. The usual evening procession. The air was pleasantly warm and lightly scented now with the aroma of freshly cooked steak and chips. It smelled good. Yet again, he got to thinking about how little he relished the life he lived back home.

The drinking had helped, at first, to combat the relentless boredom of it all, and most days, he could keep within what he regarded as reasonable limits. Reasonable for him, at least.

And he didn't drink simply from habit. It was more than that. Much more. When he got it right, and there'd been a period when that had been most times, it came close to what he imagined a religious experience might be like.

First, there was the taste. Good in itself. Then came that enjoyable, low level of inebriation. This was where most people stopped and either fell asleep on the sofa, or made love, or finished their meal, or went off to bed, or got into a pointless argument with some poor soul outside the pub and beat the living shit out of them. But it was the next stage that was the real prize. The point where he would feel himself on the very edge of bliss, his soul liberated and glowing clear and golden. That was as good as anything was ever going to get. These days nothing else even came close.

But lately, that approach to spiritual liberation was harder and harder to hold on to. He had to drink more and more in the attempt to arrive there and, most times now, would simply fall into a deep ocean of mindless drunkenness. And the binges had become bigger over time. They were beginning to make a difference.

7

The Phone Call

After two nights at Fran's place, as he sat watching from Star City, Davidson's Mercedes arrived to collect him, and he was gone. It seemed reasonable to suppose that he had returned to his finca. There was still no sign of Hamish, so there was little point in his hanging around Arrecife any longer. He packed his bag, checked out of the Diamante and got the bus down to Playa Blanca and the first available ferry over to Corralejo. The rented hatchback stood waiting in the car-park, right where he'd left it.

Someone had decorated the car with a parking ticket, which he dropped into the waste bin at the exit. He took his time with the drive to Rosario and tried to think through his next move. So far, he'd found Davidson and Davidson's woman, Fran, and he had reason to hope he'd found Keith, too.

But he hadn't found Hamish Beard or Percy or Lawrence. He considered the possibility that Fran might provide a more direct connection to Hamish than Davidson. Keith was, after all, staying at her apartment and not at Davidson's finca. But then, Harry Love had a connection both to the dog and to Davidson via the Limo Hire back in the Baltic.

Too complicated. Best put all that on one side for now. Plod on.

Either way, he'd nothing new to tell the Voice and no plan for what to do next.

Back at the hotel in Rosario, he changed and went down to the bar to drink, pacing himself, until the dining room opened for dinner. He ate well and drank sparingly. He was becoming used to the wine and thought he might even come to prefer it to whisky. Or he might when he wasn't looking for too quick a hit.

Breakfast the following morning found him no nearer to formulating any kind of plan. He drove back up to La Oliva and parked at the end of the track leading up to Davidson's place. All that was left to him now was to wait for the man to show up and then follow him again. It was what he usually ended up doing. Davidson would know it was him, but it was hard to tell which way these things would go. It might well force something out into the open.

His phone rang. Unknown number.

"Yes?"

"Hello, Jack."

"Hello. Who is this?"

"I think you should know who this is. Don't you think, Mr. Charnley?"

"Why?"

"Because you've been following me about. And, at this moment, I'd bet good money that you're sitting in that crappy little rented hatchback of yours at the bottom of my road, bored senseless, waiting for me to appear."

He said nothing, holding out for the punchline. There had to be a punchline.

"Have I got that right?" There was a pause. And then, "I don't want to see you coming to any harm, Jack. You should be careful."

A threat? He didn't know what to say. So again, he said nothing. But this was a shock. What was all this about harm? He hadn't been looking for harm, had he? Not from any direction. He looked on this as a missing persons enquiry, nothing more. Still, it had to be a missing persons enquiry with some serious intent at the back of it. Why else would someone have gone out of their way to blow away Gus Beard's legs? And why would the Voice be happy to fund his little Canarian adventure? And there was always the matter of the missing three million to consider. Serious enough for anyone.

None of that dangerous stuff had anything to do with him, though. At least, he hoped to God it didn't. But it was now evident that Davidson was taking Jack's involvement very seriously indeed. He kept quiet. He would let the man say whatever it was he'd called him to say.

"I can see this is difficult for you, Jacky boy. So why don't I help you out? Are you brave enough to drive up here and have a chat? Don't worry. I'm not intending to harm you. Quite the contrary. I've had ample opportunity to inflict lasting damage on you before now, had I wanted to. Come up and have a beer. If you're brave enough. Are you? Brave enough? Must be a bit of a bore sitting there in that little tin can all day."

The call disconnected. Now what? It was bad enough that Davidson could see he was tailing him. But how had he discovered who he was? How had he got his number? He took five minutes and considered his options. They seemed limited. Why not go for broke?

A short time after that, he stood at Davidson's front door. It was open, so he strode inside without knocking and found himself in a gloomy hallway with a door on either side. The one on the right was open. He went through it into an even gloomier lounge. A long room, with small, barred windows looking out onto a rock-strewn cactus garden at the rear. It was bright outside, but not here in the lounge. His eyes adjusted slowly. He noticed artwork on the walls, brown wooden furniture here and there, a large sofa, two couches and a few armchairs. A sizeable room.

As his eyes grew more used to the dim light, he made out a figure sitting on a couch against the far wall. Davidson.

He was holding a glass of something. No weapon. No one else in the room. He relaxed a little.

Davidson remained seated and stared across at his visitor. He stood stock-still, staring back.

"Well, let's not get off on the wrong foot, eh?" said his host, getting up. "Grab yourself an armchair, and I'll find you a drink. Beer all right? Or would you prefer something stronger?"

"A beer will be fine, thanks," he said, as Davidson ambled off to wherever he kept the drinks. When he came back, Jack was studying one of the paintings hanging on the wall.

"This one's signed 'Davidson'. I take it I have the pleasure of addressing the artist himself?"

"They're all signed 'Davidson', and we'll have to see whether it's a pleasure or not, won't we? But yes, guilty as charged. The artwork's mine. Why not sit down? We can talk and see if we can't work this thing out to our mutual advantage."

Davidson handed him a can of lager and a glass before sitting down. Jack settled into an armchair against the opposite wall.

"All the best," said Davidson, raising his glass but not taking a drink. "We appear to have a problem, don't we?"

"Doesn't seem as though I have much of a problem at the minute. Can't speak for you though, can I? Why not tell me what's bothering you, Mr Davidson?"

He was at a disadvantage on Davidson's territory and sounded more confident than he felt. The man would be well aware of what all this was about. He wasn't.

Fucking Voice. Keeping me in the dark. No cards to play now. Bastard.

"Please call me Freddy, and I'll call you Jack. Okay?"

"Okay with me. I'd be interested to know how you found out who I am, though. If that isn't asking too much?"

"Not at all. I'm happy to tell you. It was simple enough. Once I'd cottoned that you were tailing me, which was the hard part since you're so well practised, I turned the thing around and followed you to your hotel. You saw me, that is, you saw us both."

Davidson was staring at him intently now, through the gloom, studying his expression.

"I followed you in after you got into the lift and read the display to see where it stopped. Floor six. No other floors. That made it easy to guess your name from the guest list in the dining room. There were only two entries for the sixth floor. And since you aren't likely to be using the name of 'Frau Fischer', I opted for 'Charnley'. Easy really."

"Clever of you."

"And you were behaving like I imagined a professional tail might behave. So I thought there could be a fair chance that you were a private investigator of some sort. And your lack of a suntan marks you out as a visitor to the islands rather than a resident."

"Not had much time for sunbathing so far. With any luck, I'll fit some in before I have to leave."

"All it took then was a quick web search for an investigator from Merseyside. I had to guess you'd be local to my old home turf. Only one PI called Charnley showed up in the Liverpool area. So I looked at your web page and got your phone number from that. Easy, see? Nothing sinister. Nothing you need worry about."

"Right. Hadn't realised I'd become so careless. Old age, d'you think?"

"Now that we've cleared that up," said Davidson, "perhaps we should press on. First of all, let me assure you that we're effectively alone here. The housekeeper and my driver are both on the premises at the moment, but they'll be well out of earshot. And they aren't fluent English speakers. You can speak freely."

"Glad to hear it. So what's your problem?"

"You, Jack Charnley. You are my problem."

"How so?"

"You're spying on me. Like I said. You've been following me. That should bother anyone, don't you think?"

"Could be. I can see how it might make some people feel awkward."

"So can you tell me why? I assume you aren't doing this entirely for your own amusement. Or as some sort of hobby. So who's paying you? And why?"

"I'm not sure who's paying me, Freddy. And I wouldn't tell you, even if I knew. But I don't. As for why? I'm sure you must know why, even if I don't. But, to save time, let me make it clear that I'm here looking for Hamish Beard and possibly two others. And I have reason to believe you can tell me where Hamish is."

"And why would I want to tell you anything? Even supposing that I knew what you were talking about."

"Tell me where I can find him and I won't need to follow you any more. Simple."

Davidson did not answer at once. Jack could see that he was examining him, wondering just how much it would be safe for him to say and trying to decide what kind of man he was dealing with. He sipped his lager and tried to look at himself through Davidson's eyes.

He would see a man on the shortish side, stocky, possibly well muscled at some point, but now with the muscle turning to flab. His face having the puffy features that often characterise the faces of heavy drinkers. For all that, the eyes, set beneath a tangled mass of dark, even if now greying, curly hair, would seem clear and his glance penetrating. He would sense an air of dogged determination. This, at least, was how he saw himself.

He would also see someone way down the pecking order. Someone kept in the dark, following orders, and paid little enough for his efforts. Someone, in the usual run of things, of no consequence. But someone, right now, who was an inconvenient and even dangerous pest. Someone who needed to be dealt with.

Davidson took a long, thoughtful sip of his lager before speaking.

"Let's assume that you're right and that I'm aware of this Hamish's whereabouts. I might consider it to be to my advantage to keep that information to myself. I've no doubt that, before much longer, you'll get bored with your spying. I'm not all that interesting these days, as I'm sure you'll have noticed. And whoever is paying you will tire of doing that when you continue to fail to come up with anything. And I'll make sure you continue to fail."

"You could try."

"But then again, Jack, I might have no idea what the hell you're talking about. In which case you're wasting your time and your client's cash."

He took a few seconds to frame his reply.

"What can I say, Freddy? You're obviously aware of who I am and what I do. And as long as I get paid, I'll keep on doing my job. I like it over here. It's warmer and sunnier than it is back home. And the booze is cheaper. And I'm on expenses."

"That's nice."

Was the man smirking? He couldn't quite make out Davidson's expression. He went on.

"I'm sure that once I report this little meeting, my client will be even more certain that we're onto something. He could keep me here for months. Or lose patience and send someone with a more hands-on approach to deal with you. However it goes, I'm fine."

Davidson sat back and put down his glass on a small side table. Then he pulled a handgun from his pocket and kept it in his hand, resting it on his lap. Jack was shocked. This wasn't his usual territory. He was way out of his depth.

What the fuck's going on?

"A gun, Freddy? An actual fucking gun? Jesus. And I thought we'd been getting on so well," he said, trying hard to hide his nervousness.

"And if I decide it's better to kill you?"

"You told me you intended me no harm. Or am I misremembering our conversation?"

"I'm simply making it clear to you how things stand."

Davidson was definitely smirking now. Despite the gloom of the finca, he was sure of it.

Christ! No time to lose your cool. Show the bastard you aren't about to mess your pants.

"I doubt you'll risk firing that thing while your staff are in the house," he said, sounding a lot more certain than he felt. "And even if you did kill me, that would leave you with the problem of a body to dispose of. I don't think the soil up here can be all that deep. What with the lava field your property is sitting on. Hardly deep enough for a decent burial."

Davidson said nothing. He just sat there, waiting.

"And if I suddenly disappeared? Wouldn't that only make my client even more suspicious?"

"Or how about I buy you off?" asked Davidson, grinning openly now. Confident he had the upper hand. "How about that? And I'm not talking about peanuts either. There's real money involved in this. So tell me. What would it take?"

He stayed silent for some time, giving serious consideration to the question. Given what Davidson had just suggested, he doubted that he intended to shoot him. He got abruptly to his feet, drained the remains of his beer and started toward the door.

"Well?" Davidson persisted. "Tell me what!"

"I'll let you know," he said, tossing his empty glass onto an armchair as he left.

He took the rest of the day off and drove back to the Rosario hotel. Davidson's suggestion had made an impact. Suspects had offered him bribes before, and he'd sometimes, albeit rarely, taken them. But they had been relatively small scale and in situations unlikely to damage his business or his health if something had gone wrong. This time might turn out to be very different.

In this case, even though he had no idea who they were, he had to assume that he was working for dangerous people. So, following up on Freddy's suggestion would entail a high degree of risk. But serious risk often meant serious money, and maybe he'd find a chance here to bail out of a career that was taking him nowhere.

He parked up the hire car and headed back along the footpath to his hotel.

His phone rang. Tooth.

"Alan, I'm working. I told you. Is it something important?"

"It's the cat."

"The cat?"

"In the shed."

"Okay. It's the cat then."

No response.

"And?"

"There's kittens. Five of them. She's got them in an old jacket of yours. On top of a case of whisky."

"Ah. What kind?"

"Just moggies, I think. Not pedigree. Maybe a bit of Persian in there."

"The whisky, Alan. I knew I had a box of single malt somewhere. How the hell it's got into the shed, God knows."

"Says something about Highland and single malt on the side. I'd have to move your jacket and I don't want to disturb the kittens."

Back in his room, he stretched out on the bed and tried his best to think things through. No point now in continuing to spy on Davidson. The man had actually managed to learn his name. It was humiliating.

And why, in any event, was he doing this? To achieve what, exactly? It wasn't as though the financial rewards for his line of work were anything to write home about.

Taking a longer view, he had to recognise that he didn't always have a case to work on. Even calling the jobs he got 'cases' was a joke. He only did it to try to lend a little dignity to his occupation. To distance it from the unsavoury reality. But all it boiled down to, in the end, was sneaking about, spying on people. Adulterers mainly.

And then there was the pilfering from commercial premises where he would wear a set of overalls and pretend to be a relief storeman or some such, so he could shop some employee sidelining electronics or baby clothes. Someone had to do it, he supposed. And there were always bills to pay. How he'd managed it was a mystery, but after all these years he seemed to be more in debt than ever. Losing the house had begun to loom as a distinct possibility, but he knew that ending the care home fees, post Beat, would help to balance things up a little more in his favour.

But then, it could be worse still when he didn't have any work in hand. Idling his time away, waiting for something to turn up, while he eked out whatever pitiful float he might have scrimped together during the better times. He drank more then.

Had there been anyone close enough to care, they would probably have labelled his drinking as a problem. But to him it seemed more like salvation. Blotting things out. Smoothing them over. Stopping him feeling what he didn't want to feel. A failure.

And now this latest humiliation, with Freddy Davidson offering to buy him off. He'd not mentioned an amount, but was it likely to be as much as he really needed? On the few occasions suspects had bought him off in the past, he'd been surprised at how little it had taken to do it. Surprised to find out how very cheap he'd proved to be.

He could sense himself getting wound up. If he didn't watch it, he'd find the depression settling back in before long. A drink would calm him down and help him think this thing through. He got up off the bed and made his way down through the hotel to the bar, where he decided that the youngster currently serving the drinks there was far from his idea of what a proper barman should be. Squinting earnestly at Jack's desperately mangled and misremembered Spanish, he was having some difficulty in understanding the concept of a single malt.

Okay. So forget the malt. 'Una copa grande de vino tinto' was a phrase he now had off by heart. He'd pieced it together from the Helpful Phrases section in his guide book while sitting at his table in Star City watching Fran's terrace.

But the wine was good. So good that he forgot about the whisky and had several more glasses.

Early the next morning he was jolted into wakefulness by a loud snort, rounding off a surprisingly undisturbing episode of heavy snoring. He lay still for long seconds and stared at the ceiling, struggling to piece together the memory of his trip down to the hotel bar the previous afternoon. But, beyond the first couple of drinks, his memory remained a complete blank.

He checked for his wallet. Still there. His phone sat on the bedside cabinet. He looked across at the door to his room. Closed. Everything seemed okay and appeared normal, except that he was fully dressed and challenged by a raging thirst.

So, not too bad on the whole.

He grabbed the bottle of water he'd had the foresight to leave on his dressing table and drank it all. His thirst remained, undefeated.

After his shower, he eased himself into a comfortable chair by the window and gazed out at the bright emerald green of the ocean, glinting in the bay. Two small wooden rowing boats, one red, the other blue, rested at anchor.

Try to think.

He carefully cleared away the fog from inside his head, exposing the idea he had brought back from his chat with Freddy Davidson. The idea that the man was willing to bribe him to leave him alone.

He worked on the idea for a while and fashioned it into a better one. One which should appeal to Davidson. One which might help ensure that his bribe amounted to something worthwhile.

Feeling hopeful, he wandered down into the bar area and got himself a breakfast of scrambled egg, toast and coffee. He bypassed the fruit juice and the muesli. Despite his thirst, which he couldn't seem to rid himself of, he felt fine.

He phoned Davidson.

"Yes?"

"Been thinking about your offer."

"Maybe it's me, but I wasn't aware I'd made you an offer."

"Your suggestion, then. Whatever you want to call it."

"I'm assuming you're referring to my suggestion about some kind of financial inducement for you to lay off?"

"That sort of thing, yes. Can we talk about it?"

That afternoon he drove back up to the finca.

As he sat, once again, in the cooling gloom of the old house, enjoying a single ice-cold lager, he outlined his idea.

"If you simply pay me to go away, you might only be making your problem worse. If my client is still interested enough, he could well send someone else to replace me. Suppose he lost patience with the whole exercise and sent someone with a less peaceful nature to find a more direct route to the truth. You'd be dealing with an even more difficult situation."

His mouth was dry. He paused for a gulp of lager before he continued. Davidson sat and waited.

"You've explained how you cottoned on to me, but you might not be so lucky with the next guy. Maybe I got careless. Maybe he won't. But you'll never be sure of anything. You'll never be able to relax. What you need is peace of mind in the longer term. Some assurance that my client will forget about you for good."

"And this would be the deal you are about to sell me?"

"It would."

He described his idea to Davidson, who listened patiently and said nothing. When he'd finished, he said, "I'll leave you to consider that then, shall I? It's simple enough. But it should help us both. You can let me know what you think. Make it worth my while."

8

The Deal

He spent the following day back in Rosario, mooching around the neighbourhood. He was trying to imagine himself living in such a place, taking his ease. But he couldn't quite see it. Somehow it didn't feel like him. Low-key. That summed it up. Very nice but, on the whole, low-key. And this was the island's capital. It wasn't as if he could simply get a train into Liverpool like he could at home when life out on the Point was boring him beyond endurance.

In the afternoon, the moment he went out onto the sunlit street, ready to explore some more, he got a call from Freddy Davidson. He wanted to meet him in a villa over on Lanzarote early that evening.

*

The villa was easy enough to find, and he reached it earlier than he needed. It was a little way up from the beach, in a newish-looking development of similar properties in a place called Honda. It was a short distance along the coast from Arrecife and the Diamante.

Leaving the hatchback parked some blocks away from Davidson's Mercedes, he walked back to the villa. He didn't walk up to the front gate. He'd spotted a narrow walkway between the villa and the adjacent property. Weeds covered the path, which was shaded by leafy plant life from the gardens on each side. It didn't look well used, and it was easy to remain out of view while he tiptoed up to the garden wall.

From there he could hear two male voices coming from what he imagined might be the patio area. One of them was Freddy's.

Freddy was talking.

"... so at least one of your dad's old money-laundering clients was left hanging. And they'll be making efforts to recover their cash. They'll have checked out Stella and your uncle Gus already. It's likely they've drawn a blank, since they're still searching. Your disappearance will have made them suspicious about you."

"Hence this Charnley guy. Right."

Hamish!

"I'd hoped we were in the clear. But this is bad, isn't it?"

"You could put it like that."

"What do we do, Freddy? Pay Charnley off? Kill him? How much does he want?"

"Killing him would risk drawing even more attention to ourselves. It's not my thing, anyway. I don't do killing people."

"So?"

"We'd be lucky to spot the next guy they send after you. They seem determined to get their money back, and they most likely see you as a route to doing that."

"Okay. So how do we handle Charnley?"

"How about this? Charnley needs enough cash to be able to give up his current crappy lifestyle, pay off whatever debts I'm sure he has hanging over him, and fund a fresh start. That's his pitch, and he's waiting for us to make him an offer he can't refuse."

"And he gets these guys off our backs?"

"As best as he can. It's a risk for him if it goes wrong, but that's what he's offered."

"And you think we should go with it?"

"Kind of. We can improve the deal. For us and for him."

His heart skipped a beat. Was he hearing this right? They were going to offer him even more than he was expecting? He had to force himself to stay quiet. He felt more like climbing over the wall and shouting, 'I'll take it! Give it to me now!'

But he didn't. He hadn't missed the part where they'd raised the possibility of killing him instead.

"How about we don't pay him off? We cut him in. We put him on the team. Make him work for what he gets."

"And we can trust him?"

"We can trust his neediness. Charnley isn't partnered with anyone else. He's just low-paid hired help, doing the legwork for the big guys. He's a nobody, going nowhere. And skint, if I'm any judge. Or why else would he be doing this?"

"And you reckon we can turn him?"

"Should be easy. He's already told me he's willing to do what he can to help, if we pay him enough. And we're in a race for the missing money. We could use some assistance. I say we offer Charnley an equal share. Buy his loyalty."

"An equal share of three mill is a lot to give someone we don't even know that much about."

"We don't have three million, Hamish. We have a shot at three million. It's not the same thing. It's risky, and it's a long shot. Anyone who gets on board at this stage deserves an equal split."

"I see your point."

"And the three million, if we can get our hands on it, is just a start. Venture capital if you like. We'll make much more over time from restarting your dad's money-laundering operation. There's a gap in the market right now. Has been ever since your dad checked out. It'll be shrinking fast and we need to fill that gap while there still is one."

"So why don't we go through Charnley to whoever it is he's working for? Offer to work with them."

"Because these people will be big time. Most likely into drugs. Maybe worse. I don't know about you, but I'm not too confident about coming out in front of people like that."

"You think they might not treat us nicely?"

"Now you're getting it. Reality. I've tried dealing with types like that before. There's no respect. They killed my son, Jimmy."

Jack, listening from the alleyway, heard nothing but birdsong for long seconds until Hamish spoke again.

"Okay, Freddy. Didn't know about Jimmy. And you've done good by me so far. Let's try it your way. You sure Charnley's coming?"

"He should be here soon. Anytime now."

He had heard enough. He crept back down the little walkway and strolled around to the front entrance. He pressed the buzzer. He felt great. A chance at a whole new future. Who'd have thought it?

A voice came through the speaker. A voice he could now recognise as belonging to Hamish Beard. "Mr Charnley?"

He grunted in the affirmative, and the heavy wooden gate swung back.

He walked in and on through a well-stocked garden as the gate closed automatically behind him. He saw what he took to be semi-tropical plants, a little lawn and then two steps up onto a tiled terrace under an awning where a small dog growled at him before padding off to attend to more important matters inside the villa. Keith, he supposed. He looked a lot like the Yorkie he'd seen with Fran Rimmer.

Freddy Davidson and another man he recognised as his quarry, Hamish Beard, were sitting at a table. There were green bottles of beer in an ice-bucket and a spare glass in front of an empty chair.

"Hello again, Jack," Davidson began. "Sit yourself down and grab a lager. Here's the man you've been looking for. This is Hamish Beard," he said, waving his glass towards his table companion.

"Hi," said Jack, smiling. "Good to meet you at last."

"We've agreed on a proposition to put to you."

He sat down and poured himself a beer. "I'm all ears."

"I'll get right to the point," said Davidson. "We believe your client is looking for a lump of cash which has gone missing. It isn't the kind of cash you can tell the police about."

"How much?"

"Three million. Which, thanks to Hamish here, we have an excellent chance of getting hold of before anyone else does. It's a hell of a lot of dosh and time, as they say, is of the essence."

He said nothing in reply. He closed down his smile and sat there, listening impassively. He could do impassively. He could see that Freddy was trying to hide his surprise at his lack of response.

"I want to offer you an even better deal than the one we discussed. There's a downside, though."

"I'm not sure I'm in the market for a downside. How far down?"

"You get nothing up front."

"How better?"

"Join us and help us get hold of the cash and you get an equal share. Fair?"

"There's just the three of us?"

"That's right. I fund the operation. You and Hamish chase the money."

"Chase the money how, exactly?"

"We believe we know where it is. Hamish is working on a way to get to it. Nothing's finalised yet. We can fill you in on the details later, when things firm up a bit."

"When?"

"Soon. A day or two, maybe. At most."

Easy, Jack. Don't push your luck. Can't expect them to lay it all out on a plate at this point. Trust. Works both ways.

"And you do what you can to get whoever's paying your wages off our case," said Hamish.

"What d'you say?" asked Davidson, reaching across the table to offer Jack his hand. "We have a deal?"

"We do," he said, smiling again, as he grasped Davidson's hand. "Count me in."

"So now we need you to tell your client that the line of enquiry you've been following here in the Canaries is a dead end. As you yourself suggested to me when we last met. You tell them that you are as sure as you can be that the person they are looking for, Hamish, is probably deceased. And the Whites likewise. We need you to do this before you leave this villa."

Say nothing. Wait for the clincher.

"Do this, and provide us with whatever contact details you have for your client, and you're one of the team."

He knew this was dangerous. And he knew he'd be unlikely to get an opportunity like this again. He was going to do as they asked. He wanted the money. He wanted the freedom. He wanted to leave the villa alive.

"What I say is that I need some assurance that neither Hamish, nor the Whites, will give me serious problems by showing up on my clients' radar after I've told my contact that they're most likely kaput."

"Percy White's dead," said Hamish at once. "Gone."

"Are you sure?"

"Positive. I saw the body at the Warehouse. Gus has long since disposed of it. And as for Lawrence, I can't be certain, but I'm pretty sure he's a goner too. He fell into the Albert Dock on a dark night last winter. I was there, and I never saw him come out. Most likely he's somewhere in the middle of the Irish Sea by now."

"What happened? Were you quarrelling over the money?"

"Nothing to do with money. Both deaths were accidental, hard as you might find that to believe, and long before anyone knew anything about any missing millions."

"Well, that's some more information I can give to my client, at least. Two names to cross off the list. But that still leaves you, Hamish."

"The best I can do," said Hamish, "by way of reassurance, is to point out that it's as much in my interest as yours for me to stay out of sight. Your clients, whoever they are, are pretty scary people."

He paused.

"Sound reasonable?"

"I suppose. But why do you need contact details for my client?"

"It's not much," said Freddy. "But it's some sort of insurance. It's so we can shop you if you do the dirty on us." He looked at Jack as if waiting for a response. "You're okay with that?"

He let his face break into a wide grin. "Yes, Freddy. I'm okay with it."

"I can't tell you how glad I am to hear you say that. Having to kill you would have put a definite crimp in my day. Trust me. So... those details?"

"All I have is a phone number," he said. "Nothing else. Not even a name. If you ever phone that number, you could put my well-being seriously at risk. The client will suspect I snitched."

"That's just it, Jack. We need a way of making sure you stick to our deal. And we aren't likely to make that call if you don't give us good reason, are we?"

He took out a small notepad and a pen and wrote down the Voice's number. He tore out the page and handed it to Freddy.

"That's it. That's all I have."

"And how can we be sure this is genuine? Could be one of your mates for all we know."

"You can't. And I can't prove it's who I say. If it helps, I don't have any mates. That do?"

"I suppose it'll have to," said Freddy. "But you'll need to speak to whoever gives you your instructions and do your level best to get us all off the hook. Give me your phone. I'm going to call the number you gave me and pass it back to you. Is it a good time to do this?"

"Good a time as any. Usually I get an answer right away. Sometimes my contact calls back. Never takes too long though."

He unlocked his phone, brought up the Voice's number and handed it to Davidson, who checked the number against the one that Jack had written down for him. He put in the call.

"It's ringing," he said, handing back the phone. "Make sure we can hear what's being said."

The Voice answered within a few seconds.

"Yeah? Do you have something for me?"

"It's a bit mixed, I'm afraid. The word on the Percy White character is that someone bumped him off in Liverpool months ago. Lawrence White is almost certainly dead, likewise. Drowned in the Mersey. All to do with some kind of upset at the Warehouse."

"Sad. And Hamish Beard himself?"

"Hard to be completely certain, but the trail over here turned out to lead nowhere. I have no other leads. For what it's worth, my gut instinct is that Hamish is dead too. I'm sure something would have shown up by now otherwise. The guy's disappeared."

"Okay then, Jack. I suppose that'll have to do for now. Text me an amount for what you've spent, and I'll put a final payment into your account today, less the five grand you've already stung us for. Then you'd better go back to doing whatever it is you do. If we need you again, I'll let you know. Hope you had a pleasant time over there at our expense."

At that, the connection went dead.

"That's it," he said. "All done."

9

Hamish

Jack felt good. He wanted to celebrate. He would prefer not to have to celebrate alone.

After a single glass of lager to seal the deal, Freddy dug his driver out of a cafe a couple of blocks away and rode off home to his finca.

Meanwhile, brandishing a whisky bottle, Hamish invited Jack to spend the night.

"It would be useful to get to know each other a bit better, right? Since we'll be working together."

He checked out the whisky.

"Sounds reasonable. So this is your villa?"

"Rented. I can afford it for the time being."

Hamish searched out some food from his fridge, and they sat down to talk while they ate.

"Tell me," asked Jack, as Hamish poured them each a drink, "how did you get from the Blue Warehouse to here? It's a bit of a jump."

"You're one of us now, so I suppose I don't mind talking about it. Where do you want me to start?"

"You choose."

"You heard about my dad, Claude? About how he died?"

"He fell into the cellar at the Warehouse, right? I read the story in the Echo."

"My uncle, Gus, set Dad up for that fall. He murdered his own brother."

Hamish's blunt assertion of his uncle's guilt took him by surprise. He did his best not to show it.

"And someone got to Gus, didn't they? Wasn't you, I don't suppose?"

"You might think that," said Hamish, grinning. "I couldn't possibly comment."

"But can you be sure the man killed your dad? Do you have evidence?"

"Nothing that would stand up in court. Not that kind of evidence. I just know what sort of person he is.

"And who benefited from Dad's death? Only Gus. He got to marry Stella, and he got complete control over the Firm. I guess it worried him that Dad wanted to bring me in to help him run the business."

"The nightclub?"

"Not the Warehouse. Stella's always run that."

"So Claude's thing was what then? Exactly?" he asked, draining his glass and pouring them both another drink. He made sure he poured much more for Hamish than himself.

"Dad had some money-laundering going on. On two levels. There was the street level. Infrequent. Very small-time. That was where he'd started off with Gus in the old days. They'd buy in cash from a few criminal operations around the North West and clean it. But that was only a tiny part of what they did. They had all kinds of things going to help keep them ticking over.

"Dad was always in charge, but he left Gus to run things day to day. Dad had got into a much bigger game. He'd started to tell me about it."

"But still money-laundering, right?"

"Yeah. But sizeable amounts. He used a banker guy in London, called Giuseppe. Giuseppe had connections in Naples and the cash sometimes went over there before going offshore. From there it can be moved around and come back looking clean, whenever it's needed."

"And your dad wanted you to get in on all this?"

"Right."

"And Gus wanted to take this over himself, I suppose?"

"No. I think what Gus wanted was Stella, the Warehouse, and the street. His level. Dad's thing was way beyond him. But he'd always been used to being Dad's number two and me being nothing. So, when he saw me getting clued up by Dad, I reckon he got worried he might be dumped as surplus to requirements."

"And how come you got connected up with Freddy and ended up over here? It's a long way from the Baltic."

Hamish stared down at his glass. Jack guessed he must be wondering how much more he should tell him. But Hamish was a drinker. And so was he. And they were bonding over the rapidly emptying bottle of malt as the daylight faded. Some people kept things to themselves forever. Others, he well understood, needed to confide in someone. They'd keep things inside for as long as they could bear to, and then out it came.

"Well, the thing is, I wasn't too level-headed back when all this business started. It's been a short learning curve, but steep, and I'm a different person now. After all that's happened."

"So you haven't always been an international criminal. What were you before you became one?"

"A kind of waster, I suppose. Aimless. I'd flunked out of uni through boozing way beyond the limit. I was doing odd jobs around the nightclub. On a road to nowhere. I think Dad aimed to change all that."

"I overdo the drinking myself, from time to time," he said, pleased to find Hamish so talkative. He seemed to want to trust him.

"So how bad was your drinking? Exactly?"

"Bad enough. Still can be. A bit of a pisshead, really. Freddy doesn't seem to drink much, so I'm glad to have a fellow boozer on the team."

104

It was starting to get dark, and he wanted to watch Hamish's expression while he poked about in his head. He got up and flicked on the light.

He sat back down and poured more whisky. Again, he gave Hamish a larger measure.

"So you're working at the Warehouse, and your dad begins to share the details of his money-laundering enterprise with you. Then he has his fall and you're convinced that Gus has murdered him. So you put the bomb under his bed. Right?"

"I might have. It was an old wartime grenade that Dad had kept hidden away in his office for some reason, along with a handgun, a semi-automatic. I took them both."

"The gun I can get my head around. But a grenade?"

"I've no idea why he had it or where it even came from. Probably from back when he and Gus had been carving out their territory.

"I wired up the grenade behind the headboard of Gus's bed, so it would pull the pin the next time the ugly bastard sat his fat backside down on it. Didn't go off at first, though. It took quite a while for that to come good."

"But what about your mum? What about Stella? You might have got her too."

"No way. She would never go into Gus's room. Never. He had porn and a handgun and all sorts of crap in there. He even had to clean the place himself. She wouldn't let the cleaner do it."

Hamish twiddled with his whisky glass on the tabletop before draining it and grabbing the bottle to pour himself another shot. Jack put his hand over his own glass.

"And just to be clear, Stella's my stepmother. I don't have much info about my birth mum. All Dad would ever say was that she left when I was little. I don't remember much about her.

"Stella and me have never been what you might call close. But we get on okay."

"So... Gus?"

"So what happened next was that Gus decided I had to go."

"Because you were onto him?"

"Because I scared the shit out of him. By then, I'm sure, I was going a bit loopy. What with the drink and brooding about Dad and everything. I missed Dad. He watched out for me. More than Stella ever has.

"And anyway, I killed Gus's right-hand man, Percy. He had to be worried after that."

Could he be hearing this right? A confession to a killing as a throwaway line over a drink? And they'd only just met. There was obviously a lot more to young Hamish than he'd imagined.

"You killed Percy White?"

"I did. I'm sorry for it. An accident."

Hamish looked serious now. Almost sad. Jack topped up his drink and pretended to top up his own.

"Why are you telling me all this? You only met me today. How can you be sure I'm going to keep all this to myself?"

"It's just, like, you get a sense of who it's safe to trust and who isn't. Least, I do. I'm right about you, aren't I?"

"You are, Hamish. You can trust me."

As if to underscore this, he allowed himself a big gulp from his glass.

Why ration myself? I need this.

"Right now, I have to talk to someone. I have to talk about what's going on inside my head sometimes. If I don't, the pressure just builds and I get anxious."

"You often anxious, then? Is that a big problem for you?"

106

"Can be. Sometimes. It's what tends to bother me more than anything. If you discount accidentally killing people, that is."

He looked carefully at his new drinking partner. He looked ordinary enough. Gangly, perhaps, for someone in his early twenties. But that would go soon, when he learned to relax and put on some weight. Greasy hair above a suntanned face. A tendency to grin too much. He'd seemed normal, but now he was beginning to realise that his new drinking companion wasn't normal at all.

"How did it happen? This accidental death."

"Well, after Gus killed Dad, I got hold of his old pistol, like I told you. I took the clip out, so I couldn't fire it accidentally. I screwed in the silencer for effect and I walked into Stella's sitting room with the thing in my hand."

"Jesus! What the hell was that about?"

"I thought, if she saw the gun, she'd have to take me seriously. I intended to make out that I was ready to shoot Gus. I'd tried to tell her what I thought about Gus before, and she wouldn't listen. Anyway, I told her how disgusted I was that she'd married Dad's murderer, and she was crying, and I was going on a bit..."

He stopped suddenly and just sat there, staring into space.

"Go on," Jack prompted. "What happened?"

Hamish cleared his throat and seemed to tune back into the conversation.

"I heard a noise from the study next door. I thought it was Gus, listening in. Keith was there with me, growling away at the door."

"And was it? Gus?"

"No. Percy. His number two. He walked out, looking all embarrassed. The idiot probably knocked something over on the desk in there. I think he must have heard everything. Anyway, he saw the gun and got frightened.

107

I was laughing at him. Percy had always seemed more of a wimp than a gangster to me."

"And you shot him?"

"I was only teasing the old fool. I thought the gun was empty, see? Anyway, I pointed the thing at him and pulled the trigger. As a joke. And it just went off. Bang."

"Good God."

"I'd removed the ammo in the clip, but it turned out there was a round already in the chamber, or whatever it's called. Percy crumpled up and fell onto the floor, bleeding from a hole in his chest. Dead."

"That's automatics for you. You won't make the same mistake next time."

Hamish didn't laugh. "Gus went ape-shit. Then he got all serious and got some guys he knows to deal with the body."

"How?"

"Easy enough. If you have the right connections, you can get your inconvenient body dropped off a ship en route to Dublin, all nicely weighted down. You never see it again. It costs two grand a go, apparently. A bargain."

"I can see how you might have got your uncle worried. He must have been wondering if he'd be next to go."

"Could be. He sent me off to New York with a couple of his thugs. Said it was a sort of business trip. We were supposed to be seeing someone called Tony, in Queens. He told me it would be educational for me to sit in on the discussion."

"So, Gus has a New York connection?"

"He'd spent some time over there on a mission for Claude a few years ago and had got to know this Tony character pretty well."

"Tony from Queens? Really?"

"I know. You couldn't make it up. But I was happy to go. I'd never been to the US before. We got a decent hotel near Central Station, and I had a few days to get a good look round all the sights and the museums. I was enjoying the trip until I overheard part of a phone call one of Gus's men was making to this Tony guy. I could see they were planning on going back home without me."

"So you got scared?"

"Very. Anyone would've, right? Obviously, my grenade hadn't removed Gus from the biosphere as I'd hoped and they were getting ready to take me out to Tony's place. So I legged it out of the hotel and got a cab to JFK before they realised what was happening."

"Close thing."

"I got a flight to Madrid."

"Because?"

"It was available, that's all. I hung out in a little hotel near the Retiro Park for a while and tried to work out what to do. I had my laptop and some files I'd copied from the office computer at the Warehouse."

"Interesting, were they?"

"All the details of Gus's operations were on there. Interesting enough. But the best stuff was the copies of Dad's private files. He'd disguised them as photo albums."

Hamish tuned out for long seconds. Jack could hear the cicadas, suddenly loud, coming in from the inky darkness of the villa garden.

Until he began again, "While I was there, I found out from Facebook that Percy's daughter, Lily, had taken an overdose. She died. That got to me. I'd always liked Lily."

"Why do you think she did that? Because of what had happened to her dad?"

"She didn't know about that. Not exactly. Only that her dad had vanished. Mr Routine. That was Percy. No way he'd go and take off without a word."

"So she'd have known something bad had happened?"

"She would have been able to tell from their behaviour, and from some of the things they were saying, that Stella and Gus didn't expect him to reappear.

"That would have unsettled her. Big time. She was like me, an anxious type. Depended a lot on her dad. Her brother Lawrence was away, and she had no one else. I'm sure she didn't mean to kill herself. The overdose would have been an accident."

"Easy to see how that would have disturbed you." He made an effort to sound sympathetic.

Hamish paused and took another drink.

"Then I remembered the Davidsons. I remembered how they'd once had a go at muscling in on Gus's territory and had got the worst of it. Davidson's son Jimmy disappeared not long after that. Although Gus always denied he'd had anything to do with it. Some Glaswegian gangsters had done for the guy, so he said."

"So you figured you'd use Davidson against Gus, right?"

"Exactly. I emailed Freddy and arranged to come out here to meet him.

"I met up with him at his finca in Oliva. I told him I was going to fix Gus and that I could give him lots of info about Gus's operations. And I could tell him all about Claude's money-laundering business. So I had quite a package of goodies to trade."

"And he was interested?"

"Very. I don't think Freddy has nearly as much stashed as he likes everyone to think. And he got well interested in what Dad had been up to."

"So you found yourself an ally."

"Saw it that way. I was vulnerable, and I needed to be sure I had back up and somewhere safe to go."

"So you've told me what happened to Percy White, but what about Lawrence? What happened to him?"

"I'll get to that," said Hamish, with a grin. "You might as well know everything now. You already know too much."

"My lips are sealed. No worries."

"I'm not worried. Like I said, I feel I can trust you. And, if not, I have other options."

"Options?"

"Some. I've made a note of the contact number you gave Freddy, for one thing. And there's always the possibility of another accident should it come to that."

"Are you threatening me, Hamish? I hoped we were going to be friends."

"Of course we are. A joke, right?"

Another silence. An awkward one this time. Before Hamish spoke again.

"I wanted Gus dead. I was sure he'd killed Dad. But killing Gus would put me in line for attention from the police. And from any of his associates who might feel that I'd made things difficult for them."

Jack smiled across the table at his drinking partner.

Best keep this friendly.

"Freddy agreed to help me get away to somewhere safe once I'd sorted Gus. So when I went home, I flew into Manchester, so I could make out I'd just got back from New York. Like I'd simply been hanging out there, doing my own thing. I didn't want Gus to know for sure that I knew he was trying to have me bumped off."

"Right. I get that."

"Lawrence White had got himself back home by then, and Gus sent him out to the airport to collect me in the Lexus. One of Gus's thugs was driving. Frankie."

"Didn't that worry you. You'd shot Lawrence's dad."

111

"It worried me a lot. I knew right away it must be Gus's next attempt to have me killed. So, on the way up the M56, we had a tense little chat about me shooting Percy and about Lily's overdose. He wasn't going to let bygones be bygones. I mean, who would? But I realised he still had to act like he was simply intending to take me to see Gus, up until he managed to get me into position."

"Tricky."

"Anyway, we made it back down the Sixty-Two into town and he suggested that we go out to the Albert Dock for a full English. So we could talk things through."

"Didn't that seem strange? Given the situation?"

"Obviously part of some klutzy plan he and Gus had cooked up. But I reckoned I'd best play along until I found a safe way out."

"So you didn't get to the Warehouse?"

"No. Frankie dropped us at the dock to find something to eat. It was already afternoon. We ate a meal and knocked back a few drinks while I tried to figure out how to lose Lawrence."

"So you got ratted?" He poured Hamish another whisky.

"Somewhat. He would have wanted me pissed, to make me easier to handle. But I spiked Lawrence's drink every time I went to the bar."

"Eventually, he got up to leave. He said I needed to go with him. Go to the Warehouse to speak to Gus. I didn't believe that. I felt pretty sure he was aiming to get me somewhere where he could deal with me. Finish me, probably. Most likely he'd have Frankie waiting to help."

"Wasn't Lawrence getting drunk himself?"

"He was no kind of drinker. Didn't even sus that I'd been spiking his beers. He could hardly walk."

"So you managed to make a break for it?"

"No, I didn't want him coming after me again. It was late afternoon by then and it was winter, so it was dark. I wanted to surprise him and push him into the dock."

"You're not about to tell me you killed him too?"

"Sort of. Ironic, I suppose, but it turned into another accident. I struggled to shove him off the walkway, and we had a kind of drunken tussle. We both fell over the side. The water was freezing. But I was lucky. There was a type of ladder of iron staples up the dockside. I climbed out and walked into town. Still had my wallet, so I called into John Lewis en route and bought fresh clothes. I changed in the fitting room and dumped my wet stuff."

Jack could hear a car being driven slowly along the road by the villa before accelerating away into the night. And then the sound of the cicadas came flooding back.

"I checked into the Marriott and slept until morning."

"And Lawrence?"

"I don't think he got out. At least, no one seems to have seen him since. Must've drifted out of the dock and down the Mersey. Most likely he joined his dad out in the Irish Sea. To be clear, I didn't intend to kill the guy. Just wanted to warn him off."

He had no difficulty believing Hamish's story. It all fitted. And why tell him all this if it wasn't true?

"The next morning, I was up late, aching and hungover, but otherwise okay. So I set off for the Warehouse to sort Gus. Like I'd told Freddy I would. I thought I'd get a knife from the kitchen and stab him in the neck."

"No one spotted you?"

"No one. But it was close. I'd got all the way along Jamaica Street, turning the corner to the Warehouse, and I had to dodge behind a phone box to avoid Stella seeing me. She was coming out of the front door with

Frankie, making for the Lexus. Probably going shopping in town."

"She didn't see you?"

"No one did. So I lurked behind the phone box, waiting for her to go.

"Then we got the explosion. I saw the pieces of glass from Gus's bedroom window, along with something that might well have been one of Stella's cats, fly out across the yard and down onto the concrete. There was silence for ages and then some shouting before the alarm system kicked in.

"I saw Stella and Frankie running back inside. I turned around and walked off the way I'd come."

"What are the odds?"

"Odds?"

"Of you being stood outside when the grenade exploded."

"A simple coincidence, I guess. But you're right. What are the odds?"

"So, from any objective viewpoint, things were stacking up. Your dad was dead, Percy and Lawrence were missing, Lily White had overdosed and now the explosion under Gus's bed."

Hamish looked across at him. He was biting his bottom lip. He sighed.

"I'm assuming the grenade must've fallen out from behind the headboard and rolled along the floor beneath the bed. Seeing as how it was Gus's legs that got it. Unless he'd been lying there with his legs up against the wall. Which is something I don't even want to think about."

"Must have," said Hamish.

"So now the police would have been all over things, big style. And once Frankie told them you were back, they'd need to question you as part of the enquiry. So what did you do?"

"Freddy fixed it so all I had to do was phone a number he'd given me, and tell the guy at the other end the job was done. Next thing, I'm below decks on a ship getting ready to sail out of Liverpool, holding a false passport and brushing up on my Spanish."

"I take it we're not talking about a cruise liner."

"An old cargo freighter called the Speeding Star. It had a deadweight of around forty-five thousand tons. I looked that up online. The crew seemed to be eastern Mediterranean types, but I didn't recognise the flag. They gave me a small inside cabin to myself.

"I ate all my meals in there. A young boy with dark, unhappy eyes and an apron brought them. He spoke hardly any English. Just enough to make it clear that he'd be pleased to sleep with me for twenty euros."

"Cheap rate, then. Any good?"

He was disappointed when Hamish ignored his jibe.

"Interesting voyage?"

"Not so's you'd notice. I tried talking to the crew, but they had as little English as the cabin boy. Either that, or they'd been told not to talk to me. The captain and the other officers ignored me or just waved me away."

"Did you feel safe?"

"Not entirely. I had the idea that, once we were out at sea, they might drop me overboard to be rid of me. I tried not to worry about that too much."

The whisky was beginning to affect Jack now. It had been a full bottle, and the level was getting low. He leaned back in his chair and put his hands behind his head. It'd be okay, so long as he didn't drink too quickly. He'd given Hamish the lion's share, and he was sure they'd soon be opening a second bottle. He'd seen two more on the dresser. And there was wine.

Easy does it. Let the boy talk. It's all good background stuff.

"When we headed out of the Mersey and onto the Irish Sea, I had no idea of our route. We spent that first night at Dublin. After that we sailed south and it got warmer, like it does. We called at Lisbon and Malta and then trundled on down the African coast to Cape Town."

"You obviously managed to stay clear of the pirates."

"I think we must have stayed well out to sea through the dangerous stretches. Not that the Speeding Star would have been a tempting target.

"By then, no one cared if I went up on deck, so I got myself quite a tan.

"It took weeks to get to Las Palmas. The poor old Star wasn't really all that speedy. We probably averaged around ten knots, at a rough guess."

"Las Palmas?"

"In Gran Canaria. I got the ferry from there to Rosario."

"So I imagine by this point you'd have been wondering what your new friend, Davidson, was expecting you to deliver in terms of your dad's money-laundering business?"

"Exactly. I had to admit to myself that I might have raised Freddy's expectations a bit higher than I should've."

"You wouldn't be able to hand over a fully fledged, big-time money-laundering operation?"

"Something like that. I understood the outline of how the thing worked, but not much of the detail."

"But you'd got copies of your old man's files, right?"

"Yeah. Like I said, I had Dad's files copied onto my laptop. But nothing immediately useful. He kept a lot of his stuff in code."

Jack reached for the bottle. He'd been good. He'd paced himself. He was due for a big one.

The bottle was empty. He looked over at the dresser. It might be hard to concentrate now, without another drink.

"I wondered if I should make a run for it. But I was already running from what I'd done back in Liverpool. And if I ran from Davidson as well, then where would I stop? And, in the end, what would I do? The few thousands I still had access to would be spent quick enough."

Jack got up and edged toward the dresser. "Do you mind if I...?"

He gestured vaguely at the whisky.

Hamish grunted and nodded. He pushed his own glass across to Jack, who was already holding the bottle gratefully and unscrewing the cap.

"Didn't you have a Plan B? Everyone should have a Plan B."

He poured them each a generous measure and sat down again. The new bottle stood ready at his elbow.

"So? No Plan B?" he repeated.

"No Plan B. Plan B was decidedly missing."

"And so?"

"So I thought maybe it was best to continue as intended and see how things worked out with Freddy."

"And, by this time," said Jack, "back at the ranch, the police must have been heavily involved. They'd want to find out why Lily White died. Where Percy and Lawrence had gone. Where you'd got to. Who blew Gus off his mattress? And even whether Claude's death had really been an accident, after all. All that."

"So they did. But I knew they wouldn't get anywhere. They'd nothing to go on, apart from whatever Stella told them. And I knew she wouldn't say much. She'd just want it all to disappear. And she'd had years of experience of keeping her mouth shut."

"It seems to be working out like that," said Jack. "As far as I can tell, the police have had to leave things hanging. And the odds are they don't even know where you are."

10

Plan B

The following morning, waking up on the couch in Hamish's villa, he didn't feel too bad. They'd only drunk a small amount from the second bottle, and he'd made sure he'd had much less than Hamish. He knew it would be more polite to wait for Hamish to show himself and invite him to eat, but he was hungry. He went through to the kitchen to make coffee and fried himself some eggs to have with half of a stale baguette he'd found in a cupboard.

He finished eating and rinsed the breakfast things. There was still no sign of Hamish, so he sat out on the terrace on a small bench where Keith was dozing and sipped his coffee while he reflected on what he'd learned from his host the day before.

When Hamish had stepped off the ferry from Las Palmas, at the Goat Port in Fuerteventura, Davidson's driver, Miguel, had collected him and taken him to the finca on the volcanic slopes above La Oliva.

Davidson had told him that even though he hadn't succeeded in killing Gus, he'd done enough to put him out of action for the foreseeable future. And he made it clear that Junior Davidson had now got his hands on a valuable slice of the Firm's business.

Freddy had assured him that he'd already had Keith flown over from Liverpool to a secure berth in Arrecife.

He had kept his end of the deal to the letter.

In contrast, Hamish had had to admit to Freddy Davidson that his expertise and grasp of detail regarding Claude's money-laundering activities had serious gaps.

The morning sun slanted into the garden and across the terrace, causing Keith to stretch and move farther along the bench into the shade. He went back into the kitchen and got himself a second coffee.

So, he reasoned, Freddy must have been disappointed to find that his newfound accomplice hadn't turned out to be quite the expert money launderer he'd been hoping for.

But it was obvious, wasn't it, that something had turned out well? Or they wouldn't be in a position to offer him an equal share in the three million. What on earth were they going to expect him to do to earn it?

He was toying with these thoughts and trying to resist making himself a third coffee when Keith leapt down from the bench and ran off, barking, towards Hamish, coming out to join them.

He examined his host for signs of damage. A little frayed around the edges, perhaps. Not too bad, though, considering.

"I was about to call the undertaker. Thought you might have died in the night."

"Not at all, Jack. As you can see, I'm fully functional. Ready for anything. Although I have to admit that I'm not feeling too sharp right now. Did we overdo the whisky?"

"We did a bottle and then some, between us. That's all. But you did drink a wee bit more than me."

"Not that much then, really. Not in the great scheme of things. Coffee? All I'm having."

"Had two already. But as it's you, I'll risk another."

They drank the coffee and made small talk as Hamish saw to Keith's breakfast. The dog soon finished his biscuits and then sat watching Hamish intently as he took the coffee cups over to the sink. As soon as Hamish put the crockery down on the drainer, Keith began to bark and to paw at his legs.

"Time to walk Keith. Want to join us?"

"Love to," said Jack. "Which way are we going?"

"Along the beachfront. There's a wide walkway that goes all the way into Arrecife. It's quite a stretch there and back, and it'll help to wake us up."

They were heading into the sun and, even with baseball caps pulled down low over their eyes, they needed sunglasses.

He felt great. Relaxed. Strolling by the ocean on a holiday island. A new drinking buddy. Someone who was still young enough to be optimistic. Even better, he was feeling richer. A million pounds richer. Okay, so they hadn't actually got their hands on the money as yet, but he felt confident that he'd turned a corner and that life was, for once, going his way.

It would be his chance to make good, at last. It deserved his best shot.

"So, yesterday, before the whisky got to you. I was hoping you were about to explain how you plan to get hold of three million pounds worth of dodgy cash?"

"Yeah," said Hamish, grinning. "Like I already told you, it was soon obvious to Freddy that I wasn't quite the money-laundering expert he might have thought."

"Could have led to some noticeable tension, I suppose."

"Could have. But it didn't. He just asked me to describe the ins and outs of Dad's operation to him, so far as I understood it."

"And you did, of course."

"As well as I was able to."

"So why not explain it to me in the same way? Me being part of the gang now and all."

There was a brief halt on the hot pavement while Keith did his thing. "Glad to see you're so well prepared," he said, as Hamish got to work with a plastic bag and a bottle of water.

"Not like back home," said Hamish, tying off the bag. "Over here they expect that you don't only pick up, they want you to rinse off the paving too. In the tourist areas, anyway. I like that. I like things to be clean."

"Me too," agreed Jack, as a sudden flash of memory recalled the stack of washing-up waiting in the sink back at the semi.

They started off again, toward Arrecife, Hamish swinging the plastic bag at his side as they walked.

"So, the money-laundering?"

"Okay," said Hamish. "Right. So the thing Gus was into was pretty basic. Your criminal has his pile of loot in cash. If the pile is big enough, he can't just bank it or spend it without drawing attention to it. He risks getting into trouble when he can't explain how he came by it.

"He needs some way to turn his dirty money into clean money. So he'd go to Gus, who'd feed it through one or more of the cash businesses he was in cahoots with. Splitting up the money keeps the amounts relatively small and inconspicuous. It comes out of the other end looking like regular cash income. It gets banked and accounted for.

"Your criminal might then invoice the business for some made-up service or goods. Consultancy of some kind or something like that. And he gets what's left of his money back. Clean.

"It costs, though. The guy who put the cash in at the start wouldn't expect to get more than forty or fifty percent of it back. But at least now he can spend it and not create problems for himself."

"Seems expensive."

"It is. Cheaper to claim you won it somehow. But you can't use that one too many times without looking suspect.

"But it's all pretty much small scale. There has to be a lot of it to make any kind of significant return. So you have to get your customers from far and wide."

"So Gus wouldn't have relied on that to make his money?"

"No way. That was just a sideline. Gus and Dad had all kinds of stuff going."

"Couldn't they have used the Blue Warehouse to launder some of the cash? Keep things simple?"

"Dad had the nightclub in Stella's name. She still has it. Stella wouldn't have had anything to do with that sort of thing. But Dad did the books. So I'd guess at least some of Gus's suspect loot got put through there."

"So if that was how they dealt with the petty cash, what about the other side of it? The big money?"

"Well, from what Dad told me, I know that if you're dealing with large enough amounts, it's good to have a bent financial type, a broker or a banker, you can use to take care of things. The money might end up offshore, in some shell company accounts or whatever."

"So how do you ever get to spend it?"

"Easy. It can be placed back with the criminal as and when it's needed. As fake fees, for example. Or as a loan at virtually non-existent interest rates. A loan which never actually gets repaid. See what I mean?"

"I see. Simple really."

"Can be."

Simple? Really? Sounds complicated enough to me.

"Or it might be put through some intermediary to buy assets. It's no secret that money-laundering operations have funded quite a few of the pricier properties in London."

"And this kind of thing is common?"

"Very common. The whole point of the exercise is to make the trail too confusing to follow and the money itself appear legit. It doesn't take much imagination to see that there are lots of ways that could work."

"Okay. I get that. But where did Claude fit into all this? What was the operation he was introducing you to before he had that fall?"

"Dad's operation was bigger, simpler and much more lucrative than anything Gus ever did."

"Tell me more," he said, hoping that, at last, they were getting to the point.

"Dad provided a specialised kind of conduit for the cash. He was funnelling sizeable amounts of dodgy money, in banknotes, into the banking system so that it would end up somewhere where the authorities wouldn't ask too many questions.

"And once it's in the system, you can move it around from account to account, country to country. Becomes impossible for anyone to trace."

"Your dad was doing all this?"

"No," said Hamish. "He was doing the front-desk stuff. He had a drop-off point for the banknotes at the Warehouse. Once he got the cash, he would move it along the chain. He had a contact in London."

"A contact?"

"A financial type he used to move it into some bank and then offshore."

"And that's where the real money's made. I get it."

"Right. But it's dangerous. You can't afford to make a slip up with some top gangster's drug receipts. Dad made sure I understood that."

"So why continue to bother with the small-time stuff? Even if he did farm it out to Gus to run? All those people. All those transactions. Risky."

"He wouldn't have wanted to disturb Uncle Gus too much. Gus was very good at dealing with any people issues that cropped up. The bastard scared everyone shitless, so no one would risk taking against him. Anyone ever looked like they might cause the Firm problems, they simply disappeared. Or they had a very nasty accident of some sort."

They walked for a while in silence. It was a still day with little cloud and no shade on their route. They were walking under a strong sun, and Jack wasn't used to the heat. The pace was getting to him.

When he got home, he'd sign on at one of the gyms in the village for sure. Cut down on the drinking. Get back in shape.

Like a pig in flight.

"Long walk, isn't it?"

"Long enough. About two miles down to Playa Reducto. We can get a coffee and a rest before we walk back. Reckon you can make it? You're not looking too sharp."

He bridled a little at this, remembering how he used to do ten miles easily in his army days. With a full pack. A rifle, even. But the boy had a point. Maybe he really would sign himself on at a gym after all.

Get the conversation on track again.

"Freddy isn't worried about Gus trying to get in on the act?"

"No. I told him Gus never knew a lot about how Dad's side of things worked, and he's strictly small-time. He'll find it difficult to get back on board with anything now, in any case."

"How so?"

"Now that Dad's gone, he'll struggle. He always needed Dad to direct his efforts. I just can't see him having what it takes to make a comeback from his wheelchair. The fat bastard is history."

They walked on in silence again for a while. Then he tried a new question.

"I'm not looking to be negative, but won't your Dad's old customers have gone elsewhere by now to get their cash dealt with. And we're going to need them, right?"

"Maybe some will have moved on, but it's not that easy. A lot of them won't have known where else to go. Some might have tried to move the cash themselves.

But they're not likely to have the right contacts, so there'd be a risk.

"Some of them will just be stockpiling their surplus while they figure out where to go next."

"Could be. Like Pablo Escobar, burying his cash in the woods."

"Escobar? Not quite. But they'll need some time to get anything up and running anything like smoothly. There'll be enough dirty cash left hanging around for us to deal with. We can take it from there."

He was relieved to reach Arrecife. They stopped at the first cafe they found, opposite Reducto beach, and sat outside, breathing traffic fumes, and watched the winter-sun tourists taking a stroll along the shore. The waiter brought coffee and croissants, one of which Hamish broke into small pieces to feed to Keith, while Jack poured some water from the bottle into a saucer for the dog to drink.

"So there you were, then," said Jack, sliding his double espresso towards him, "with Freddy picking your brains about the money-laundering. Where were you living then? At the finca?"

"Freddy got me a place in a storeroom above a cafe, up the road from here. I helped out doing odd jobs while I worked through Dad's files. He parked Keith just around the block with his woman, Fran. I could visit him there and take him for walks."

"Convenient."

"It was. And now it means I have a safe place to leave Keith when I'm away."

"Right. So do you think you can tell me how we're aiming to get our hands on all this money Freddy says is waiting for us. I really would like to know exactly what I've signed up for."

"It's simple enough. I'd spent time on board ship going through Dad's records on my laptop, so I'd already figured out that there might be three million or so hanging fire somewhere. I told Freddy that. And I said that the key to everything had to be the London contact. The one responsible for moving the dodgy cash offshore."

"The next bit of your dad's conduit."

"Exactly. I told Freddy our best way forward would be to reconnect with this same contact and build on what we found out from him."

"Sounds straightforward enough. And was it?"

"No. It wasn't. I didn't have any details for this guy. So it wasn't actually much of a contact in my case, was it? I didn't even know his name. Dad would often use codenames rather than real ones."

"A very cautious man, your dad."

"He was. Goes some way to explaining how he survived untouched for all that time."

"So you had a problem."

"And I had two possible solutions. I could either spend what might be quite a long time digging around some more in Dad's files, trying to put two and two together. Or try to contact the courier."

"What courier?"

"Dad hadn't physically moved the cash along himself. He'd had someone he trusted to do the legwork. I was pretty sure I knew who. The same guy who'd sorted Keith's care for me when I was away."

"And this guy was?" He already knew the answer. He could sense the dots starting to connect.

"A friend of mine, sort of, called Harry Love. And, because of the thing with Keith, I had his email address. So I emailed him."

"You couldn't have phoned?"

"Couldn't get through that way. He'd changed his number. But I got through on the email. There was a bit of to-ing and fro-ing until we'd each made sure of the other's identity."

"So where was he, this Love? Back in the Baltic?"

"No, he had been there, working for Junior Davidson, but he'd moved on. To Naples."

"Italy?"

"Napoli. Yeah."

"He wouldn't give me his new number until he was sure it was safe. I told him I wanted to get in touch with one or two of Dad's old money-laundering contacts. Try to pick up on things."

"And he was helpful?"

"He will be. He's willing to help. But he won't tell me any more by email. He wants me to go out there and speak to him face to face. He says he's handling something to do with Dad's last contract. One that's been left hanging. He thinks that maybe I can help move things along."

"So he wants you to get involved?"

"He does. Which is why you and I are going out there tomorrow. Freddy's booked us a flight via Madrid."

11

Naples

The airport taxi dropped them off in front of an old concrete high rise, fronting onto the main road by the docks.

Hamish had emailed Harry their ETA and his mobile number before getting the flight from Madrid. He'd taken the opportunity to tell him that he wouldn't be alone. That he'd be bringing extra, qualified help. Harry had sent him the address and told him to text when he got there.

"You sent the text?" asked Jack.

"I did. Just now."

They waited on the roadside. Their travel bags on the pavement next to them.

God knows what this place is. Looks like some kind of cross between a warehouse and a commercial centre. Some residential stuff, too. Dilapidated.

Busy, though. A lot of people in and out. Four lanes of traffic. Nose to tail with horns blaring. Trams. Docks over the road, stretching off in all directions. Big cruise liner at the quayside.

Suddenly Harry was there, rushing them inside.

"This is where you're living? Here?"

"You expected the Hilton, at least, right?"

"Something like that."

The place was all locks. A different key for each. One key for the door from the street into the entrance hall. Another to get into the central courtyard. Yet another to get into the main section of the building. Then up four floors in an ancient cage lift. The lift had a slot meter, which you had to feed a few cents at peak times to make the thing work. It seemed surreal.

Then, a long, dark corridor. A lot of doors. Offices for various commercial outfits. Import/export, lawyers, accountants. Then a reinforced steel door with two separate locks. Through that, into a tiny hall and through another locked door.

Harry's place. One room. An ancient kitchenette. A shower cubicle in the corner. A balcony in crumbling concrete overlooking the dock road. There was air conditioning at least, functional and effective.

A pullout under the bed and an old sleeping bag for Hamish. An inflatable mattress and a new sleeping bag for Jack.

Harry worried about being spotted and wanted to keep a low profile. But, once Hamish had introduced Jack and explained how he had come to be recruited onto the hunt for the missing millions, they risked a walk around the corner to a restaurant.

Over the meal, they learned that Harry had often acted as Claude's courier. It had been one of his regular jobs during the last couple of years. He told them that, at the time Claude died, he had already set him up to do another run.

"I was supposed to leave that same night. I usually drove down overnight. Easier driving."

"So what stopped you?" asked Jack.

"I hadn't had the okay from Claude. The usual thing was that he'd book me into a hotel. Never the same one twice in a row. He'd give me the details I needed, and cash for petrol and expenses. The hotel was always in the Euston area."

"Because that was where your money guy was?"

"That's right. Meant I didn't have far to hump the cash. Once I'd done the delivery, I could relax. I'd go back to the hotel, get something to eat and get some sleep. I'd drive home the following day."

"But this last time you didn't even get started?"

"No, it didn't work out. Usually, once he'd given me the money and everything I needed, he'd do a final check with Giuseppe, the banker, and I'd go right away. This time, though, he put me on hold. He couldn't get through to Giuseppe. Sometimes the phone signal was tricky inside some parts of the Warehouse. He said he'd take his drink out to the yard and try from there."

"So you never got the okay?"

"I didn't. I'd dumped my bag in the car, ready to roll, and I was sitting in the reception with the cash. The Boss went off with his whisky. Told me to sit tight, and he'd keep trying and let me know."

They paused the conversation while the waiter cleared the table and served the coffee. The restaurant was only half full, with no one close enough to overhear.

"So did he connect with Giuseppe in the end?"

"Dunno. He never came back. I sat there for nearly an hour."

"Then what did you do?"

"I got worried. The Boss seemed to have disappeared. There was no way he could have gone upstairs without me seeing him. So I looked around the bar and the dining area and the kitchen. No show. The cellar stairs were locked off. The door to the yard was open, but I couldn't see him out there anywhere."

"So you must have thought he'd gone out through the yard? Gone off into the night?"

"It didn't make sense. Didn't feel right. I tried phoning him from outside to try to get a better signal but got no response. I tried twice."

"And?"

"I took the cash and drove home to my gran's, in town. I reckoned the Boss would phone me."

First impressions? The guy's telling the truth. So, the money?

"So where's the cash?"

"It's not far from here. In a locker in a left luggage place."

"You've got a million in used notes in the left luggage?"

Unbelievable. We have a million pounds waiting in a locker down the road? Could this get any better?

"I do. It's all there. I can get it out whenever."

"What made you think you should just walk off with it, Harry?" asked Hamish. "It's good that you kept Gus out of it, but why not tell me? We're friends, aren't we?"

"I was confused. I wasn't sure what was best. I mean, the next morning they found Claude dead in the cellar, and I knew the guys who'd left their cash with him would be pretty heavily pissed when they saw it hadn't got as far as their offshore account."

"So what did you do?"

"I didn't know who to trust, and I didn't want to be the one who'd nothing to offer when whoever it was came looking for it. So I stashed it on top of the wardrobe in my room at my gran's and kept my mouth shut.

"Next thing, you'd gone loopy and shot Percy and I was having to help shift the body. Accessory to murder, I think they call that, right? Then Gus has you flown off to New York and I'm left there, minding Keith. I was feeling unsafe, to put it mildly, so I thought I should put some space between myself and the Warehouse."

"So you left Keith at the boarding kennels and went to work for the Davidsons," said Hamish. "And you were still there when Freddy got in touch to ask you to get the dog onto a flight over to the Canaries."

"That's right. But not long after that, Gus gets blown across his bedroom. So I'm thinking I have to get away from all this."

The restaurant was emptying now. Harry signalled the waiter for more coffee and poured them each a fresh cup.

"Long story short," he said, "I managed to get in touch with Giuseppe, at his Naples business address. I got myself and the money over here and found myself a room, the one you've just seen, in the same building as Giuseppe's office."

"You were planning to hand over the money to this Giuseppe?" asked Jack. "You might as well have left it at your gran's."

"Not really. By that time I had a plan to get out and get myself safe."

"Let me guess," said Hamish. "You intended to steal Dad's million. Am I right?"

"Not to be picky," said Harry, "but it wasn't your dad's money. It was gangster money. I was due to deliver it to Giuseppe. I'm here trying to do exactly that."

"Because you're a moral sort of guy?" asked Jack. "Doing the right thing? You should have turned the cash over to Gus or Hamish here. Much easier."

"Look at this from my point of view. I'd no idea what was going on, had I? Claude was dead. Hamish had killed Percy and then disappeared in New York. Someone had put a bomb under Gus. Sounds dangerous, doesn't it? Who should I trust?"

"So you thought you'd pop over to Naples and hand the cash in. That it?"

"Honestly? No, it wasn't. By then I couldn't even be sure giving Giuseppe the money would put me in the clear. I wanted to do a deal. Split the cash somehow with Giuseppe and persuade him to move my share into some safe account, offshore. Half a million or so would keep me afloat for quite a while. I could disappear."

"Well, that makes sense. You'd have stood out like a sore thumb if you'd tried to spend the money back home," said Jack.

"Still looks to me like you were stealing from the Firm," said Hamish. "But I can see how that might be debatable. And you took good care of Keith while I was away, so, so far, I'm willing to call it a draw."

"Nice of you," said Harry, his tone lacking conviction.

"How about this?" asked Hamish. "We talk to this Giuseppe character and tell him that my partners and I want to continue the family business where Dad left off. We make sure the million you have stashed gets to where it's supposed to go."

"And that leaves me where, exactly?"

"You come and work for me. Or go back home and drive for Junior Davidson or whatever. I could even ask Stella to take you on again at the Warehouse if that's what you want."

"There's something else. Something you don't know."

"Like?"

"Like I already talked to Giuseppe. He'd agreed to help me out with the money. We were going to go fifty fifty. I'd get the offshore account. He'd keep quiet about the entire thing."

"So what happened? Why were you so agreeable to me and Jack coming over here to help?"

"Because now someone else is over here looking for the money. They'd already been to Giuseppe's London office and made threats. Giuseppe's no gangster. He'd got scared and moved back to Naples."

"So, it's all getting a bit tricky. Why don't we go and see the guy and get all this sorted?"

"Because he's gone missing. I've been trying his office for a week, on and off. And I've phoned. I've sent texts. Nothing."

"So you're stuck. Squatting out here in Naples, with your stolen million stashed in a luggage locker and nowhere safe to go."

"I admit it. I'm way out of my depth."

The waiter came and took away the coffee things. He left the bill with Jack, who passed it straight to Hamish.

"Okay," said Hamish. "Enough chat. Show us where Giuseppe's office is and if he's still not there, we'll go back to yours and figure out what we do next."

Hamish paid at the bar, and they made their way back into Harry's crumbling tower block and up in the cage lift to Giuseppe's floor. Harry led them along the corridor and into a small, dark hallway, at the end of which stood Giuseppe's office.

The door swung open at Harry's touch. The place was in darkness. He flicked the light switch.

Just a single room. No window. They could see that someone had ransacked everything. Filing cabinets and drawers broken into. Papers strewn about. They'd forced the lock, splintering the doorframe.

"This is new," said Harry. "This is getting to be even more worrying."

"Take a few snaps of all this on your phone," said Hamish. "Then we'd better get out of here."

They hurried down, through empty, gloomy corridors, back to Harry's place where Hamish looked through the images of the ransacked office.

"Okay," he said. "Send these to Giuseppe and let him know you've just found his office wrecked and that you have some friends here who can help. Get him to meet us somewhere he feels safe."

"You think he'll agree?"

"It's worth a shot. He must be thinking he's pretty much cornered by now."

A few minutes later, there was a reply naming a place they would be able to meet sometime during the next hour: an art museum, a couple of stops along the metro line.

They went out into the sun-drenched Neapolitan afternoon and the blaring traffic.

Why do these people find it necessary to lean on their car horns all the time? Don't they have radios to listen to?

It was only a short walk to the station, but he baked in the heat. He thought about the cool gloom of the lounge in his semi, back home. Had he turned down the heating before he left? Maybe not so cool after all. At least now, there was hope that he'd have no trouble paying the bill.

Half an hour later, they arrived at the museum, the Madre. There were a few art lovers inside, walking through the galleries, looking serious. They found Giuseppe standing alone in one of the rooms, and he seemed to trust Harry enough to join the group as they walked around the place, keeping clear of the other visitors and pretending to appreciate the artwork.

Harry explained who Jack and Hamish were and why they were there. That they were aiming to take over where Claude Beard had left off.

"But," said Giuseppe, "I'm not so sure I'm in a good position to be helpful right now."

They were standing in front of an abstract painting, which took up most of one wall of the room. Behind them, a large window gave a view of the flat roof of the ancient apartment block across the street. The painting, Jack decided, wasn't worth too much attention, and he turned to look out through the window, happy to leave the conversation to the others while he listened.

136

He found that the rooftop on the far side of the narrow street had been set out as a kind of living area. An iron-framed bed, complete with mattress. A battered chest of drawers. A rusting metal chair. The whole arrangement, separated from the rest of the roof by a rickety chain-link fence, stood open to the elements. There was no sign of the occupant.

An art lover, perhaps? Down on his luck?

"A man came to see me in my office in Euston, recently. An Englishman. He talked like you guys."

"From Liverpool, then?" asked Hamish.

"Maybe. Sounded like that."

"Who was he? What did he want?"

"Money. A million in cash, most likely the same million Harry's got hold of. And then a lot more."

"And you didn't have that kind of dosh lying about the office to give him, I imagine. So how did this guy know about you? And about the cash? Who do you think he was?"

"I have no idea. But he told me he knew I had the cash, and that if I didn't give him what he wanted, he'd drop me down the stairwell. And he was big. Dangerous looking."

"So you came here to escape?"

"That was what I hoped. But he just followed me. He'd even got my home address, here in Naples."

"Probably he'd been watching you and followed you there."

Jack thought it was time he got more involved in the conversation. He turned to face the others.

"So how did you get away from him?" he asked. "Did he just leave?"

"I had to threaten him with a gun I keep in my desk drawer, as a sort of insurance. I'd never had to use it before. Turns out I hadn't even loaded it, but when I got the thing out and waved it at him, the guy backed down."

"So you managed to scare him off?"

"I don't think I scared him. He didn't act scared. More like careful. He told me I was asking for trouble and that he'd be back when I wasn't expecting him. And if I didn't have the money ready for him by then, I'd be sorry.

"As soon as the guy left, I locked up and went out through the service door at the back. I made sure I wasn't being followed. I decided to stay with a friend while I tried to work out what to do."

"And?"

"And I put some bullets in the gun."

"Smart."

It was a slow afternoon at the Madre. They still had the room to themselves.

"And you said the guy wanted more than just the million?" asked Jack.

"He wanted three million, not just one. Said he knew for a fact that the last three consignments from Liverpool, a million each, hadn't got beyond my control. And he wanted it all."

"That true? You had three million?"

"I had two. The other million was the one Harry was holding in cash. The two million that had already reached me were being held in one of my offshore holding accounts. Still in transit."

"In transit?"

"Both lots got paid in through a banker I often use and then moved into a shell company offshore. It's where I leave the cash until the client tells me where to move it to next."

"Your clients, Claude Beard included, must have trusted you a lot."

"We're talking about London here. The money-laundering capital of the world. And Naples, even! I do what I'm told. That's how I keep my good reputation and stay alive."

"But how could you know that this guy who threatened you wasn't Beard's client, or someone acting on his behalf? Wouldn't that be the most likely thing?"

"If he'd been acting for someone like that, he'd have been more relaxed about the whole business. He'd simply have given me the usual instructions about where to put the cash."

"You mean he was behaving as though he didn't have the full picture?"

"Exactly. He acted as though he didn't know the ropes."

"So what about the actual client then?" asked Hamish. "Isn't he going to be getting anxious about what's happened to his money?"

"He might well be doing just that. Don't forget that I've no idea who it is. I got all my instructions from Liverpool. At least I did until everything went quiet. Until Claude Beard's death."

"So, is it someone who's picked this up from the Liverpool end?" mused Jack. He scratched the back of his head and gave Hamish a puzzled look. "Any ideas?"

"Not sure. The best I can come up with is that Gus and Kevin have worked something out about what was going on. Gus could be getting low on cash. And he would've had access to Dad's files, just as I did. So I reckon that the guy bothering Giuseppe is possibly Gus's man, Kevin, but, obviously, I can't be certain. It could just as easily be Dad's client if they've managed to make the link to Giuseppe."

"So," said Jack, "we've no means of knowing who actually owns this money. We don't know who your dad was working for. Big problem?"

"Looked at one way, you might well think so. Looked at another way, this all looks more like a big opportunity."

"You reckon?"

"Well, it appears to me that we have the whole three million up for grabs just now. Two of which Giuseppe already has banked along with the million Harry here has safely stashed. And from what Giuseppe's told us, most likely the actual owners aren't able to make the link to Giuseppe. They'd probably got used to leaving it all to Dad. Careless, really. But some people are like that."

"So?"

"So we have a couple of options. We can keep two million in the holding account with Giuseppe, let him pay in Harry's million on top and leave things at that. The owners will then, eventually, either manage to identify Giuseppe as the man in the middle, or they won't.

"If they don't, we could just leave the cash there until we reckon it's safe to grab it. But we won't know how long to wait. A year? Two years?"

"Tricky," said Jack. "I see that."

"Of course, if the clients do find their way to Giuseppe, then he could simply move the money on as directed. And everything would revert to normal. This has the major disadvantage that we would lose any hope of holding onto any of the cash ourselves."

"Freddy wouldn't be too happy with that. Neither would I. I signed on for a share in three million, remember?"

"None of us would be happy with that, Jack. I'm just going through the possibilities here."

"And?"

"And whatever we do, we still might need to deal with whoever's bothering Giuseppe in the meantime. Especially if we intend to carry on with the money-laundering business ourselves. Which we do."

"Deal with?" asked Jack. "Deal with, how?"

"If we're to be sure of keeping Giuseppe here alive and well and on the team, we'll probably want to kill the guy who's threatening him. Right? We don't know if

140

he's going to come back armed, or whether he'll be alone next time. Only Giuseppe knows what he actually looks like. And even if we do kill him, we'd have no way of knowing whether someone else is going to follow up later."

"But that isn't what you're about to propose, I think. Given the way you're talking."

"Well, we have an alternative. What if we decide that this is the best chance of such easy money that we're ever likely to get? We grab it and run. Just like we planned. Take the risk that neither the money's owners, or the guy threatening Giuseppe, will be able to find us."

"What about it, Giuseppe? Want to sign on with us? Do you have anything tying you to Naples? How would you feel about leaving the place behind?"

He didn't hesitate for more than a second or so before responding.

"There's a girl I've been seeing. Sort of. Nothing serious. No kind of problem. And my immediate family are all in Rome."

"And, if you think about it, you could set up your operation more or less anywhere. You'd still have your contacts."

"The way things are right now, I'd certainly consider the idea of moving somewhere else."

"So how about this? In the short term, we get a flight to anywhere we fancy. We disappear for a while, along with the cash, and we take it from there. I have a partner who's keen to take on my dad's part in the business and more besides."

"Suits me," said Harry at once. "It'd be a load off, to be honest."

"And you, Jack?"

"Seems to me there's nothing against me going back home for now. No one's chasing me for the cash, are they?"

"Just leaves you, Giuseppe. No pressure, but I reckon it could be your best way out of this and you might not have a great amount of time. You keep control of the two mill until we get the chance to talk about how we all want things to go. Sound feasible?"

Giuseppe glanced at Harry. "Tell me, is this a good idea?"

"Well," asked Harry. "What else is there?"

Giuseppe stared up at the ceiling as if hoping to find inspiration there. Then he sighed. "Okay," he said. "I can appreciate that my options are limited. So we'll see how this goes. And where do we go, actually?"

"You come to the Canaries with me. A safe haven. It'll make a good base."

Nice move, Hamish. This is looking promising.

Hamish didn't wait for a response. He simply took charge. Jack was impressed.

"Where's your passport? You got that with you?"

"It's in my apartment. About thirty minutes walk from my office."

"Okay, so here's what we do. Jack, you go with Giuseppe and watch his back while he gets whatever he needs for the trip.

"Harry, you go and collect your cash and get it over to your room. I should come with you."

"I'll be fine. It's not far and I'm used to moving money around. No worries."

"If you're sure. Might be best, anyway, if we split up. So I'll get back to the room to book us all onto the first suitable flight I can find. I'll call at a supermarket en route and get us some food for later. We're in danger of looking a bit conspicuous as a group, and we can't risk the restaurant again with Giuseppe along."

"You'd better take these," said Harry, handing Hamish a set of keys. "Spare set. In case you get there before me."

Giuseppe's apartment was up on the hill at the back of town.

"It's in an area called Vomero," he said, as they walked across from the metro. "You know it, Jack?"

"First time in Naples. So no, I don't. First time in Italy, actually."

"It's a nice neighbourhood. You'll see. Probably cooler for you up there too. You don't look comfortable."

"Not used to the heat, that's all. Is it far?"

"To walk? No. We take a sort of railcar up the slope. Easy."

Twenty minutes later, they were at the apartment. It was on the ground floor of a well maintained, if elderly, block at the very top of the hill.

Someone had forced a kitchen window and searched the place. Drawers and shelves had been emptied out, and Giuseppe's possessions had been strewn everywhere. It was lucky that the searcher hadn't found the passport tucked into the pocket of one of his large collection of tailored jackets. Giuseppe packed a bag, and they were on their way back down in under fifteen minutes.

"Pity about all your stuff. Having to leave it all behind like that."

"Don't worry about it. I'll get my friend to come and secure everything. It'll be okay. They won't have found anything useful in there. I always encrypt any sensitive data and store it online."

"So you're good to get that plane?"

"There's some paperwork in my office I should pick up. Nothing that would be any use to anyone else, just

143

admin. But it'll help me set up my operation again wherever we end up."

When they got back to the tower block, Hamish let them into Harry's one-room apartment. A stack of ready meals and two bottles of wine were waiting on the little worktop in the kitchen area.

"I see you got the food in, then," said Jack. "And you even remembered to get some booze. Did you book the flight?"

"All booked for tomorrow. I need the passports to finalise the check-in and we're done. See anything of Harry on your way up?"

"Nothing. Is he okay, do you think?"

"Maybe not. There's been no sign of him. Or his million."

"Think he's done a runner?"

"You tell me. Obviously something hasn't worked out quite as expected on the Harry Love front."

"So what? We just wait?"

"We can check out the streets between here and the left luggage. I looked online. There are two within an easy walk. I was only waiting for you to get back, so I'll do that now. You get everything you needed from your apartment, Giuseppe?"

"Enough. Someone had searched it, like the office, but whoever did it wasn't a pro. They didn't find my passport."

"So you're all set?"

"There's a file I could use, upstairs. I'm going to fetch it."

"You sure? Might not be too safe up there."

"Jack can come with me. We'll be careful. And I have the gun, remember. It'll only take a few minutes."

They pushed open the office door at the end of the gloomy corridor and flicked on the light. Giuseppe went inside first, holding the pistol. It surprised them to find

Harry Love sitting in a chair by the desk. His back to them.

"Harry?" asked Jack. "What are you doing up here? Everything okay?"

Even as he spoke, he realised that everything was most probably not 'okay'. Harry made no response to his questions.

*

"And there he was," said Jack, "sitting with his back to us. No sign of any money. I thought he'd dozed off. Sitting there like that. But when I sat down opposite, to wake him, I saw the blood soaking into his T-shirt and all the way down his chest to the top of his jeans."

"Dead?" asked Hamish, already knowing what the answer must be.

"As a doornail. Someone had cut his throat wide open. I've never seen anything so bad. I nearly threw up."

What, in the name of all that's holy, have I got myself into?

12

Finger Food

No one saw them carry Harry's bedsheet-wrapped body down a floor and along the dimly lit corridor to his room. They had no choice but to leave it there, pushed in under the bed. That was bad. But at least whoever murdered Harry had left the rest of them alone. Most likely, thought Jack, they didn't even know where he had been living. Didn't know they were all hiding out in there. They'd have been watching the approach to the building on the off-chance and waylaid Harry on his way back up.

They would have taken him into Giuseppe's office, under threat, and relieved him of the cash. Then slit his throat.

Why do that? Once they had what they wanted, why kill the guy? Had he recognised his assailant? Known him? That would maybe put this Kevin in the frame. Gus's man. Or is the killing simply aimed at frightening Giuseppe?

They got a taxi to a hotel near to the airport, where they spent the night. They dumped Giuseppe's gun in a bin in the street, on their way to the departure lounge early the following morning. It was too big a risk to take the thing through security.

Their flight took them to Madrid, where Hamish and Giuseppe were able to find a connection to Lanzarote, and Jack could get a plane back to John Lennon.

They had lost Harry Love, along with a million in cash, but gained two million in an offshore account and found Giuseppe. And with Giuseppe and his banker connections, they foresaw a lucrative, if illegal, future in the international money market.

There was a good chance, now, that they might all be able to stay out of sight for long enough for those who were hunting for the money to tire of the search.

In the family room they shared in the hotel, Giuseppe divided up the two million. He set up a secure offshore account with a deposit of five hundred thousand for each of them and another for Freddy. For Hamish and Jack, and for Freddy too, five hundred thousand was less than they had hoped for. But it was still a lot, and the golden future they now could see, through the lens of Giuseppe De Lorca, was more than enough to compensate.

Jack was amazed at the sudden transformation of his fortunes. In a life-changing last few days, he'd gone from being one of life's also-rans to being someone to be reckoned with. Cash in the bank, a purpose and membership of an international money-laundering gang. An amateurish sort of gang for the most part since, Giuseppe apart, they were making it up as they went along. But they would learn. He felt sure of it.

He'd crossed a line and needed to settle his mind to his new mode of being. The quickest way of doing that was to get himself back home and take a view of things from the late winter gloom of his semi, out on the Point. He wanted perspective. A few days in the quiet solitude of familiar surroundings would give him that.

He thought about the line he'd crossed. He might have worked for criminals before but had always told himself that the criminality was someone else's business. While he'd been nothing more than a private investigator doing a job. It didn't seem much like that now.

He couldn't generate much enthusiasm for becoming a criminal. It wasn't how he liked to see himself. He tried to tell himself that money-laundering was a victimless crime.

But he knew that there would always be victims further upstream. The dirty money had to come from somewhere. From drug dealing, from people trafficking, from all kinds of unpleasant activities. Tax dodging, perhaps, at the kindlier end of things.

If he wanted to justify himself and his plans for the future, then how about what the fat cats did in the city? Didn't they launder billions for Russian gangsters in full view of an establishment that did little or nothing to prevent it?

And then again, what about those who made their fortunes from legalised, life-destroying addictions like tobacco and gambling? Not to mention the God-given booze. Didn't some of those gentle souls even get knighthoods?

There was no getting away from it. There had been casualties en route to his half a million. And now someone had murdered Harry Love. He remembered that he'd dreamed of Harry last night. Sitting there on his own in the gloom of Giuseppe's ransacked office, his throat sliced open, his clothing blood-soaked.

Harry might lie lifeless under his bed, decomposing in the heat of the Naples climate for a while yet. The neighbours beginning to wonder about the unpleasant smell, and the flies, edging unexpectedly into their lives.

He was aware of his tendency to keep things at a distance. Or to try to, until reality became overwhelmingly present. Just like reality always did. But now, all at once, the thought of Harry's death was unavoidably real.

Harry had been the closest thing Hamish had had to a friend back at the Warehouse. It was Harry who made sure Keith was safe until Freddy flew him out to Fuerteventura. Harry who had led Hamish to Giuseppe and who had housed them in Naples in relative safety.

Harry asked for Hamish's help and followed his advice. And now he was dead.

So? Should he jet back home and hang out in his semi, waiting for his new-look bank statements to show up online?

He harboured few illusions about how much booze he'd get through sitting around there. He would have to hope that Freddy would be quick to deliver on his proposals for picking up where Claude had left off, and that he kept him involved.

On the flight to Madrid, he took the opportunity to put a few questions to Hamish.

"Hasn't Stella been in touch with you? Or anyone from back home?"

"No one over there has my new number. Gus's thugs took my old phone on that last morning in New York, before I got away. And Stella isn't much of an online type of person. Dad used to handle all that kind of thing for her. She wouldn't even know my email address. And I'm Billy No-Mates, remember?"

"And you haven't considered calling home?"

"No. Can't say I have. There's nothing useful I can tell Stella right now. And I don't want anyone knowing where I am unless they really need to."

Obviously, he thought, Hamish and Stella aren't exactly close. Best not to tell Hamish what he knew about events at the Blue Warehouse. Better to keep that to himself and see how things turned out.

*

He got back to the Point in the grey half-light of early evening. He was missing the sun already. And he missed the colour. No leaves on the trees yet, he noticed, as he dragged his luggage out from the rear of the hatchback. Not much showing in the gardens round

149

about, beyond the odd clump of daffodils braving the chill.

A text from Stella:

need to talk sometime… please?

That was all it said. He dumped his bag in the house and went straight to the Merseyrail station. Simpler to take the train into town. He was too tired to drive.

He hadn't planned on visiting Stella. He could have phoned, but he had nothing else in mind for the evening ahead, so why not use the diversion to keep himself away from the drink?

An hour or so later, he was in her apartment, sitting across from Stella in her private lounge. The nightclub wasn't yet open for business, and she had still to glamorise herself, ready for her stint in the bar. But even in jeans and a shirt, he thought, she was looking good. She had worn well. Better than him. No doubt about that.

"Is that the start of a tan you've got there, Jack? Been somewhere nice?"

"Just business, you know. The usual. Must've caught more sun than I realised."

He considered telling her he had been in contact with her missing stepson but decided against it. If Hamish wanted to stay hidden away for now, then that might be safer all round. Not his place to interfere.

"Thought you would have phoned, actually. Didn't mean to drag you all the way down here. Pleased to see you, though. Of course."

"Nothing else on this evening. Just fancied getting out for a couple of hours. Hope you don't mind?"

"Like I said, I'm pleased to see you."

She'd been surprised to see him at the side door, turning up unannounced like that. She'd expected a phone call.

But he often found a surprise approach of this kind to be a quicker way to the truth. Although it did sometimes have the opposite effect and make people clam up. Not tonight, though. Stella was wound up, and she was anxious to talk.

He saw Stella as a very competent individual. A person to be relied on to keep up her end of the business. But a person who needed to feel that someone she could trust and depend on had her back. For her, that would always be the man in her life. It had been Claude. And then Gus. But now, her husband had become the problem. She wanted to talk about that.

She explained to him how Gus had become even more unhappy with the way things were after Kevin disappeared. The carer she'd hired had not seemed particularly sympathetic. He was big enough, to be sure, to move Gus off and on his wheelchair and see to his needs. But he wasn't there twenty-four-seven like Kevin. And didn't have so much time to wheel him out into the streets to enjoy the cheerful uplift that a sunny day by Liverpool's waterside could provide.

"And he wouldn't have been able to discuss his business problems with his new carer, as he'd been used to doing with Kevin. I'm sure he would have found that hard to deal with."

"Sounds likely."

"And what must have made him unhappier still would have been getting the phone call he'd been expecting from the men wanting to talk some more about Claude's financial arrangements. He tried telling them that while they might want to talk, he didn't. He told them he probably wouldn't even let them into his apartment."

"Worth a try, I suppose."

"They said they'd get in anyway, whatever Gus said. Later that night, perhaps. Or in a few minutes, if they felt that way inclined. They told him if he didn't cooperate, the consequences would be very unpleasant."

He had nothing to contribute to the story, so he listened while Stella unburdened herself.

She explained how Gus, feeling sick at the prospect, had told his callers to come on up. His new carer was out, and he was alone. Even worse, he'd left his handgun stashed back at the Warehouse. An enormous mistake.

The same two men who had visited Stella at the nightclub were soon sitting on Gus's sofa. The small, dapper man was accompanied by a colleague, a very much bigger individual who looked as though he might have enjoyed a lengthy career as a punchbag in some backstreet gym.

The smaller of his visitors, who appeared to be the one in charge, assured him that everything would be fine, just so long as he gave them the information they needed.

Gus told them about the set of transactions that he and Kevin had found, and the pair agreed that they did, indeed, sound like they referenced the missing cash. But they were, after all, no more than transactions on a list. Whereas what they wanted was a sure route to the three million.

He'd seen no alternative to telling his visitors that he was unable to help them. He was sorry, but he simply didn't have the information or the cash they were looking for.

The dapper man sighed and said that that was a pity.

Listening to Stella, he realised how difficult all this would have been for Gus. He was unused to being the one on the losing side of the argument. His life had been spent inflicting pain on others. To Gus, this would all have seemed the wrong way round. A grotesque mistake.

He must have wondered how events could have turned against him so quickly. First, the grenade exploding under his bed, then his removal from the Blue Warehouse, and now this.

*

The bigger man, the punchbag, had reached into a hold-all he was carrying.

"We brought you a present," he'd said, pulling out a brand-new food slicer.

"Bought it from John Lewis on the way over. I do like that store, don't you? They have pretty much everything you could want in the kitchen department.

"And oh, yes," he'd continued. "Got you something else to go with it."

He had produced a roll of gaffer tape. "Mustn't forget this."

Gus had found his heart rate quickening and a wave of panic rising through his chest.

"Don't want to have a mess in here, do we?" the small, dapper man had said. "The kitchen area is probably best. Let me help."

He'd wheeled Gus through his lounge and into the kitchen-diner.

"Much better in here. Got some bread somewhere? A loaf?"

He had clutched at the only straw in view. "You want to make a sandwich? Please, go ahead." He had found it hard to control his breathing. "There's loads of stuff. Bread in the cupboard."

"Just the bread, thanks." The small, dapper man had taken a fresh, unsliced loaf from the shelf and given it a squeeze and a sniff. "Crusty wholegrain. Excellent choice."

Then Punchbag had joined them and placed the slicer on the worktop. He'd plugged the machine in and fiddled about with it for a few seconds, setting it up, ready for use.

"There's roast beef," Gus had said. "Or pork. And there's mustard somewhere." He had felt himself beginning to perspire heavily. He'd had a lifelong problem with excessive perspiration.

"I always find this kind of thing distressing," the small, dapper man had said, sounding as though he meant it. "But business is business and needs must."

"Try the bread, Eric." He'd passed the crusty wholewheat to Punchbag. "Just a slice."

The machine had emitted a high-pitched whine as it cut quickly and evenly through the loaf.

"Marvellous. Hold Mr. Beard's arms down, would you, Eric? I'd better get the tape over his mouth. Looks like he might be a screamer."

*

Stella wasn't telling him much that he didn't already know. She was simply filling in the awful details. She had told him before about the two visitors, over the phone, as he sat in his rental car at the end of the track leading up to Freddy's place. But he let her talk, and he listened.

She had been engaged in some frenzied thinking. She told him how her nightclub, her pride and joy, had been a gangster-free zone after Claude and Gus and all their henchmen had gone. She had intended to keep it that way. But now the gangsters were back with a vengeance, and this time they weren't on her side.

Maybe Claude had been right all along, keeping Gus and his heavies around the place. Those two thugs would not have dared to come tramping about, searching through everything, if Gus's men had been here. They had even searched her bedroom. All her personal belongings. She hadn't mentioned this before.

154

She'd felt violated, she said. Her life shouldn't have to be like this.

"I considered calling the police. But that would most likely lead to some troublesome questions."

Questions which she would find difficult to answer. Things would come out. Things which a reasonable person might expect her to be aware of, having lived here for all these years, in a house full of crooks. And wasn't there something about being an 'accessory' to a crime, even if you weren't one of those actually carrying it out? Something about the authorities being able to confiscate the assets of criminals? And whilst the Warehouse and Claude's investments were all in her name, Claude had provided the funding. In Stella's opinion, calling in the law simply wasn't an option.

"Obviously, I'll need to find some other way to protect myself from these people, these thugs. But what?"

She now realised, she said, that all those years with Claude had been years of peaceful prosperity. Peaceful and prosperous here in the Warehouse at least, whatever Claude and Gus and their little gang had got up to elsewhere.

"Things only began to take a turn for the worse after poor Claude fell into the cellar and died, and that dreadful bomb thing exploded under Gus's bed."

It was clear now, she confessed, that she'd been foolish to think she could leave matters to Gus. Claude had been the brains behind the years of peace, maintaining tight control over his brother and directing him along the right path.

Then she described the call from Gus after his visitors had left. He'd seemed distressed. She'd asked him if there was something wrong.

"Yes," he'd said. "Something's wrong. Something is very much fucking wrong."

His breath had been coming in quick pants, and it had sounded to Stella as though his voice was actually shaking.

"As if I haven't suffered enough already," he'd said, so shaken up that he was having difficulty speaking. "I want you over here, Stella. I'm in trouble. You're still my wife and I need you. Right now. There is no one else."

Gus had ended the call.

Twenty minutes later, she had let herself into Gus's apartment with the key she had held onto when she'd moved him in.

He was beginning to feel the need for a drink. A small measure. To tide him over. He risked a furtive glance toward the tray of bottles and glasses on the sideboard.

Stella hadn't spent years in the hospitality business without knowing how to read the signs. She continued to tell him her tale as she waved him over to the drinks. He poured a very large whisky.

Best pour a big one. Save getting up again and looking greedy.

He offered the drink to Stella, but she shook her head and carried on, so he sat down, nursing his glass. He'd just sip. He would make this last.

She described how, once inside Gus's place, she'd found her husband in the kitchen, sitting, shivering, in his wheelchair. His left hand holding a bloodstained towel over his right. Then she saw the slicer, standing in a pool of blood on the worktop.

"My little finger," Gus had wailed. "The bastards sliced it off. I've called an ambulance. Should be here anytime now."

At the hospital, the surgeon had explained how lucky Gus had been. It was a nice clean cut, and they had got to it quickly enough. It would heal well.

With some skilled surgery, the finger could have been re-attached. Unfortunately, neither Stella nor the ambulance crew had been able to find it. Gus had told them that as far as he could recollect, through the mist of pain he'd been experiencing at the time, the missing digit had fallen into the waste disposal unit, been ground up and flushed down the drain.

The medic had done what he could to repair the damage, but Gus's right hand would be without its little finger, leaving him with a small stump.

"A bit like the rest of me," he'd said.

When he'd recovered enough to be discharged, Stella was surprised to find that she couldn't quite bring herself to send him back to his apartment to live alone.

If Kevin had still been on the scene, it could have been different. But Kevin was gone, and no one had the faintest idea where he was. So she'd had the ambulance deliver him to the Warehouse where she installed him in his old bedroom, now completely clear of blast damage and fully refurbished.

"I told him he could stay here," she said. "I've arranged for his carer to come in every day, to do the necessary until he learns to do things for himself. He gets all his meals provided, and I'm keeping him supplied with booze."

He sat and listened and nursed his drink. It was all very interesting, but why did Stella want him to know all this? Him in particular? She obviously needed to get it all off her chest to someone. But why choose Jack Charnley? But then, hadn't he often found himself to be the one people chose to tell their secrets to? He took another sip of Stella's excellent whisky. A slightly larger sip than the last.

"I've told Gus that he needs to realise that everything will be different around here in future. He'll have to accept my way of doing things. From now on, I'm going to be totally in charge.

"And I followed your advice, Jack. Told Gus I needed his expertise and his contacts to recruit some security staff. And I made it clear that there mustn't be any more of the gangster stuff. Nothing criminal. The place has been completely legit since he got blown out of bed and I want it to stay that way."

"He agreed?"

"He did. Said he'd help me with recruitment. And with some man management. I'll need some help with that, at least for starters."

"So you're recruiting a few heavies? That's good."

"A couple. Like you suggested. They'll have to double up as doormen, bouncers, drivers and general odd job types or whatever. As and when."

"And you can afford that?"

"I have the money. It's obvious to me now that I need protection to keep the Warehouse intact. I've been naïve to think I didn't. But I've got too much of myself invested in the place to let go of it at this stage.

"So I told Gus that if he helps me with this, he can stay on here. I'll see to it he's looked after. Beyond that, it will be purely a working relationship."

Why tell me this? Why do I need to know about her sex life?

"So we have a deal. He's been dragging it out a bit, but I know he's been making some calls. I suspect he's embarrassed about the situation he's in. Shouldn't be too difficult with all the contacts he has, though. And I told him I want quality operatives. The best he can get."

Sitting in Stella's lounge, listening to her explanations, he wondered again why he was doing this. He didn't have any interest in the Blue Warehouse or its personnel. Not now. The Voice had already paid him off.

But then there were still a few loose ends that might come back to haunt him. Those two characters who'd been so unpleasant to Stella and Gus? They could turn into a problem. And what about the thing with Kevin? Had it been Kevin who had got to Giuseppe in Naples? Kevin who had killed Harry Love and taken the missing million?

And then there was Stella. Why had she called him, Jack Charnley, when the trouble showed up, when there was a nightclub full of men of all kinds right downstairs? Why make a point of telling him she and Gus were now husband and wife in name only?

Was the woman genuinely interested in him? Was he being played? He'd maybe go along with things for the time being and see where the flow might take him. His usual approach. It wasn't as though he possessed some neatly packaged life-plan he needed to keep to.

He tuned back into what she was telling him. Something about how, after an afternoon of phone calls, Gus had arrived at a shortlist of four heavies who fitted Stella's specification. It was just a matter of negotiating the right rate for the job.

"Looks like it's all turning out as you'd hoped, then, Stella. That's good."

But there was something more she wanted to tell him. About Gus.

"He's behaving strangely, Jack. I catch him giggling sometimes, quietly, to himself. It's disturbing, to say the least. I think he's losing it.

"He used to have a thing about roadkill. He'd cook it up for himself and eat it. Quite disgusting, actually. Of course, since he lost his legs, he's not had the opportunity to go out foraging for dead squirrels and delicacies of that sort."

159

He resorted to an even larger sip of whisky in an attempt to hold the image of a panful of dead squirrels firmly at bay.

"Sounds lovely."

"But today, just before you showed up, I went to talk to him about the new recruits. I found him in the kitchen in his wheelchair. Finding him back at work at the stove was a good sign, or so I thought. There was something on the go in his favourite frying pan. So I wandered across to take a look. He'd got a couple of eggs in there, some mushrooms and another thing that looked like a sausage."

"Looked like?"

"His finger. I took it away from him. He was planning to eat it."

13

Gunter Roth

He spent the remainder of the week back at his semi. He didn't do much other than think about the way things were going and try to imagine what might come next.

He took over the feeding of the cat from Alan Tooth, who had cut a small hole in the bottom of the shed door to allow twenty-four-seven cat access. He went for a walk along the beach each day. The Irish Sea coast could be bracing at this time of year. In fact, he reflected, it could often turn out to be pretty bracing all year round.

And he tried to exercise. Push-ups, squats, and similar challenges. He managed only six push-ups. Perhaps he wasn't quite ready for the gym. On the plus side, and against his expectations, he kept away from the booze.

The phone rang. Hamish.

"Hi, buddy. How's it hanging?"

"It's hanging good, Jack. How are things your end?"

"Oh, you know. Quiet. Went down to see Stella at the Warehouse. I wanted to check on the situation down there. See what info I could pick up."

There was a brief silence from Hamish, as if he was carefully considering Jack's words. And then, "That's good. Stella okay?"

He told Hamish about the two visitors and Gus's take on finger food and all the rest of it. Hamish heard him out without interrupting.

"So Uncle Gus is going crazy, but at least Stella's got the security she needs?

"It's pretty much sorted. The Warehouse has two new bodies in place. Hogan and Barry. They've their own room, behind the bar area, and at least one of them will sleep there every night. Both of them sometimes. They're tough guys. Gus specials."

"That's good. You've been keeping an eye on things. Did you mention me?"

"Wasn't sure you'd want me talking about your doings, Hamish. Happy to leave all that to you."

There was a pause.

"Been considering coming back myself for a while. There's a job in the pipeline we can talk about. Not over the phone. And I'd like to see for myself how things are over there."

"You're not worried that someone could recognise you? The police would, most likely, still want a word. And I'm sure those troublesome bastards Stella's fending off would bust a gut in their rush to get to you."

"I'll need to take a few precautions, that's all. For starters, I can use the ID on my fake passport, Gunter Roth."

"German?"

"Sounds German. That's one issue you can have with false passports. Apparently."

"But why German in particular?"

"Probably because the guy Freddy bought it from is a German. There are quite a few over here. I'll make up some story about being born and raised in the UK."

"So it's a UK passport, is it?"

"It's a fake UK passport. Just the name in it is German."

"Nothing's ever simple."

"Could help, if you think about it. Plus, I've been growing a beard, and I was clean shaven when I left. I have a deep tan now and I've let my hair grow. Add a change in my clothing and a plausible backstory and I should be fine."

"Might work, I suppose. Do you want to stay at mine? Less obvious than Stella's place."

He was waiting as Hamish came out of the arrivals hall at John Lennon. He saw at once that the person he was looking at would be hard to recognise as the old Hamish. He looked little like the Hamish Beard he remembered from the photographs he'd seen hanging in the Warehouse bar and in the media reports he'd found online at the start of his search.

It was clear that, with care, he should be able to do the new identity thing without breaking too much of a sweat.

"Lucky you," he said as he led Hamish to his car. "The weather's good at the moment. Nowhere near as hot as over there in Honda, but warm and sunny all the same."

"Might be nice to escape the heat for a while, actually. It can get to be boring."

"You've not brought the wee doggie with you?"

"Don't need the hassle. And Keith wouldn't enjoy the flight, so it's better he stays with Fran. She says she's more than happy to have him."

"Probably best. I seem to have cats now, myself. Six."

He lifted Hamish's bag into the back of his brand-new Nissan Qashqai and prepared to drive off. He'd considered getting a more expensive car, but why draw attention to himself? And anyway, he'd never been any kind of poser.

"Don't be expecting the Ritz. My place is nothing like luxurious. 'Spartan' would sum it up. So don't expect too much."

"No worries, buddy. Won't bother me, whatever. The main issue is to keep a low profile until I've got things sussed."

They pulled out of the car park and headed off in the direction of the Expressway and the M57.

"We'll get you settled in at my place and then take a walk over to my local, if you feel like it. Have a steak? Couple of pints? What do you say?"

"Don't see why not. No one likely to know me in there. It's miles from the Baltic."

"Not what we'd call a keen gardener, then," said Hamish when Jack parked the Qashqai on his driveway, next to the ancient grey hatchback he sometimes used for surveillance.

The front garden was mainly paving and gravel, the only plant being a single ornamental tree, of a type Hamish couldn't put a name to, standing opposite the bay window. The tree was dead.

"Didn't always have the time really," he said, stepping aside to wave his guest into the hallway. "It's the same at the back. I was often away for weeks at once, working. I didn't want to have some jobbing gardener snooping about when I wasn't here."

"And now? Now that you have the time?"

"Now I have the time, I really can't be bothered."

"You weren't exaggerating when you said it was Spartan," said Hamish, as Jack showed him around. There were no rugs or carpets anywhere but on the staircase. The rest of the flooring was a mix of bare laminate and painted wooden floorboards. The furniture was utilitarian. The minimum needed to serve a single occupant and the occasional guest.

"Did you have a burglary or a flood or something?"

"Not quite. Wasn't like this until my wife died. Back then it was a fairly normal looking, well-furnished place. Over furnished, if anything."

"So, what happened?"

"After what happened to Wendy, I planned to relocate. I was aiming to get a short-term rental while I decided where to go. I was trying to move away from the grief, I suppose. So I got a house clearance firm in to strip out most of the stuff before I put the place up for sale."

"Obviously you didn't follow through with that."

"I just lost heart. Lost any sense of purpose. And I was drinking more and more. I wasn't very clear-headed back then."

"So I'm guessing you don't entertain a lot?"

"No one comes here these days. I realised a while ago that, apart from Wendy, I've never been that good at relationships. If I want company, I go down the pub. Not that I actually talk to anyone much while I'm there.

"Speaking of which, how about I let you get your stuff sorted out and then we can wander down to the Railway. Steak and chips and a drink or two. Okay?"

Less than an hour later, they were sitting at a table in the Railway Hotel. The nearest thing he had to a local.

"Had enough?" he asked when they'd finished eating. "Nice steak tonight. You're lucky."

He poured himself another glass of wine and topped up Hamish's half-empty one.

"Never thought I'd make a wine drinker. It was always beer and whisky with me. Up until the trip out to the Canaries."

They drank slowly until dusk and then made the half-mile trek home to Jack's darkened semi.

Jack opened a bottle of whisky. "Nightcap?"

"Love one," said Hamish, his voice already slurred.

"And what's the plan then? You said something about a job in the works."

"It's something you might want to do for Freddy. Watching Junior's back while he moves some cash to Amsterdam."

"More millions?"

"Not millions. Not yet. A sizeable amount, though."

"Sounds like the kind of thing I could help with. Stop me getting bored."

"Just the start, Jack. There'll be other jobs down the line, and you can be as involved as you feel you want to be. There's a world full of dirty money that needs to be moved on."

"And you?"

"I need to check things out for myself at the Warehouse. Speak to Stell. Shouldn't take long. I've phoned her already and told her I'm staying at yours. She's happy to go along with the new name."

"Didn't she ask if you knew anything about the missing cash?"

"She did. But don't fret yourself. I said it was news to me. You can drive me into town tomorrow, if you want, and we'll go see Stella together. Best we keep all that stuff about the money to ourselves, I think. For now, at least."

*

"It's good to see you, Hamie," said Stella, as she met the pair at the door of the Blue Warehouse and ushered them inside. "I've been worried about you. But are you sure it's safe for you to be seen around here? We've been having some problems."

"Don't bother yourself about that, Stell. No one here is going to recognise me. This is one situation where being Billy No-Mates pays off. There was Harry Love, I suppose. But he's not around anymore."

"I sometimes wondered if you'd gone for good, Hamish. But I think I always knew you'd turn up when you felt safe enough. You might have kept me posted, though. A text would've done it."

"Sorry, Stell. Maybe I wasn't actually thinking straight, but I didn't know whether it would be better for all concerned if I simply disappeared."

*

It was another two days before the small, dapper man and the punchbag returned.

He got the story from Hamish that same evening.

"It was mid-afternoon. So the place was closed and Hogan and Barry kept them penned in the reception area, while Stella went down to speak to them. They'd been looking for Gus and when they found he wasn't staying at his apartment any more, they assumed he was back at the Warehouse."

"So what was their pitch?"

"They said they needed another chat with Gus. That was all. But it would have surprised them to find Stell's two minders in their way.

"She told them that if they wanted to talk to Gus again, they'd have to arrange that with the man himself. But that she wasn't able to put them in touch. She said she was too busy just then to concern herself with their problems."

"That must have pleased them."

"Well, they did tell Stella they were trying to keep things friendly. Which was rich. But said that they didn't feel that she was being very accommodating. They offered to call back later. When she had more time."

"And what did she say to that?"

"She told them she didn't seem to have a window free anytime soon and that Hogan would see them out."

"Call me an old worrywart if you like, Hamish, but I wouldn't take these guys so lightly. They've already sliced off Gus's finger and turned over Stella's apartment."

"Well, I'm not sure whether you should be more worried about them or about Gus. Stella seems to think the fat, murdering bastard could be losing it."

"Not that you'd want to gloat at all."

"I probably do. You've probably put your finger on something there. But don't worry. I'm not going to slice it off.

"Stella still won't believe he killed Dad. And I can't prove anything. So really, for the time being, gloating is all I've got."

"Well, I don't want to add to your concerns, but we might have a bigger problem than Gus right now."

"Like?"

"Like while you were in town today, I had a stroll down to the newsagent and got myself a paper. I was coming back along the footpath, enjoying the sunshine, when I found a person of interest dozing in a car across the road from here. Under the laburnum."

"What kind of interest?"

"A cop. A policewoman. A certain Sergeant Styles. I know her by sight from years ago. Used to be run of the mill CID, but I believe these days she's attached to some special investigations outfit based in town."

"A coincidence?"

"Unlikely. Most of my neighbours are fairly upright citizens. Librarians and retired teachers and suchlike. No one the cops would be all that interested in. Anyway, the woman had an unrestricted view of my front door."

"And she was sleeping?"

"Like a log. Dozed off in the sun with a paperback on her lap. She had the window open a bit, and I could actually hear her snoring."

"Not a gripping read then. So what did you do? Go off to the pub until she'd gone?"

"I knocked on her window and asked if she needed medical assistance. She wouldn't have known I'd recognised her. She looked flustered. Said she'd simply been resting her eyes."

"You must've surprised her."

168

"I'm sure I did. But I couldn't help laughing, just a little. Spoilt it. Anyway, she got all embarrassed and drove off."

"You sure she was a cop?"

"I'm sure. Like I said, I know of her from way back. Plus, the dead giveaway was the blue, clip-on roof-light gizmo lying on the rear seat."

The following morning he got a phone call from someone called Slaughter, a detective inspector.

DI Slaughter asked, politely enough, if he wouldn't mind calling into the office for a chat sometime soon.

"Or maybe you might find it more convenient, if I came out there in the next day or so to talk to you?"

"I'm in or hereabouts most of the time," he said. "You can text me and let me know. What's it about? Am I in trouble?"

"I really can't say, Mr Charnley. You might be the one best placed to answer that. Are you? In trouble?"

"Not that I've noticed. See you whenever, then."

It was two o'clock on the following afternoon when Slaughter and Styles arrived. He was stretched out on the couch, peacefully digesting a Railway Hotel lunch, when he was roused by some insistent rapping on the windowpane. The doorbell, lacking a battery, hadn't worked in years.

Hamish was at the kitchen table, fiddling around on his laptop. Jack told him to stay out of sight and keep quiet.

He opened the front door to find DI Slaughter and Sergeant Styles standing on the path.

"What the fuck is this?" He tried his best to sound annoyed. "Can't a man enjoy a sleep in his own home? And if you're from the Jehovahs, you can bugger off right now. I've warned you lot before about wasting my time."

Slaughter ignored the unfriendly greeting and showed his ID.

"I'm DI Slaughter. This is DS Styles. We spoke on the phone yesterday, in case you've forgotten. We're with the SIU."

"The what?"

"The Special Intelligence Unit."

"Oh."

"Might we come inside for a chat?"

"Up to you," he said with a shrug. "Weren't you supposed to text me when you were on your way?"

"We did. Obviously you were sleeping too soundly to spot it. A late night, was it?"

"Not especially. I was sleeping off a pub lunch, if that's all right with you."

He led the way into the lounge.

"Have a seat, guys," he said, adopting a friendlier tone. "Can I get you a hot beverage or anything?"

"We'll skip the drinks, thanks. I'd just like to ask you a few questions."

"At your service," he said, collapsing into an armchair. "But could you tell me something first?"

"If I can."

"Can you tell me why my house has been under police surveillance lately?"

"What makes you think that?"

"Ask your sergeant there. She was the one I found sitting, or I should say sleeping, in her car over the road there a couple of days ago."

"DS Styles has told me about your meeting. My sergeant had simply been checking out your location."

Styles reddened.

"She was asleep."

"She had been working late the previous night. We maintain a fairly hectic pace. Plays havoc with one's sleep patterns."

"But DS Styles must have already known my location, as you put it. Or she wouldn't have been here, would she? But if she really didn't know where I was, and her sleeping outside my house was a pure coincidence, then why not simply phone?"

"I beg your pardon?"

"Why didn't the detective sergeant just phone me if she wanted my address? You obviously have my number. And it's there online for all to see."

Slaughter's patience had its limits. "Look here, Charnley. Let's not worry about the good sergeant's doings. We have a case to investigate, and I believe you might well be able to help us."

"Really? How's that?"

"Because you've been asking around about someone who happens to be on our radar at the moment."

"And who might that be?"

"I'd appreciate it if you'd let me ask the questions."

"Go ahead. What can I tell you? Sure you wouldn't like some tea?"

"No tea, thank you. What we would like is to hear about is the nature of the interest you've been showing in a certain person by the name of Hamish Beard."

"That was weeks ago. And why are you lot worrying yourselves about him, anyway? What's he done?"

"We only want to talk to him. That's all. In connection with a matter we're investigating."

"The explosion at the Blue Warehouse? Would that be it?"

"It might be."

"And you think it might involve this Hamish character?"

"As I said, Mr Charnley, I'll ask the questions if you don't mind. So, what's your interest in Hamish? You're a private investigator. Who's paying you to track down Hamish Beard?"

"No one."

"Then why are you interested?"

"Because I'm getting old and being a PI is no fun. Even when you're young. And I want to do something different with my life before it's too late. So I thought I'd try my hand at writing a book. Something in the true crime genre. See?"

"You're telling me you've become an author?"

"No law against that, is there? Anyway, I thought this guy Hamish might well know about the explosion and all the other stuff that's been going on."

"And how's it going, then? Do you have a manuscript?"

"Not yet. Still trawling for facts."

"And what have you come up with, thus far?" asked Slaughter, frowning. "Anything which could be of significance to the police?"

"Nothing. So far I've unearthed nothing in any way interesting. Very discouraging, I have to say. Is there anything you could tell me, since you're here? Anything that might help me get the thing going?"

"Mr Charnley, what was the purpose of your recent visit to Fuerteventura?"

"Holiday. I needed a break. We all need a change of air from time to time. Don't you think?"

"So you won't help us?"

"Can't. Not won't."

"If I find out you've been withholding information, I'll personally see to it that you suffer the consequences."

"And so you should, Inspector. Anything else I can help you with?" he asked, getting to his feet.

"No? I'll see you out then, shall I?"

"Good luck with the book," said DS Styles as they left.

14

Options

Junior Davidson was busy at his desk in the cluttered office above the garage. The garage housed the two stretched limos which he made available, complete with uniformed drivers, to anyone, so Jack imagined, with money to waste.

"Is there much call for this sort of thing?" he asked as he took a seat opposite. "Really?"

"You'd be surprised. Hen parties, school proms, any kind of special do. People like to impress their friends. Even did a funeral last week. Both our cars have bars in the back, so you can get yourself in the mood on the way to your event."

A bar? Could be good.

"A lot of competition these days, though. It's beginning to take the edge off. But never mind all that. We've got this money thing now, right? Got to shift a bag full of the stuff from here to Amsterdam. The Old Man says you're here to help."

"That's the plan."

"Can't figure out why I'd need you really, but Grandad must have a reason. I've booked us on the overnight ferry from Hull to Rotterdam tomorrow. Friday. A two-hour drive from there will get us to Amsterdam by lunchtime. We've a room sorted in a Ramada on the edge of town.

"Better get here earlyish, right after lunch, and we'll load up and go. It's mainly motorway to the boat. Shouldn't be a problem."

"In a limo?" asked Jack, hopefully. "I could ride in the back."

"Not in a limo. I need to keep those cars spotless."

"And we're planning to come home when? Just so I know."

"We'll drop off the cash on Saturday and get the night ferry the same day. Should be back in time for lunch on Sunday. Okay?"

"Sounds good to me."

"Well, you can fuck off now, Jack. If you wouldn't mind. Things to do. See you tomorrow lunchtime."

After he left the Limo Hire, he set off along Jamaica Street, heading towards the Warehouse. He told himself it wouldn't hurt to maintain some kind of presence in the establishment where the Beards' money-laundering operation had originated.

He reached the car park in the front yard and phoned Stella's number.

"Stella."

It was Stella's voice, but sounding firmer and more confident now than when he'd last heard it.

"It's me. Jack. I'm outside. Want to come down and let me in?"

Less than a minute later, she appeared at the side door and waved him inside. Alone in the darkened corridor, she took him by surprise and gave him a hug. He hadn't thought of her as a hugger.

She led him up the backstairs to the family apartment and into the lounge. They sat side by side on the sofa, and she surprised him again by taking hold of his hand.

"Where's Gus?" he asked, beginning to feel at once nervous and excited at this unexpectedly touchy-feely approach.

"In his room. He hardly ever leaves it during the day. Comes in here sometimes in the early evening, or after we've closed up for the night, for a chat. Do you want to see him?"

174

"Not right now. Probably never. Hamish told you he's sure Gus murdered Claude, didn't he? He says you don't believe him. He's convinced Gus tried to set him up to be killed too."

"I know what Hamish thinks. But it's hardly likely."

"No?"

"No. The shock of losing his dad like that must have made him see things kind of oddly. But then, he's never been entirely normal. Why would Gus even want to do such a thing?"

"I'm not certain he's wrong about the guy, Stella. I prefer to keep an open mind on that one."

"And he still hasn't told me where he's been hiding himself all this time. What happened to him? What's he been doing?"

"It's a long story. But basically, he was out of the country. And he's here under a false identity."

"I know about that. He makes me call him Gunter and treat him like some new acquaintance whenever anyone else is around. But where's he been living? And why? I can't seem to get much out of him, and I don't want to badger him for the details."

"I'm not sure he wants anyone to learn about where he's been hiding out."

"But why?"

"Perhaps, at first, he was trying to stay out of Gus's way for the sake of his own safety. But now, maybe, he's looking to avoid being interviewed by the police after Gus got all blown up like he did. I think he felt it would be better all round if people thought he was most likely dead."

"Well, he's back now. That's what counts. He told me he's staying at your place, but he can use his old room here whenever he wants."

"Could be he's not quite ready to stay here just yet, Stella. He only came to visit you to let you see he was okay and to make sure all was well with you. And how are things with you at the moment, anyway?"

175

"All right, I suppose. Though nothing's as it was. Not since Gus got 'all blown up', as you put it. It's disrupted everything."

"Bound to, really."

"Those bullies who came here to search. They've been here again, looking for Gus, but we had our security in place by then."

"Hamish told me all about it. You saw them off, I know. But what if they come back mob-handed? What then? You still aren't completely safe here."

"Don't we have enough protection with these two guys Gus has found? They're costing a lot more than minimum wage."

"You can never have too much security. You should keep both for as long as you can afford to. Until the danger's passed."

"Claude left me well provided for, so I'm okay cash-wise. It's more that I'm not getting any younger, and I don't want to waste whatever money I have."

She still had his hand in hers, and she began to stroke the back of it, very lightly, with her free hand as she spoke.

"And if I weren't holding out here, then where exactly would I go to be safe? I'd hate to have to go away and hide like Hamish."

She was looking at him now almost pleadingly, as if she believed he had the answer.

"This place is my life. I love it here."

"Keep yourself safe, Stella. That's what's important. Right?"

"I have an old pistol of Claude's. Hamish left it behind when he went to New York. And I have Hogan and Barry. I'm safe enough for now."

Stella moved closer to him and gripped his hand more firmly. She rested her other hand on his thigh as she turned towards him.

"Especially now that you've come back into my life like this, so suddenly."

"Whatever I can do to help."

Not knowing quite how else to handle the situation, he followed through on Stella's invitation. It had been years since his last sexual encounter, and he was clumsy and awkward at first. But Stella seemed to know exactly what she was doing. She made sure that he wasn't clumsy or awkward for long.

An hour later, he made ready to leave. Stella needed to get dressed for the evening opening, and he didn't want to be hanging around, getting in the way. And he wasn't sure precisely what kind of situation he might be being drawn into. Despite Stella's assurances that she would love him to stay the night, he said he really had to go.

"Business to attend to," he lied.

"Did Hamish tell you that he killed Percy White, Claude's right-hand man?" she asked, as she repaired her make-up at her dressing-table mirror. "He shot him. Here, in this apartment."

A serious subject. Casually raised. Odd.

"He did kind of mention it. It surprised me. He doesn't look the killer type."

"He'd been behaving strangely right after Claude's death, and he only had the gun to frighten Gus. Probably had no idea the thing was loaded. An accident."

There was a slight tremor in Stella's voice, and her eyes were glistening with tears. Was he being pulled into something he wouldn't be able to handle?

"I wish there was some way I could help, but I can't see how right now. You've got my number. And don't hesitate to call me if there's ever anything I can do. How about I come over from time to time, to check on how things are going?"

Should I be saying this? What am I getting myself into?

"That'd be nice," she said with a smile. She took his hand and squeezed it. "It's a bit like old times, isn't it, Jack?"

"More than a bit," he said, smiling. "Anyway, I'd better go."

She came down the stairs with him and gave him another hug and a lingering kiss before letting him out of the side door.

On the walk back toward the town centre and the train station, once again in charge of his own emotions, he considered the situation at the Warehouse. He was looking for an angle that might come in useful somehow. He didn't find one.

He walked on, into the centre and up to Central, to get the train out to the Point. The city was as lively as ever. Passing the buskers giving their all on Church Street, he realised just how much he'd miss the place if he left.

It was sunny today, though, and warm. That made a difference. Was he, on some unconscious level, thinking about leaving, moving out to some bolthole in the Canaries to live alongside his new business associates and his new friend, Hamish? An apartment in Arrecife? Somewhere like that?

And there was Stella to consider. He had little doubt now that she had him in view as a replacement for Gus. Someone to be there whenever she needed. Someone she could rely on to take care of her security and help her run things safely.

Not so long ago, he realised, he would have leapt at the opportunity. She was an attractive woman. The Warehouse would be an interesting place to live, and being there with Stella would have meant that he need never again trudge home in the rain to a cold, empty and lonely house. But times had changed. He now had money, a future, ambitions to fulfil, and a like-minded band of brothers to help him fulfil them.

Could he have Stella and a role at the nightclub and keep his new gang member activities to boot? Was that possible? Claude and Gus had both run their lives along similar lines. But then, events hadn't worked out all that well for either of them, had they?

And then again, Claude and Gus had been running their own operations, whereas he still seemed to be at the bottom of the pecking order. Playing second fiddle to Freddy's tattooed and be-studded grandson.

Clearly, these were things to think about.

Back at the semi, there was no sign of Hamish. He made himself a coffee and got busy packing a bag for the Amsterdam trip.

It was two hours later when he heard the front door close and Hamish came into the kitchen to find him sitting at the table, staring at his hands.

"Hi," he said, glancing at the bag parked by the doorway. "Just had a long hike up on the dunes. All along the beach and then home through the pines. You should come with me sometime."

There was no response.

"Been getting ready for your trip?"

He grunted a reply. He was aware that Hamish was looking at him a little more closely than usual.

"You okay?" Hamish asked. He sounded concerned.

"Yeah," he said, looking up only briefly and scratching the side of his head.

"I suppose I am. Don't worry about me."

"Been to the pub?"

"I have. Got a meal there. And, when you think about it, where else would I go? There's an art group exhibition at the church hall and an introduction to computers class at the library. And there's the Railway. So, of the three?"

"Well, you don't sound too happy about it. What's the problem? If you don't mind me asking."

He noticed the whisky bottle at Jack's elbow. The glass waiting, half full.

"I don't mind at all, Hamish, old pal," he said, reaching for the bottle and waving it towards the empty chair opposite. "Want a glug?"

"A small one. To be sociable. So what's up?"

He got himself a glass and put it on the table for Jack to fill as he sat down.

"Don't worry about it. I just seem to have too much on my mind at the moment. Too much at once. So I decided I'd try to drink my way out of my mental thicket before I got to be too depressed. As it happens, I'm starting to feel better already."

"You sure about that? You might think you're feeling better at the minute, but what you're actually feeling is drunk. If you're feeling better about anything at all, it's probably the fact that I'm here and that now you have someone to drink with."

He knew Hamish was right. The booze would leave him feeling even more depressed in the end. He'd do better next time around. Right now, though, he needed to drink himself to sleep. Sleep was important, wasn't it?

They sat and drank steadily on into the evening. They talked about the upcoming Amsterdam trip and about how things were down in the Baltic. Somewhere along the way, a new bottle was opened.

"It may be," said Jack, speaking slowly and deliberately through the whisky, "that I'm having what they call a midlife crisis. Heard of that, have you?"

"I might have."

"It's what happens when you start to wonder just what you did with the first half of your life and begin to realise that, all in all, you've been something of a twat. And it gets even worse, when you realise that the

180

rest of your life is going nowhere either, and you don't know what to do about it."

"I find it hard to get my head around that," said Hamish. "You have money in the bank. Your mortgage problem is sorted. The world's your oyster. You're free to do whatever you want."

"Like what? Exactly what do I do now? I'm a paunchy, middle-aged git with a drink habit. I'm not complaining about the cash. But look at me. I've no real friends. Beyond, hopefully, your good self. No family. No meaningful relationships. I'm not even sure I have what it takes to risk one of those."

"So you're a loner. So am I. So what?"

"So I'm a good deal older than you. It's beginning to feel a little bit desperate, that's all. Don't get me wrong. I've always made my own decisions in life, bad ones mainly, and I am where I am.

"I should get myself some sort of hobby. Like collecting antique jam jars or something. Something totally fucking pointless."

Hamish wanted to help. He tried another tack.

"I can see that the money might not be a total solution. I get that. Maybe that's actually making your problem even worse, in the short term. Now you have no more excuses. You have the freedom. More choices. Isn't our money-laundering operation a purposeful enough project for you?"

Jack made no response.

Hamish sighed over his whisky and tried again. "What if you never had any choice but to do what you did. What if it just felt like you did?"

"What?"

"Try looking at it this way. I know we're both a bit pissed already, but tell me, was it true yesterday that we would be sitting here today, drinking together?"

He thought hard, the effort showing on his face.

"Yes," he said at length, "sure it was."

"Right answer. So if it was true yesterday, it must have also been true the day before that. Yes?"

"So?"

"So you can track that back all the way through time, see? In fact, it's always been true that we would be sitting here like this, drinking, just as we are."

"And?"

"And so we had no choice but to do it, did we? If we had done something else today, we would have had to falsify an existing fact, a truth, in order to do it. And that would be impossible. Truth is truth. Get it? It's all like that."

He felt himself sliding, quite gracefully it seemed to him, from his chair. And then he was lying, peacefully enough, on the kitchen floor. He could hear himself snoring.

"Suit yourself," said Hamish, as he poured himself another.

The following morning, with pale sunlight leaking in through the window of the lounge, an insistent ringing brought him back to consciousness. He was stretched out, fully clothed, on the couch. He made the effort to fish his phone out of his pocket.

"Where the fuck are you?" shouted Junior. "I said early, didn't I?"

15

Amsterdam

The journey to Amsterdam was uneventful. On the ferry, they ate sandwiches in their cabin before Jack wandered off to spend a couple of hours drinking in the bar. After the whisky he'd guzzled with Hamish the previous night, he wasn't feeling at his best. He was careful to drink no more than he needed to keep himself painlessly afloat.

The following morning Junior drove them up from Rotterdam, under grey and overcast skies. When they arrived in Amsterdam, it was already beginning to rain. They went straight to the Ramada, checked in, and took their luggage up to their room. They each had an overnight bag and a large wheeled case.

"One at a time," said Junior, heaving his case up onto one of the twin beds and opening it up. "We'll do mine, then yours."

At first glance, the case contained nothing more than a stack of unframed paintings on canvas.

"Got these from an acquaintance at the art school. Redundant stuff the students have finished with. Some of it's quality artwork, though."

"On the off-chance someone checked our bags, nice."

"I looked into some of the methods they use," said Junior, peeling off a few layers of artwork to reveal neat bundles of banknotes packed underneath.

"A scanner can show up a large lump of organic material like the notes, and that could make the guys on the border suspicious. So if they wanted to take a quick look, they'd see the paintings. For an exhibition. Yeah?"

He suspected that the people staffing the border could well prove to be a little cannier than that if it ever came to it. But they'd got this far, so why knock it?

"Works for me," he said. He watched Junior emptying the artworks and the banknotes onto the bed. He stacked the bundles of notes on one side.

"Now yours," said Junior, dropping his own case onto the floor. "Unpack it."

Jack followed a similar procedure with his own luggage.

"Okay. Stack all the canvases back inside your case and close it up. That one goes home with us."

"Let me guess," he said. "We put all the money into the empty one."

"Right, smart-ass, while I do that, maybe you should get yourself showered and spruced up a bit. You look like shit, and I can't say I'm sold on your personal fragrance either."

"Lucky we didn't go for a double bed, then. All things considered."

"You got yourself hammered the other night, didn't you? Judging by the state you were in when you managed to turn up at the limo hire. You still stink of booze."

"So? I'm here, aren't I? You simply can't please some people."

"Getting pissed up the night before a job? This is important. You have a drink problem, Jack. You should deal with it."

"I prefer to see it as more of a solution than a problem, snowflake. So what's next?"

"Next is that you get to have lunch in town while I stay here and guard the cash."

"I think I should be able to manage that."

"You get the tram from the stop over the road. It takes twenty minutes to reach the centre. Get yourself to the central railway station. Ask for directions. Most of the natives speak English better than we do.

"You'll find an eatery called Loetje." He spelt it out, making sure Jack understood. "Grab yourself a table in there. The reviews say the food's good. And, if you choose to sit by the window, you can watch the tour boats cruise the canal. Might take your mind off the whisky."

"And?"

"Relax and enjoy your meal. I'll text your number to the contact the Old Man sent me. Make sure your phone's turned on. Okay?"

"Think I can manage that."

"When our guy there contacts you, he should give you a business card belonging to someone called Giuseppe De Lorca. You already know him from your Naples trip."

"Right. I do. I know Giuseppe."

"But this isn't Giuseppe, it's some Dutch money guy. If he checks out with the card and he's on his own, you tell him which hotel we're at and ride back here with him in his car. He should be alone. Okay?"

"I think I can manage that too."

"And it's important that he doesn't get to use his phone once he knows where we are. He shouldn't even try to, if he sticks to the rules."

"Got it."

"And make sure no one follows you on the drive back."

"Okay, boss."

"And don't drink. Coffee only. All right? Alky? Give me your mobile."

He handed over his phone and waited while Junior punched in a new contact before handing it back.

He liked the Loetje. It had a peaceful atmosphere, good views over the canal and excellent food. He was finishing his coffee and wondering if Junior would be able to tell if he followed it with a large whisky when his phone began to vibrate. 'Money Guy', the screen said.

He turned to look across the restaurant. Over the heads of the diners, he could see a man standing in the entrance, holding a phone. When he saw he had Jack's attention, he jerked his head and moved out through the door. Jack got up, paid his bill at the counter and followed.

The man, middle-aged, medium height and nondescript, was wearing a waterproof and a cap against the rain. He stared at Jack for a few seconds.

"You?" he asked. His accent said he was a local. So far, so good.

"Me," he said. "And?"

The man showed him Giuseppe's business card.

"Okay," he said. "Take me to your car and we'll go."

"To where?"

"You give me your phone and I'll tell you. It's not like we don't trust you or anything. Procedure, that's all. You'll get it back once we're done."

The contact said nothing as he handed over his mobile. Jack powered it down.

"Ramada Apollo. You know where it is?"

"I do. No worries."

On the walk to the car, he phoned Junior to tell him they were on their way.

Despite Jack's attempts at small talk, the man said little on the drive out to the hotel. So he gave up on the idea of having an interesting chat about the pros and cons of the dirty money business. Instead, he sat there, staring through the window and checking to make sure they weren't being followed. When they reached a roundabout, he got the contact to double back on himself for a few hundred yards, just to be certain.

They parked right by the Ramada's front entrance, and he waited while the contact took a large bag from

186

the back of his car. Then he led the man up to the room. Junior let them in, checking up and down the corridor as he did so.

"Everything okay?"

"So far. No problems so far. Our friend here doesn't say much. He hasn't even told me his name."

"You don't need it. I'm a courier, that's all. I should count the money now."

They sat, side by side, on the window seat as the contact pulled a counting machine from his bag. He set it down on the dressing table and plugged it into the wall socket. Then he took out a sack and placed it on the floor next to him.

"I'm going to count it and do some random checks for fakes," he said, without even a glance in their direction. "And I have to concentrate. So you two keep quiet until I'm finished, okay? You can make me a hot drink. This place does sachets of lemon tea. Just keep them coming."

Three lemon teas later, the contact had completed his work and dropped all the money into the sack by his side.

"Close enough," he said. "We're good."

He replaced the counting machine in his bag and tied up the neck of the sack holding the notes.

When Jack returned the man's phone, he powered it up and sent a text.

Two minutes later, Junior got a text in response. He checked it and nodded to the contact. "Okay. Everything's squared off at the other end. You can go."

"Nice meeting you," said the contact, without the slightest hint of sincerity, as he struggled through the doorway with the bag in one hand and the sack in the other.

"You too," said Junior, standing up and stretching. "It's been fun."

"We'd better go soon, ourselves," said Jack. "Just about enough time to make the ferry."

*

They were disembarking in Hull on Sunday morning when he found a text from Stella.

> Don't want to speak over the phone – something terrible has happened – I need help x

"I don't like the sound of this."

"What?" asked Junior. "What is it?"

"It's Stella Beard at the nightclub. Can you step on it a bit? There's a problem."

Back in the Baltic, Junior dropped Jack outside the Warehouse.

"Till next time then, Alky. Hope it's all okay with your Mrs. Beard. Do let me know if I can help at all."

It was lunchtime, and on Sunday the bar area was usually open for business. But today it was closed. A worried-looking Stella opened the side door almost as soon as he phoned to tell her he was outside.

"What?"

"Come in," she said, glancing around the yard. "No one about, is there?"

"Didn't see anyone. Why are you closed? It's Sunday."

"Because I daren't open the place. And anyway, there are no staff. I sent them home."

"Even the heavies?"

"Heaven knows where they are. I haven't sent them away. They've disappeared. Both of them. They aren't answering their phones. There's only me, Gus and Hamish here."

She led him into the room behind the bar and pointed at a chest freezer. It was where the ice cubes were kept.

"It's in there. It's horrible. I couldn't look at it again."

"What is it? From the expression on your face, I'm not sure I want to see."

"Kevin."

He steeled himself and slowly raised the lid of the freezer. There was a plastic carrier bag sitting amongst the packs of ice cubes. He reached in and pulled, tentatively, at the side of the bag to open it. There was a head inside, the face contorted and set in an agonised grimace. He took a step back, slamming the lid down. He felt sick and dizzy.

"For God's sake!" he said. "What the hell is going on?"

"I've no idea. It came by special delivery earlier today. It was bubble wrapped, inside a cardboard box."

She wrinkled her lips as if she was about to sob. Then she recovered.

"I'm terrified. What do we do?"

"Where's Hamish?"

"Upstairs, keeping watch through the windows. He wanted you here with us before we made any kind of move."

They climbed the stairs to the apartment and found Hamish standing by the lounge window.

"You'd better all come with me," said Jack. "Anytime now would be good. Goes without saying, we have to get away from here as fast as possible."

He turned to face Stella.

"Pack a bag, right now. And leave the Lexus out front. It might fool them for a while if they come sniffing around. We'll go via the rear exit and walk into town through the back streets. We'll get the train out. No taxis, no cars, nothing traceable."

"What about Gus?" asked Stella. "He's holed up in his room and he's got his hands on a gun from somewhere."

"Looks as though he knows what's coming. What's he told you?"

"Nothing. He's been acting weird ever since I moved him back here. He used to like to chat, but he's stopped speaking to me. I have no idea why."

"What do you mean, 'what about Gus'?" asked Hamish. "Is there an issue?"

"Well, we can't leave him here. On his own."

"Yes, we can. We're not taking the murdering bastard anywhere. None of this would have happened if it weren't for him. Dad would still be here running things, and no millions would ever have gone missing."

"But they could kill him."

"And that would be bad how?"

*

"I'm sorry, Jack. But I couldn't think what else to do," said Hamish, following Stella into the lounge of Jack's semi.

"I waited for you to get back so we could bring Stells out here. With the Warehouse being targeted like it is, I needed somewhere safe to take her and yours was the best place I could come up with."

"I don't want to stay in the apartment now they've scared off my so-called security," said Stella. "Or maybe they bought them off. Either way, they're gone. And look at what they've done to poor Kevin."

"Who did this?" asked Jack. "Do you know?"

"Looks like Dad's clients caught up with somehow," said Hamish. "What do you reckon we should do?"

"Have they made any new demands?"

"They phoned me," said Stella. "They just want to find out where their missing money is. Like always. I've told them I don't know. Neither does Gus. What else do they expect me to say?"

"You sure Gus can't tell you?" asked Jack, peering between the window blinds at the road outside. "Does he have no idea at all?"

"I'm sure he didn't enjoy having his finger sliced off. He'd have told them whatever he knew."

He turned to Hamish. "You didn't tell him where you were taking Stella?"

"We didn't even let him know we were leaving. He's still in his room at the top of the Warehouse. You needn't worry, no one knows we're here. I owe you. I've put you on the spot. I'm sorry."

"Don't fuss yourself. I've nothing else on at the moment, have I? It'll give me something to think about. And I couldn't leave Stella at risk, could I? Tea anyone?"

"Tea?" asked Hamish, laughing. "Are you serious? No booze?"

"No booze. Not until we get this sorted."

He went off to the kitchen feeling good. For now, at least, he had a worthwhile purpose - keeping all three of them safe.

He brought the tea things in on a tray and placed them on the low table in front of his guests. "Help yourself to milk and sugar," he said, smiling.

"So you really are on the wagon."

"Well, I'm not a full-time drunk. That's just a hobby of mine. I like to straighten out sometimes. This is one of those times."

Stella's phone rang. She put down her cup and reached into her pocket to retrieve it. She glanced at the screen, then she hesitated, looking in turn from Hamish to Jack.

"Unknown number."

"Better answer it," said Jack. "Might find out something useful."

She took the call. "Yes?"

"Don't say anything. Just listen," said the caller.

She sat on the sofa with the phone to her ear, neglecting to turn on the speakerphone. The call did not take long.

"It was someone who didn't give his name. Told me they'd got one of their missing millions back. Something to do with poor Kevin. But, since they're still two million down, they've decided to take a controlling interest in the Warehouse in lieu of the rest."

"How?"

"Nothing official. They want to act through me and skim off most of the profits. They'll leave me with the equivalent of a salary, and I'll stay on as manager."

"Shit!" said Hamish. "It gets worse."

"On the plus side, though, I don't get to end up like Kevin. With my head in the freezer. Or get cut up with a meat slicer like Gus."

"Always a bright side to everything," said Jack, smiling again. "Anything about Gus?"

"Never mentioned him at all. Maybe they've written him off."

"So what are you going to do, then?" asked Hamish. "You could leave town. Leave the country, even. Disappear. Or go to the police."

"Or I could do what they want. Run the Warehouse, just as I always have. The gangsters would let the place be. Gus could go back to his apartment, and I wouldn't have to worry about him, beyond making sure the care was there when he needed it."

"I can't see why you concern yourself about Gus," said Hamish. "You know what I think."

"I'll never believe he had anything to do with your dad's death. It was an accident."

"But I just know it was him. He was even planning to get me bumped off in New York."

"You've been deluding yourself. No one else believes any of this. You never liked Gus, and you made no attempt to get on with him."

"So I'm nuts then, am I? Is that it?"

"Troubled. You're troubled. That's all. Don't you remember how, after your dad died, you thought you could talk to his ghost? That was when you began to imagine Gus was a murderer."

"I can see how you find it hard to understand, but I did talk to Dad's ghost. I still do sometimes."

So, Hamish talks to the spirit world. Not exactly normal, then.

"So if you don't believe Gus killed Dad," asked Hamish, looking at Stella, "how do you explain what happened?"

"An accident. Someone left the trapdoor open, and he fell through it in the dark. He'd been drinking and simply didn't notice."

"But the trapdoor's always kept locked. The padlock was missing. No deliveries that day. No reason for it to be open at all. So who opened it, and why?"

"I don't know. But I'm still sure it was an accident of some kind. And even if someone had been trying to murder your dad, why blame Gus? Why not the same people who killed Kevin? They might even have been the ones who tried to kill Gus by putting that bomb under his bed."

She turned towards Jack, who was sitting to one side, following the discussion between the pair.

"What about it, Jack? Which of us is making the most sense?"

"I do feel Claude's death is suspicious," he said. "But there's no evidence that anyone murdered him. And none at all to point to the identity of the murderer, should he or she exist."

"But Dad told me himself that it was Gus," said Hamish, sounding exasperated.

"In a dream," said Stella. "You were dreaming, that's all."

"It was his ghost. A genuine ghost. Not a dream."

It was evident to Jack that the conversation was going nowhere and that it could take quite a while, possibly forever, to get there. He brought Stella a duvet and his last spare pillow before excusing himself and heading off to bed.

He considered inviting Stella to join him. But Hamish's presence made that feel awkward, so he left Hamish and Stella to say goodnight.

"Looks as though you'll have to make do with the sofa for tonight," said Hamish. "I'm already set up in the guest room. It's a big sofa, though. You'll be fine. I'll swop with you tomorrow if you like."

By the time they were all sitting down to a breakfast of scrambled egg and toast, early the next morning, she had reached her decision.

"The way I see it, I've got no choice. I don't want to lose my role at the Warehouse. And I don't see myself spending what would probably be a very long time hiding out, God knows where.

"If I go to the police, I might still end up dead. And explaining exactly how the Warehouse got into this situation is likely to result in the place being confiscated as proceeds of crime. Or whatever the term is. And my pension fund is liable to go the same way."

"So you're going to accept the gangsters' offer?" asked Hamish.

"I am."

An hour and a half later, the three of them re-entered the eerie silence of the Blue Warehouse. And as soon as they opened the door to the apartment on the top floor, they could smell the danger.

"It's gas!" said Stella. "Whatever you do, don't flick any switches!"

They moved quickly through the rooms, pushing windows open as they went. Hamish ran back downstairs to turn off the flow at the mains while Stella checked out Gus's bedroom.

She didn't know how, but she was aware at once that Gus was dead. She was sure of it. She went over and touched his forehead. Cool to the touch. She let her hand brush his cheek, surprised at the sudden flush of emotion she felt. Her eyes were filling with tears. 'Not the time for that,' she told herself. 'Get a grip.' Even as these thoughts formed, she realised that the moment would never come again. No one would mourn Gus's passing.

"You won't have to trouble yourself about Gus anymore," she said, coming back out to find Hamish and Jack in the kitchen, turning off the gas taps on the cooker. "He's gone."

"Where to?"

"He's dead. He's sitting by the window in his room with a cigarette lighter in one hand and a gun in the other. As if he was planning to take half of the Warehouse with him. Along with anyone else who might happen to be inside. I knew we shouldn't have just walked off and left him like we did."

"You sure he's a goner?" asked Jack.

"Feel free to look. I don't think he's faking it. The gas must've got him."

"Looks pretty well dead to me," agreed Hamish, as they viewed Gus, slumped in his wheelchair. "You going to try mouth to mouth?"

"Do you think I should?" asked Stella. "I don't really want to."

"Only joking," said Hamish. "But you should phone for an ambulance. And the police. Jack and I should go. You'd best tell them you'd been out shopping and came back alone."

"And the complete absence of staff? The place closed up? How do I explain all that? The police already have the Warehouse under suspicion."

"Try to find a way to put all that on Gus. I'm sure you'll come up with something, if you think about it. And hide the gun somewhere no one's going to find it."

She began to cry. For herself, this time. Not for Gus.

"I'm not much good at this, am I? That's two dead husbands in a row."

"It's not ideal, I'll give you that," said Hamish. "And I don't mean to sound cruel, but maybe he's better off like he is, in that big nightclub in the sky. He wasn't coping too well with his new situation, was he? And we really couldn't have taken him with us. There was no way it was practical in the circumstances."

"Perhaps you're right," she said, dabbing at her eyes. "Nothing we can do now, anyway."

16

Champagne

Jack was sitting with Giuseppe and Hamish in Hamish's sunlit kitchen, waiting for Freddy to arrive from La Oliva. It was mid-afternoon when he strode in and placed an expensive-looking bottle of champagne on the table.

"We did good," he said. "Got some glasses, Hamish? We should celebrate."

Hamish set four wine glasses in front of Freddy, who made a show of uncorking the wine and pouring them each a drink.

"Our first client's well pleased with our performance and, you'll all be getting a cut of our commission in due course. Our operation is now officially up and running."

"Have you spoken to Junior?" asked Hamish.

"Spoke to him on the way over here. He's happy to do another run as soon as we can arrange the business."

"And we can get more?" asked Giuseppe, accepting a glass of champagne. "More business?"

"Sure as eggs," said Freddy. "As you know, better than any of us, the world is full of dodgy cash waiting to be moved on. Word gets around. You'll see.

"Salud!" he said, raising his glass. "To our new enterprise and a golden future."

"The thing is," he continued, once the glasses had been drained, "we'd best not keep repeating the same run to Amsterdam. We're not on our own territory over there. And we risk attracting the wrong kind of attention if we show up repeatedly on the same route. It's not quite the same as trundling up and down to London and dealing with someone we know well. It's not the same operation Claude Beard was running with Giuseppe here."

"So where, then?" asked Hamish. "What did you have in mind?"

"That will be up to Giuseppe. Wherever he can line up a suitable banker for us to do business with. Shouldn't be too difficult, do you think, G? Not for a man with your talents and connections."

"I have links to a few people we could use. And, as you say, the way things are at the moment, it's probably better not to keep putting everything along the same track. Safer to spread our operations around and leave our options open."

"Junior will provide our focus on the money-laundering from now on. The limo hire is an excellent cover. It even makes a bit of cash. We're going to hang onto that.

"I want you and Junior to continue to work together, Jack. It worked well for Amsterdam, and I don't want either of you going solo just yet. Maybe never. We can't risk losing a consignment, and two heads are better than one if things get tricky."

Jack couldn't help but notice that it was the money that Freddy was worried about losing, not his grandson. And certainly not him.

17

The Smiths

"I'm not sure," said Vincent, as he stood on the wide back porch of the large, converted barn that two-thirds of the Smith Clan called home. He looked out over a sunlit valley of pastures and woodland to where the far fell-side sat blue on the horizon. No unwanted sound intruded. There was only birdsong.

"We don't know how much we can rely on this Beard woman, do we?"

He spat out the matchstick he'd been chewing and turned to face his brother, Craig.

"She's accepted the deal, anyway," said Craig. "Those guys we hired to work on her and that husband-on-wheels of hers have scared the shit out of them both."

"I think having someone's head delivered to your place in a cardboard box would scare most. A nice touch."

"Yeah, poor old Kev," said Craig, smiling. "How dim can you get? Trying to unload the cash back here wasn't the smartest thing he could have done. Idiot.

"So what do you want to do now? About the Warehouse situation?"

"We'll just have to try her out, I suppose. The Beard woman. Once she's got her hands dirty, she'll be safe enough."

"Want me to stash some product there?"

"Why not? Let's start that way and see how she reacts. Keep a close eye on things for a while."

"You know me, Vince. Keeping a close eye on things is what I do best."

"What about the guy you put onto it? The investigator? Do we take him at his word or what?"

"Charnley? I think so. For the time being, at least. He's been reliable enough in the past, and he's strictly small time. No way he'd try to play us. We should leave him be for now in case we need to use him again. See how things turn out."

Craig took his younger brother, Michael, along and drove the ninety minutes down to the Warehouse with a bag of coke. They had wrapped the bag in three layers of plastic, placed it inside a plastic crate, and stood the crate on a groundsheet in the back of the Discovery. It was all to help guard against the sniffers spotting a trace if the police ever examined the car. Not that they'd ever found cause. The Smiths were careful that way.

He had taken the trouble to phone ahead and tell Stella Beard to expect them.

She was waiting and let them in quickly when Craig rang the bell. She led them upstairs, to the meeting room, with Michael carrying the crate.

"My name's Craig," he said. "This one here's my brother, Mike. You'll be seeing me or Mike from time to time, now that you're working for us." He grinned.

"Call me Stella, then," she said. "If we're on first-name terms." She was trying hard to keep things civil, even if she felt anything but.

"And how's Mr Beard doing, Stella? Is he around? Are you going to introduce us?"

"I doubt it. Gus's dead. Left the gas on and fell asleep."

"Oooh!" said Craig. "That's bad. Condolences."

"Yeah, right. So you wanted to see me?"

"Just brought a little something here for you to take care of. It's product, so be careful with it. It's valuable."

"Product?"

"Coke. As in the white powder you can snort. You must've used it yourself on occasion."

"Never touched the stuff. Ever. And I don't allow customers or staff to use that kind of thing anywhere on the premises. The only recreational drug in use around here is alcohol."

"Whatever you say," he said, grinning again. "I'm sure you're right. But put it somewhere safe. Like I say, it's valuable."

"How long's it going to be here?" she asked, a note of anxiety creeping into her voice, despite her best efforts.

"Until we move it. Get used to it. There'll be more. You planning to reopen soon? The place looks deserted."

"Yes, soon. But there was Gus's death to deal with, and there've been some staff issues. Was it you who scared my security away?"

"Gave them a little break and a small bonus for being so cooperative, that's all. Everyone deserves some time out now and again, don't you think? They'll be back tomorrow. Be ready."

"Not sure I want them back. They weren't much use with you lot, were they?"

"They're okay, Stella. Talented guys. Trust me. They had no choice. We were armed. They weren't. So no contest, see?"

"If you say so. But before I forget to mention it, apart from everything else, there's a severed head in the freezer. That's going to make things a bit awkward when the staff come in."

"Right," said Craig. "Not to worry. Allow us to deal with that for you."

18

Paris

Two weeks after the Amsterdam run, there was another client in the frame, and Freddy was back in Hamish's kitchen sounding out Jack, Hamish and Giuseppe about the next job.

"We'll be moving a bit more on this trip, G. Seven hundred and fifty grand. What's our best option if we don't use Amsterdam again this time?"

"Just now, I'd say Paris."

"You're sure using someone in London wouldn't be better?" asked Hamish. "Why keep risking crossing borders? Dad used London exclusively for his bigger deals, and no one bothered him, as far as I know."

"Claude Beard was an established player," said Freddy, "operating on his own territory.

"We aren't in that situation yet. Apart from which, we also want to be able to help people who simply need to move cash from A to B. As in crossing a border or two with the actual banknotes. Sometimes they'll need to use the notes at the other end to finance a deal."

"It's pretty common," said Giuseppe. "People don't always put their money through the banks."

"But we're going to run additional risks at the borders, aren't we?" asked Hamish. "This isn't something we know how to do."

"So we take small, careful steps and learn as we go," said Davidson. "I don't have time to wait years for all this to happen. Or to spend any of it inside. Cautious, steady growth is the way forward. Trust me. This is our opportunity to make it rich, big time."

"Just looking to minimise the risks."

"Soon we'll find someone trustworthy we can pay to take the risks for us. And remember, people smuggle money all the while and they rarely get caught. We have to be smarter than those that do. That's all."

"And luckier, too," said Hamish.

"So this time we're shifting more cash than before. I'll make sure you have all the details. Talk it through with Junior when you see him."

Jack and Hamish walked out of the arrivals hall at John Lennon and collected the Qashqai from the long-stay carpark.

"I'm hoping to stay at yours again," said Hamish as they climbed into the car. "And just so we're clear, are we going out for a drink tonight or are you still on the wagon? You hardly drank at all over in Honda this time. I'm impressed."

"I'll never be completely tea-total, but if I can keep big enough intervals between the binges, I'll be happy with that. Tricky, though, now I'm not working like I was. Never imagined I'd miss work, but I do. I can get to being a bit aimless sometimes."

"Well, it looks as though things are moving your way, in that case. With this run to Paris scheduled for you and Junior. He should have the cash ready by now."

"I never thought I'd be going back there. Swore I wouldn't. But I guess it's time."

"What do you mean? Time for what?"

"How about I tell you about that later? We heading straight to mine or what?"

"No. You'd better drop me in town. I need to speak to Junior about the Paris thing. And see Stella. I'll catch up with you tonight."

They spent the evening, as expected, drinking in the Railway. On this occasion, though, the pace was measured, and they stuck to beer.

"So what's this mysterious thing about it being time for you to go back to Paris? You obviously have some history there. Want to tell me the story?"

"Not sure," said Jack, sipping at his pint. "I don't usually talk about what happened. In fact, I never have. But maybe there's no harm."

"Better out than in. Isn't that what they say?"

"It's where I lost my wife, Wendy, all those years ago. In some ways it seems like a lifetime. And then, in other ways, it can sometimes seem like it was the day before yesterday."

Hamish said nothing, waiting for him to continue.

"I spent a few years in the Army in my younger days and finished up in Berlin. My career in the military wasn't very exciting, and I got bored. By the time I left, I'd developed the impressive drink habit you've been privileged to witness on occasion."

"And it's been a pleasure," said Hamish.

"It was a way of dealing with the boredom, I think. And when I left, the drink habit came home with me.

"I was young and optimistic enough, back then, to imagine a comfortable and well-adjusted future. Marriage to the right woman. Nice house. Possibly even kids."

"Sounds fairly normal."

"Well, life turned out not to be like that for me. I was still reasonably personable and, some might have said, good looking at that point. I had no problem finding suitable women to explore my options with."

"Never heard it called that, Jack. But I get your drift."

He gave Hamish a discouraging look. "I'm trying to be serious here," he said.

"Sorry. Didn't mean to sound flip. Please go on."

"Anyway. None of the ladies stuck around. I was drinking too much. And it turns out that the vast majority of women in the market for some kind of commitment aren't too keen to commit to a part-time drunk."

"Yes. I can see how that might be."

"And then I found Wendy. A nice girl. Good sense of humour. Similar future in mind. And, crucially, she liked a drink herself.

"On the downside, her parents weren't drinkers, and they strongly disapproved of our going out together. They'd been hoping she'd bag herself some strait-laced accountant or whatever, who'd keep her in line."

"Tricky."

"Yes, tricky. In the end, we got married in secret. We even drove up to Gretna Green to do it. Imagine that. She had an office job in Liverpool at the time, and I was working as a PI. So we had enough coming in to land ourselves a mortgage on the house I'm still living in."

"What happened to Wendy?"

"I'm getting to that. We had a routine. We'd keep on the straight and narrow during the week while we were at work. But at weekends, we took the opportunity to let our hair down, have a glass or two, and enjoy ourselves.

"And whenever we could manage it, we liked to have a few days off and take a trip somewhere. We made city breaks our speciality. We enjoyed exploring. Thing was, we'd always over-drink on those weekend trips."

"So, one of these outings was to Paris, yeah?"

"It was. We'd found an affordable hotel, fairly central, and we were having a nice time. Our usual plan in the evenings was to have a meal out somewhere close to where we were staying. We'd share a bottle over dinner and wander back to the hotel and finish our drinking there. So we stayed safe.

"But this particular trip was unusual because a couple of Wendy's friends happened to be in Paris at the same time. So we arranged to meet up for a meal. It was someplace miles away from where we were staying. We had to take two Metro trains and walk some distance to get there."

He was sounding serious now, and Hamish gave him his full attention.

"Problem was, we met this couple in a bar first off and had quite a few before we even reached the restaurant. And we drank more with the meal.

"When we left, we were all pretty far gone. The girls in particular. The others had a hotel in a different area to us, and they got a taxi. We decided, I decided, that it would be easy enough to use the Metro to get back."

He fell silent, staring into his pint glass.

"So what then?" prompted Hamish. "What did you do?"

"We'd been walking around, trying to find the Metro station again, but I soon enough realised we'd got ourselves lost. Wendy had drunk far too much. So much her legs gave way, and I was struggling to pull her up off the pavement. Some student types came along and took pity on us. There weren't many mobile phones around at the time, if any, so one of the students went to a bar nearby and phoned for a taxi.

"I was on autopilot. Everything was a blur. But I remembered the street the hotel was on. I still can. The Rue de Malt. Not far from Republique. Ironic, now that I think of it, given that malt whisky became my beverage of choice."

"So you got back okay?"

He ignored the question.

"I gave the street name to the driver, but I couldn't remember what our hotel was called.

"Anyway, he took us to the Rue de Malt. I managed to pay him and pull Wendy out onto the footpath and get her upright. She was holding tightly onto my arm. It had got to be very dark by then.

"I was so drunk I could barely see. Just a blur of lights and noise. We were standing at a busy junction, and we were on the wrong side of it. I led her across.

206

She was still clinging onto me for all she was worth, but she was staggering. It was a wide road with a lot of traffic."

He was silent again, for a few seconds, staring down at his hands. Hamish didn't interrupt.

"A car hit Wendy before we reached the other side. I don't think she ever knew what happened. She was dead before the ambulance arrived."

He drained his glass. "I've never really got over it. I feel so guilty, even now."

There was a long silence while Hamish tried to find a suitable response to his story. After a while, he got to his feet and grabbed Jack's empty glass.

"I'll get another round in," he said and strode off to the bar.

*

The next day, they took an early train into town.

They called at the Warehouse first. The place looked like everything had returned to normal. And Jack felt reassured when one of Stella's muscle men stopped them at the door and checked their credentials with Stella on his mobile phone.

"You can go up," said the heavy. "The boss is expecting you." And he went back to humping crates of lager from the cellar.

They found Stella in the apartment's kitchen, making coffee.

"Here," she said, handing them each a cup. "Colombian. It's good. I ground the beans myself, five minutes ago."

They sat at the breakfast bar with their drinks.

"So, how're things, then?" asked Hamish. "Looks like everything's going okay."

"The nightclub side of things is no problem, Hamie. I'm working for the drug gang now. The Smiths. But I can get used to that. They seem happy to leave me to get on with it. And they've taken Kevin's head away. Thank God."

"To where?"

"I've really no idea."

"Well, that's good, anyway. I was beginning to wonder if I'd have to drop the thing over the side of the ferry in the carrier bag. So everything's okay?"

"Not entirely," she said, frowning. "They're using the place to store drugs."

"Ah," said Hamish, putting his cup down on the worktop. "That's bad. And you're worried. You'd be mad not to be."

"Of course I am. It's not easy to see how best to deal with this."

"As long as you're here, under their thumb, there's probably nothing much you can do, Stell. But do tell me if you ever want to do a runner. I can help. There's a guy who could fix you up with a change of identity too. Think about it."

"I think about my future all the time now. But I can't bring myself to leave. It could come to that, I suppose. But not yet. And, while we're on the subject of doing a runner, you've never told me where it is you disappear to. Judging by your suntan, it isn't Jack's place."

"He has a sunbed."

"No, he doesn't. He's not the type."

"Wherever it is, it'll need to stay a secret for a while yet. Especially knowing who you work for these days. They'd be after me in search of their missing millions if you let anything slip. Best you don't know for now.

"And what about Gus? How are the police viewing that?"

"Looks like they could be buying into the suicide idea. So that's a relief, at least. There could be a few formalities before I can have the cremation, but there's no real rush with that. I'll probably be the only mourner."

"Had a similar thing with my mother-in-law, Beatrice, not too long ago," said Jack. "Had the care home manager and a couple of coffin carriers to help me fill a pew, but it still felt sad."

"Don't worry," said Hamish. "I'll be sure to show up when it's your turn. You won't be playing to an empty house."

Not long ago, no one would have noticed if I'd left the planet. Tooth, maybe. Things are looking up.

19

The Fire

Hamish was still at the semi when Jack got back from the Paris run.

"Paris go well, did it?"

"Pretty much. We got the Shuttle from Folkestone and things went as planned. More or less."

"More or less? Was there a problem?"

"Not this time. But there very nearly was. When we were leaving the Shuttle at Calais, the customs pulled the car a couple of places ahead of us out of the line into a search area. If they'd searched us instead, we'd have most likely been fucked. Big style."

"Like I've been telling Freddy. Crossing borders with a bagful of banknotes is always going to be risky."

"Tell me about it," said Jack. "Things have gone well for us on our first two runs. But I think that's more due to good luck than anything. We're just making it up as we go along, trying to learn the ropes. Anytime the guys at the border decide to search the car, we're done for."

"So what's the alternative? Do you have a better plan?"

"The way your dad did it. Safer and simpler. No tricky borders to cross. No dodgy strangers to deal with. Why can't we do that?"

"You know why."

"Because Freddy says it's still too dangerous with those guys looking for their money. But I doubt that's the real reason we're having to move cash abroad by car. I think the reason is that Freddy wants to do that anyway. He's probably looking to build a network capable of moving actual cash across borders, gangster to gangster. It's his old-style thinking.

"Even now we're dealing with strangers every time and relying on Giuseppe getting things right with his banking contacts. We're asking for trouble."

"And when you think about it," said Hamish, "you're lucky no one's tried to rip you off at the handover. We need to cut these one-offs out of the picture and try to resurrect Dad's old operation. Or maybe think about using a digital currency, like Bitcoin."

"So, what should we do?"

"I think we should get over to the Railway right away, before they close.

"How are the cats? You've kept them fed?"

"They're fine. The kittens have been practising hunting each other, out the back. Pretty scary, really."

The following morning he called at the Warehouse and spoke to Stella.

"These guys giving you trouble here at the nightclub? They're also a problem for me and the people I work with."

"For you? How?"

"Let's just say they're distorting our business model. We need to get them out of the picture. You interested in helping me do that?"

"Is it likely I'd refuse? What's the plan?"

"Can't claim to have a plan, as yet. I'm working on it. A good first step would be to get some more information. Find out exactly who it is we're up against."

"So what can I do to help?"

"Next time one of them arranges to come over here, for any reason, you tell me right away. Then just leave the rest to me.

"By the way, I've got something for you."

He reached into his pocket and pulled out a kitten.

"I know you like cats. There's more where that came from if you're interested."

He dropped the kitten into Stella's lap. "I'll let myself out."

*

Back in Honda, in Hamish's kitchen, Jack and Hamish tried to talk Freddy and Giuseppe around to their point of view.

"I have to say, Freddy, I've talked it all through with Jack and I'm not too comfortable with the way we're doing things."

"Seems like you should be. We're making money, aren't we?"

"Yes, some. But how long before Jack and your grandson get pulled over at some border and searched. That crate of artwork won't do it. They'll be screwed."

"You're exaggerating the chances of being searched. People smuggle stuff across borders every day. They always have, and they always will. And where there's no risk, there's no profit. Remember that. It's a calculated risk and we can handle it."

"You might have done the calculation, but it's me and Junior taking the risk," said Jack. "Not you."

"And a better idea would be? What exactly?"

"Claude Beard's way. No borders. One simple move to a known contact."

"Haven't we already had this conversation? It'd be even more dangerous to keep making the same moves under the noses of these old clients of Claude's. They could have been the ones who did for Harry Love, and this Kevin character. We should stay off their patch for now."

"But why should London be their patch?" asked Hamish. "It's just London. It's anybody's. There are Russian Mafia operating there, for pity's sake. And what do we know about these guys you're so afraid of upsetting, anyway?"

"We know they've killed Kevin and possibly Harry too. And they've worked on Gus with a meat slicer. So they're ruthless. We know that we relieved them of two million pounds. So they're feeling pissed off. We know they were using your dad to move money. So they're going to be local to our home area. We also know that they have sizeable amounts of cash to dispose of. So maybe they're big-time."

"I hear everything you're saying," said Jack. "And I understand your concern. We should be careful. But what we need right now is more info about who these people are, where they are, how they operate. That sort of thing."

"I can't see any harm in you taking an interest in all of that," said Freddy, with a shrug. "So long as you're cautious. Just how do you propose to find all this out?"

"I'm already on it. I only know them as a voice on the phone. I've never met any of them, so far as I'm aware. But my stock in trade is finding out things, so I'm going to do my stuff with our friends."

"You do realise, don't you," said Freddy, "that if anything goes wrong with your little scheme you could lead them right back to us?"

*

At his semi, up on the Point, two days later, he got a call from Stella to say that the one she knew as Craig was due at the Warehouse within the next hour and a half, to drop off another of the packages he referred to as 'product'.

He was in position, in the hatchback, a hundred yards back up Jamaica Street, when he got a text telling him that Craig and another man were about to leave. He managed to get a few shots of the pair as they came out

213

of the Blue Warehouse and climbed into a Rover Discovery waiting in the car park.

Craig had been careless and had complained to Stella about a traffic hold up on the M6, on the drive down, saying he would be late. She had passed this information on to Jack and made his job a whole lot easier. As soon as he'd finished his photo shoot, he dropped the camera onto the passenger seat and took off through town. He drove as fast as he dared, heading for the motorway.

She had also told him that Craig had a broad northern accent. Lancashire, rather than anything remotely Liverpudlian. That fact, together with his driving 'down' the M6, made it seem likely that he was coming from the north. So it was odds on that he'd be going north along the same route, heading back.

He was driving the grey hatchback he always used for surveillance, chosen because it looked much like the multitude of other little grey hatchbacks using the road network every day. It made it easy to blend into the traffic whenever he was tailing someone.

But it would still have been tricky to follow the Discovery through town without being spotted. And if Craig was taking care to check for possible tails, it might have been impossible. Easier to get to the motorway first and then go north slowly enough for Craig to catch up and drive right past him.

And when Craig's car did pass him, as expected, whoever was driving the Discovery was being careful to keep his speed down. No point in attracting the attention of the traffic police.

He got into position two cars behind the Land Rover and stayed there all the way up to the Longridge turnoff, where the Discovery left the motorway. It was easy enough to follow his target through the small market town, and then they were into the network of winding country lanes, moving farther north and east through the fells and valleys. Here it wasn't such a simple matter to remain inconspicuous. So when the Discovery turned right, onto a lane running up along the hillside, Jack drove straight on. After a few minutes, he turned around in a gateway and followed the road back to join the lane Craig's car had taken.

The lane took him through fields and woods for a mile or so, with the occasional stone-built cottage or farmhouse coming suddenly into view as he negotiated the twists and turns of the route.

Rounding a bend, he saw the Discovery standing in the yard of a converted barn. The car's tailgate was up. He briefly glimpsed a man leaning inside, brandishing what appeared to be a vacuum cleaner, as he sped past.

He had just enough time to notice the name of the place, displayed on a board hanging by the gateway. Heaven's Gate. Then he pulled away and out of view.

He drove on until he found a spot on the narrow lane where he was able to turn around and drive back past the property again. When he came to a country pub he had noted on the way in, he parked up and went inside.

"I'm looking for an address around here," he said, as the barman set his pint of beer down in front of him. "I reckon I'm lost."

"You wouldn't be the first," said the barman, smiling. "Where is it you're after?"

"Well, that's the problem. I must be losing it, but I'm not even sure what the house is called. Something Gate is the best I can do."

"Ah, that would be Vince's place. The Smiths. Heaven's Gate. It's not far."

"Could be that. Is there a business there? I'm supposed to be talking to someone about a computer system. Bookkeeping. Stock control. All that."

"Could be the Smiths, then. They do antique furniture. They bring it in from abroad to their shop down in Longridge."

"No, not antiques. Crafts. Wholesale. That's the thing. And I remember now, it wasn't Heaven's Gate. It was Cow Gate."

"Well, then I'd say you are lost, after all. There's no Cow Gate around here. Not that I've heard of. Sorry."

"Not to worry. I'm probably too late, anyway. Have to be next time out. So I may as well line up another of these. Have one yourself?"

Later, having kept his drinking down to the two pint limit he favoured when driving, he drove into Longridge and left the hatchback in a car park while he tracked down the Smiths' antique store. He found it on the main road. It was an imposing, detached building and, like much of the older part of town, constructed of stone, darkened by decades of weathering.

By now, the afternoon was labouring under heavy cloud, and a fine drizzle was beginning to fall. Inside Smiths Antiques, the glow of yellow electric lighting was already visible. He didn't risk going in. He'd pushed his luck as far as he felt was sensible on this first foray, and the day had gone well.

That evening he called Hamish to tell him what he'd discovered and to talk through the next move.

"My best guess," he said, "for what it's worth at this stage, is they're shipping in drugs for wholesaling around the UK. They're using the antiques business as a front."

"Makes sense to me. A good result for the first time out."

"Problem is, though, I can't take things much further without risking being recognised. It's possible someone there knows what I look like, and even more likely they could recognise my voice."

"You need a partner."

"I do. But I don't have one. I can't use just anyone on a case like this. It's too sensitive."

"You have me, Jack. I'll get the next flight over."

The following evening, sitting in Jack's lounge, Hamish took a look at the Smiths' website.

"Looks fairly kosher, doesn't it? Impressive in a way. All that classy antique stuff they've got. And we have the additional benefit of a screen-full of mugshots."

He was viewing the page which introduced the people involved in the antique furniture store. Three men, two women. All looking to be in their thirties or early forties. All called Smith.

"A proper family business," said Jack. "Nice."

"So how do we play this? How can we use what we've found out to get these people out of our hair?"

"As in?"

"Well, for a start, how do we get them out of the Warehouse? Get them to leave Stella alone?"

"An anonymous tip to the police?"

"But they couldn't act without evidence. We need them to be caught red-handed."

"We could tip off the cops when we know Craig is heading for the Warehouse with a fresh batch of stuff."

"That risks getting Stella involved. And it wouldn't necessarily mean that the law got all of them. And it might look obvious to the Smiths that the tip came from the Warehouse end."

"Then what?"

"Frankly? I've no idea."

*

Later, coming out of the shower with a towel around his waist, Hamish was startled to find someone standing at the window in his bedroom. His visitor, a man, was looking out over the garden with his back to him. He knew at once who it was.

"Dad?" he asked. "It's you, isn't it?"

The man turned to face him. "Hello, Son. How are things?"

"I'm glad to see you, Dad. As always. It's been a while. And things are going well, thanks. I do wish, though, that you could give me some warning when you're due to visit. It's not exactly normal to have your dad's ghost appear unexpectedly. It can be a bit of a shock."

"Sorry, Hamish. Thought you'd be getting used to it by now, and I haven't worked out how to warn you when I'm about to arrive. Not yet, anyway. It might not be possible."

"Well, don't worry about it. It's a tad unnerving, that's all."

He grabbed another towel and draped it around his shoulders before sitting down on the bed, facing his visitor.

"I saw what you did to brother Gus there," said Claude. "Nice try. Even if you didn't manage to kill the murdering bastard, you did cause some considerable damage."

"Yeah," said Hamish, "sorry I didn't actually finish him. I know that was what you wanted. But it might be that this way turned out even better? He didn't have a happy time after the explosion. And he's dead now, anyhow."

"So he is. But is there anything in particular you want to talk about? My grip on this manifestation business is a bit uncertain."

"Well, I'm not sure what you'll think about it, but I'm working with Freddy Davidson now. We're putting together something like the money-laundering operation you had going at the nightclub."

"And what's Davidson doing for you in return?"

"He already got me safely out of the UK, after the grenade exploded under Gus. And he helped me find a safe berth over on Lanzarote. The thing is, though, we seem to be having big problems with some of your old clients. They're fretting about their missing millions."

"And you don't want to hand the money back to them?"

"No chance. Finders keepers and all that. Anyway, it's too late. I don't have all the cash to give them, even if I wanted to. And things have got way too complicated."

"Because?"

"Because they're trying to get Stella and the Warehouse tied into their drug dealing."

"And what do you intend to do about that?"

"That's where I'm a bit stuck. Any suggestions?"

*

"I don't see what you're getting at," said Freddy when Hamish phoned him.

"I'm suggesting some direct action, that's what. We intervene somehow. Mess up their operation. And do it in a way that means the authorities find out what they're up to. How about a fire?"

"How would that help?"

"Let's assume they keep their product at the furniture store. That would seem reasonable if we're right and the stuff comes in with the antiques. So why don't we just arrange a nice fire? That way, we get to destroy their stock, disrupt their business and involve the law too if we're lucky. We could make it look like an accident.

"Sound promising?"

"If anything went wrong, we could get ourselves involved in a gang war. We'd be in way over our heads."

"Not if we're careful. And how hard can it be to start a little blaze?"

"Are you sure that's where they stow the drugs? You can't just go around torching buildings on spec. One fire can seem like an accident. Any more than that would be too much of a coincidence."

"Well, they do have a sizeable place out in the sticks, out by Longridge. I got Jack to drive me past it. Looks like they live out there. Some of them anyway, so far as we've been able to find out.

"Their other place is the antique furniture store in Longridge itself. I went in there acting like a customer, browsing around."

"You think that's where the stuff is?"

"Of the two, the store is the more likely. There's a bay at the rear where stuff gets moved in and out. The drugs must come in hidden in the furniture and get shipped out in separate lots in the back of Craig's Discovery."

"And how would you start the fire so it wouldn't look suspicious?"

"Needn't be too hard. There's old electrical wiring in there. Really old. I could plant some kind of incendiary somewhere."

"Yeah. Maybe," said Freddy, sounding more interested now. "A small one with a timer. Leave it inside a piece of furniture. Close to some dodgy cabling. You think the building would burn easily enough?"

"It's an old storehouse. Lots of rooms and stairways. A lot of wood. It should go up nicely. The fire'll turn most of it into toast before the fire brigade can even get their helmets on. The bonus will be if there's evidence of drug dealing left behind. Either way, it should put them out of action for the foreseeable."

"You know what, Hamish?"

"What?"

"I think maybe you should do it. Can't see why not, and it might just work. Do you have any idea how to build an incendiary?"

"Oddly enough, I don't. But Jack used to make his own fireworks as a kid. He's sure he could cobble something useful together. He reckons he can use potassium nitrate."

"The stuff they use in fertiliser?"

"The same."

"How about their security? Any cameras?"

"Only outside. Nothing inside that I could see. They probably won't even be recording during the day, when I go in to plant the device. I'll look inconspicuous enough.

"Michael Smith and his wife, Annie, seem to be in charge there. But there's no one with eyes on the furniture most of the time. I can be in and out in minutes."

"It's not as if you need my permission, Hamish. You should go ahead. Get these Smiths out of our way. Just don't get caught."

Hamish used the hatchback, which Jack had fitted with false plates for the occasion. He parked in a side street across the road from Smiths Antiques and sat in the driver's seat, and watched as the store closed up for the day. He saw Michael and Annie doing what must have been their usual rounds over the building's three floors. They were turning off lights and making sure everything was secure.

On his earlier trawl, he'd spotted sensors on all the windows and doors. And there were the cameras outside. Obviously, the Smiths felt that the building warranted a reasonable level of protection.

Their stash of drugs would be another concern entirely. He had seen a brick-built area by the loading bay with a heavy steel door and no windows. That area had its own separate alarm system, cameras on every aspect and was well lit after dark. Far too much security for petty cash and paperwork. No one could hope to break in there without immediately activating the alarm, set up, no doubt, to alert the Smiths directly rather than the police. Anyone brave or foolish enough to try anything would be risking violent retribution, and they would know it.

He saw the pair come out and lock the door behind them. Michael and Annie would then, he imagined, drive back to the family home on the other side of the hill. There they would enjoy a peaceful meal together, confident that they had done all that might be considered reasonably necessary to secure their business premises.

This would, most probably, be their daily routine. A routine that would be unlikely to involve checking the water valve on the sprinkler system. Most likely, they would always leave that open. But today, unknown to Michael and Annie, the valve had been closed.

Hamish settled down in the car seat, prepared for a lengthy wait.

A little after midnight, the incendiary he had positioned did what Jack had designed it to do. He had left it, wrapped in a scrap of old sackcloth, inside an ancient pine dresser at the bottom of the staircase. The device sputtered into life and then became a molten ball of fire. It was more than enough to set the dresser well alight within two minutes.

He watched from the hatchback as the first flickers of light from the blaze began to play against the ground-floor windows. After that, it was a forgone conclusion. The store was bonfire paradise. Furniture, floors, stairways, doors, all made of wood. Some of the walls were even covered with wooden boards instead of plaster. The smoke sensors did their job, and the alarm sounded, but to no avail. He stayed, watching, for longer than he'd planned. Until it was obvious that there was no chance that anyone was going to save the place.

*

The regional lunchtime news carried the story as their lead item the following day, and Jack had turned on the old tv set he kept on his kitchen worktop to watch the program.

The newsgirl explained, in the same monotonously regretful tone that she had used when reading the weather report, that the fire brigade had tried their best. But by the time they had brought the blaze under control and then damped down the remains in the early hours of the morning, most of the building was a ruin. The area which had suffered least damage was at the rear, on the ground floor, where there was a brick-built room with a fireproof door. A conscientious fireman checking through what was left of the store forced the door open. Behind it he found a charred but still recognisable lab of some sort. Much of whatever the lab had been used to process was melted, burned, or evaporated. But the brigade's speedy response had saved enough to arouse the suspicions of the firemen on the scene.

The police, declared the newsgirl, were investigating.

It was another couple of days before the same newsgirl was able to update the story. He switched on the tv as he sat at the kitchen table waiting for Hamish to come back with the takeaways for their evening meal.

As he waited for the news to begin, he reflected on just what it had taken to get him to engage fully with the world again. Drug money, money-laundering, and now this. Arson. All of this had been in store for him all along, had he but known it. He had simply been too blind to his own nature to realise the fact.

The newsgirl got into the Longridge fire story right from the start. The tv cut to a video of a reporter standing outside the burned-out ruin. The reporter told viewers that it had not taken long for whatever had been found inside the smouldering remains of the Smiths furniture store to come to the attention of the police.

The proprietors, Michael and Annie Smith and Michael's older brother, Vincent, were not, said the newsgirl, available to comment. But the police had indicated that three people from the locality were currently helping them with their enquiries.

At this point, the news video switched to the scene at Heaven's Gate, showing several police vehicles and a bored-looking constable guarding the entrance.

Careless, he thought, smiling broadly. So very careless.

Hamish drove over to Longridge to get a street-side view of the results of his handiwork. He arrived back at the semi, clutching a copy of the local paper.

"Read this," he said, offering the paper to Jack.

"The entire story's here in print. It's worked out even better than we hoped."

Not a hundred percent as I would have liked, thought Jack, as he read further into the article.

"And the dosser they found dead in the waste skip in the alley? That's not good, is it? Suffocated inside a melting plastic bin. Not such a great way to go."

"Yeah, pity about the dosser guy," said Hamish. "Must've been hammered or spaced out on something to just lie there in all that heat. Probably knew nothing about it. Tough luck really, but what can you do?"

20

Dealing

"I can't tell you what a relief this is," said Stella, giving Hamish a hug. "You've got me my freedom back. The Smiths won't be in any position to bother me now."

"That might well be true, Stell. But we'll have to see how things work out. The fire and the police interest will be a huge setback for them, for sure. And as long as they're out of the way, it could be safe for me to show my face around here again. I could use a base here in town sometimes. My old room still on offer?"

"You're not worried someone will recognise you?"

"No, I'm not. Nobody has up to now, have they? And I'll only be staying here for the odd night or two at a time.

"And if I am recognised, so what? There's no one and nothing left to link me with anything that went on here. So, even if things get as far as the police asking me a few questions, there's absolutely no evidence to connect me to any of that."

"And how would you account for your disappearance and your change of name?"

"Fresh start. I'll explain that I'm a sensitive soul, and just had to get away. Went travelling for a while. Now I'm back. Not a crime, is it?"

"And the fake passport?"

"That might be a bit harder to explain. I might have to put that down to some sort of mental/emotional breakdown. I'd busk it."

"Well, the room's yours whenever you want to stay, Hamish. It's been waiting for you ever since you left. And the stash of drugs? What do we do about that?"

"I'd been thinking about asking you to drive me down to Otterspool Prom with the stuff tonight, so I can dump it in the river. But perhaps that's not such a brilliant idea."

"Sounds good to me."

"And if the Smiths decide to send someone to collect it? They aren't all in custody."

"I was hoping we'd seen the last of that bunch of gangsters."

"Most likely we have in the longer term. Let's hope so. But they won't want to lose their drug stash. It could be all they have left. Where've you put it?"

"I've got it locked in the spirit store down in the cellar. I'm the only one with a key."

"You know Dad had a false wall down there, where he would hide the money?"

"He never said anything to me about that."

"He only told me about it a few weeks before he died. I checked it out back then, and it was empty. We can keep the Smiths' stuff in there for now. Maybe we should try to sell it."

*

"The way I see this, Freddy," said Hamish into his phone, "we shouldn't have any problem doing things just as my dad used to. With some minor changes."

"Like?"

"Like we use Junior's Limo Hire to store the cash. Giuseppe reopens his London office, and we use the Limos to run the cash down there.

"Me and Junior do the delivery runs. You find the clients and Giuseppe takes care of the banking. Everyone has a job. We all make money. Simple and safe."

"Okay, then. We could try it your way. Now that you've dealt with the Smiths, it might work out."

"And there's Jack to consider," said Hamish. "He'll be hanging on to his semi for the time being, but I've asked him to keep an eye on things at the Warehouse when I'm away. He can use Gus's old room. I'm putting him on a retainer, paid out of my share of what we make. He's going to come in useful from time to time."

"Excellent idea," said Davidson. "He's been okay so far, but he's going to cost you."

"He'll cost me. But not much. He's been used to working for peanuts on his day job. And he's got what's left of his half a million in the bank. So he's hardly short of cash. And if I'm paying him, he'll be my man. Might need him for the nightclub more than anything else."

*

"It's Craig," said Stella. She was frowning.

"He phoned me. He says someone's coming over to the Warehouse this evening to pick up the product they left here. All of it. I'm to hand over the stuff and take the money. Twenty thousand. Then he'll tell me how to get the cash to him. I thought we were free of all this, and now it's getting to be even worse than before. Thank God we didn't dump it all in the Mersey."

"What can I say, Stells?" said Hamish. "It'll be all right. Really. Just let me think about it."

He'd kept up with developments via the papers, the tv, and all the chatter in the social media. He was aware that Craig and his wife, Monica, were the only Smiths who had avoided being charged. They had their own place, a cottage higher up on the fell. Nothing incriminating had been found there, and unlike Michael and Annie, they appeared to have no actionable connection with the ruined drug lab. So for now, at least, they were in the clear and, after being questioned, had been turned loose.

227

Apart from the burned-out lab, all the evidence uncovered so far, including some carelessly concealed drugs and a large store of unexplained cash, the police had discovered in and around the converted barn.

And the barn conversion was home to Vincent and to Michael and his wife, Annie. The evidence found at that location and in the lab had placed all three of them in the frame.

Hamish was sure that Craig would have contacted the shippers at the other end of the drug smuggling operation and put future shipments on hold. Likewise, he would have needed to stay clear of any cash coming in from accounts offshore. At least until he was certain the police no longer had eyes on what he was doing.

He could guess that there would still be customers wanting drugs that Craig would want to find ways to supply. The police would be watching, just waiting for him to make a mistake. But he would need some way to keep the family business alive. And, most likely, lawyers being so expensive, he would want to put his hands on some finance.

That evening, when Craig's man came to collect the cocaine, they had it ready in two plastic charity bags behind the bar. Stella sat perched, as usual, on a barstool with a glass of Prosecco to hand. She sat well away from the first few early customers in the place and away from the girl tending the bar. Hamish was close by, leaning on the counter and nursing a beer.

They watched the man come in, carrying a briefcase. He looked around, spotted them and walked over.

"Stella Beard?"

"That's me."

He put the briefcase down by her barstool. "The cash is in there. You'd better take a look. Then you can give me the stuff."

Hamish came across and picked up the briefcase. He took it into the small preparation room at the back, taking the charity bags with him. The man followed him in.

Hamish waited until Stella had joined them and closed and bolted the door before putting the briefcase on a table and opening it.

"I suppose I should count this," he said. "Want a beer while you wait?"

Stella opened a bottle from one of the crates stacked against the wall and put it on the table next to the courier.

"Don't think I know you, do I?" asked Hamish.

"I'm John," said the man. "Usually I get this directly from Craig, but he's worried the law could be keeping tabs on his place. So you get to be the stand-in."

"So you know Craig," he said, working through the bundles of fifties, counting them. "He's the guy who supplied this stuff. There's been some trouble at his end. Maybe you heard?"

He handed each bundle he'd checked to Stella, who stacked them in neat piles.

"I heard about the fire they had. And about the police interest. But Craig doesn't tell me much and I don't ask. He isn't what you might call approachable. And I'm only a courier, that's all," he said, between gulps from the bottle.

"Must be interesting," said Stella. "You must get about a bit."

"You're joking," said John, laughing. "Driving up and down the motorway network and parcelling up coke isn't my idea of interesting. Could be worse, I suppose. The pay isn't bad."

"Do you cut it?" asked Hamish. "The coke? That's the term, right?"

"Yeah, they sometimes get me to bulk the stuff up with baking soda. Makes it go further. Use it to make crack too."

"You sound like some kind of chemist."

"Ha! I wish. I just do what the man tells me."

Hamish finished counting the cash and gave John the bags of coke to sample and weigh, using the scales he'd brought along for the purpose. He seemed satisfied.

"That's us done," said John, picking up the charity bags. Hamish unbolted and opened the preparation room door.

"Before you go," asked Hamish, "do you want to leave me your number? I might have some work for you in a few weeks. If you're interested."

"Always interested in making some money. Want to hand me your phone?"

He passed the man his mobile and waited as he keyed in the number.

"It's under John D," he said, handing back the phone. "Call me, whenever."

"Like I said, it'll be a few weeks. You should hear from me then."

"Be seeing you," said John, as he strode out of the bar with the bags. "Thanks for the beer."

So that's it, he thought. That's how it's done. Simple as that.

21

The Drug Business

From the way Hamish had been talking lately, it was apparent to Jack that the boy had been thinking hard about how their project was going.

"I never used to be too comfortable with the idea of drug dealing, Jack. But shouldn't people have the freedom to do their own thing? I mean, it's really all about market forces, supply and demand, and all that."

"So is human trafficking and contract killing, and a few other things we could mention."

Hamish ignored the comment.

"Can't say I ever had any inclination to try any particular illegal drug myself. Not beyond a couple of experiments with some weed at uni."

"And how did that go?"

"Not hugely well. Pretty unrewarding, really. If I smoked a little, then nothing much seemed to happen. If I smoked a bit more, I'd find myself reduced to crawling around the place on my hands and knees. There didn't seem to be any middle ground with the stuff. Not for me, at least. I got absolutely no pleasure from it."

"But you feel others should be free to make their own decisions on these things. Is that it?"

"In principle, yes. After giving the matter some serious consideration, I've come to hold that opinion."

They were sitting at their usual table in the Railway, nursing a glass of lager each.

"I mean, what's the difference between the business Stella runs at the Warehouse and the drug trade? It's just that one area is legal and one isn't. And exactly how does being legal equate with being morally superior? I can't see how that works."

"Well, as I see it, the crucial difference is that the government gets a cut of the take on the stuff that's traded legally. Simple. But why worry your pretty little head about it? What's the problem? Does it bother you that a lot of the cash we're laundering is likely to be drug money?"

"No, not really. I'm trying to find my way through a few issues, that's all. I mean, people have made a fortune from selling tobacco, right? And that's perfectly legal."

All cash, everywhere, has passed through dodgy hands at some stage. Nothing to be done about that.

"So why do you imagine it is, that we draw the line at dealing in recreational drugs? If we're happy to deal with the money that's made from them, isn't that just as bad? Isn't it a bit hypocritical?"

Obviously, he realised, Hamish wasn't about to let this go any time soon. And he knew him well enough by now to realise that he was leading up to something. He only needed to wait. The boy would get to the punchline, eventually.

"Wouldn't want to argue with you on that, buddy," he replied. "Not something I'd use myself, but each to his own. As long as it doesn't involve kids. And as long as the product is as safe as it can be."

"The thing is," said Hamish, "I've been toying with the idea of trying it out. The drug trade, I mean. Doing an experimental deal or two on the side. Keep Freddy and Giuseppe out of it for the present? Just the thought of it would make Freddy anxious, I'm sure, and I'm not certain G would be interested. In any case, it needn't involve anyone else."

"Why would you want to do that? Now that we've got this cash operation set up. Don't you have enough to do?"

"It isn't a question of that. If I'm going to be involved in breaking the law to make my money, then I'd like to make it and get it stashed. So I can bail out while I'm still young enough to enjoy it."

"Provided you don't end up in clink in the process."

"Of course. All business propositions need a proper evaluation, legal or otherwise. Cost Benefit Analysis, Risk Assessment. All that stuff. It's all about maximising profits while reducing risk. But also, importantly, it's about being prepared to take advantage of opportunities as and when they arise."

"I'm sure I wouldn't want to give you an argument on any of that," said Jack, who was feeling disturbed at the serious turn the conversation was taking.

Drug dealing? Jesus. This is supposed to be a drinking night.

"Another glass? It's time we moved on to the whisky. All this beer's giving me gas."

"Yes," said Hamish. "The thing is that just at this point, right now, we have a golden opportunity to increase our range of activity and give an enormous boost to our profits. So why shouldn't we grasp it?"

"What is it? This golden opportunity?"

"Coke," said Hamish with a grin. "One of the most popular recreational drugs in the country. It's so simple."

"Since when was getting into the coke business simple? Unless you're talking about standing on street corners selling it at a few pounds a go. Which can't be what you mean."

"You know I'd never want to get involved in any kind of low-level operation. I'm talking wholesale."

"Like the Smiths?"

"Exactly. Like the Smiths."

"But most of the Smiths are now on remand. And the pair who are still free-range aren't in a very good place."

"Okay," said Hamish. "I grant you that things didn't end well for them. But that was down to us. That and the fact that they got careless. If they'd attended more carefully to business, and hadn't wound up on the wrong side of us, they would never have ended up in the mess they did."

"And we wouldn't make any mistakes if we tried it?"

"Not if we're careful. We're smarter than that."

*

Craig wasn't waiting in the beer garden of the pub, off Hope Street, that Jack had suggested as their meeting place. It was too hot out there, and the bright sunlight bothered him. So he walked through the place, carrying two pints of bitter. He found Craig sitting in a secluded corner, as far as he could get from the bar itself and from the few other midweek drinkers who preferred the indoor shade.

"All right," said Craig, frowning. "I'm doing what your buddy asked. I'm sat here waiting for you to bring me a beer. Now where's my cash? And who the fuck are you, anyway? I'd like to know because I think you've got a fucking nerve, interfering in my business like this. It was Stella Beard's job to drop the cash in Longridge."

"You should know who I am, Craig. I'm the PI you lot used to hire on the cheap. It was probably you who used to phone me my instructions."

"Thought I knew your voice," said Craig, with a sneer. "Well, listen to me, Charnley. I don't approve of your attitude. You should remember that you're just the hired help around here and watch your manners. I don't think I need all this pissing about right now."

"There, there," said Jack, putting the drinks on the table and sitting down, facing Craig.

"Try to be nice. I have your cash in this little backpack I'm wearing. If you can bring yourself to hear me out, I'll put it on the floor between us. You can take it with you when you leave."

"And if I just take it from you now and go?"

"You won't. Because I'll make ever so much fuss if you make any moves in that direction. And you must have more sense than to draw attention to yourself or you'd be inside with the others. So how about you shut up and listen?"

"This had better be good."

"It will be," he said as he took off the backpack and stood it on the floor. He made sure that Craig could see him placing his leg through one of the straps.

He had only known Craig Smith up close for a few minutes, and already he disliked him a lot. Strange, he thought, how you can take an instant dislike to some people. But no matter, this was business.

"There's no one within earshot here, so I'll come straight to the point. As I see it, you're in a mess. Most of your little gang are already behind bars, and you are a person of interest to the police. If they had the resources, they'd be watching you right now. But I'm pretty sure they'd find that a stretch too far."

"I thought you were getting straight to the point."

"Your operation is finished. You can't restart it because of the police interest. The authorities will most likely come after the rest of the family property just as soon as they can get the paperwork in place. And if they dig deep enough, then you could end up on the inside yourself."

"So you're trying to cheer me up, then? Is that it?"

"What it is, is that we, my associate and I, have an idea that can help you."

"Which is?"

"Which is that we resurrect your defunct operation while keeping your good self out of the frame."

"Who's this associate?"

"Someone you can call Gunter, for now. He'll be in touch at some point. It's just me and him."

"So. Go on."

"We see the news. We're pretty sure that you've been using the furniture you were selling up there in Longridge to bring the stuff in. So my partner and I propose to set up a salesroom in the Baltic, here in town, and import the furniture ourselves. There's lots of that sort of thing down there, new start-ups and so on, so it's not likely to attract the wrong kind of attention. And you, personally, can stay well clear of the whole shebang and out of trouble."

"I dunno about that. I'm not sure I'm looking for any hired hands at the minute."

"Well, you can relax on that front, good buddy. I wouldn't dream of working for you again. Or anyone else, for that matter. Nor would my partner. We'd split the take."

"You can't be suggesting we go fifty-fifty? You must be joking. This is my business. Not yours."

"What business would that be exactly? From where I'm sitting, you aren't doing much business right now. Neither you nor any of your associates can go anywhere near your old operation without having the authorities take a keen interest. Your only options are either to look upon the whole thing as a memory of happier times or work through a third party. Someone clean. Someone like me and my partner.

"And just to be clear, I'm not offering you fifty percent. We were thinking more in the region of twenty."

"Well, you know where you can stick that. Get your foot off my money. I'm going. Thanks for wasting my time. Tosser."

What a lovely chap, he thought, releasing the backpack from his leg as Craig snatched it up. Can't wait to get to know him better.

*

"Nice cup of tea?" asked Jack that evening. "Your noodles are ready. Bombay Bad Boy or Jamaican Jerk? I don't mind which myself."

"Tea tonight, then?" asked Hamish. "All right. I'll try the Jamaican."

"There's whisky if you'd prefer? But I'm going dry for a while."

"Tea's fine. So how did it go with our friend today? Your text said he turned up and took the money. So that gets him off Stella's case. But how about the other thing?"

"Let's just say we opened negotiations. I bought a spare phone and put a note of the number in with the cash. I expected to hear from him when he'd had time to consider our offer in the round."

"Past tense? You're no longer expecting his call?"

"No. He phoned me around two hours ago. Hadn't moved from his car in Hope Street. So I went back up there for a chat. He offered sixty to forty in our favour. We negotiated, insofar as a string of offensive expletives mixed in with a few numbers counts as a negotiation."

"And?"

"And we're in. He settled for a third of the net. We have something to celebrate."

"I'll get the whisky, then, shall I? It'll add a sense of purpose to the tea. You can go dry tomorrow."

"I'll make an exception. Just this once."

"Let me tell you how I see this working," said Hamish, moving a pair of pouncing kittens to one side as he sat down on the sofa. "Then you can have a think

237

about it all and about how you might want to fit in with our new operation."

"Explain away," said Jack, putting down two teacups. "Don't forget the whisky."

Hamish fetched the bottle from the sideboard and poured each of them a generous measure.

"First, we need to get ourselves some space in one of those old buildings in the Baltic, like we discussed. It'll be cheap enough down there. We'll have to make the place fit for purpose, and hire some very trustworthy help. In the meantime, we get Craig to restart his shipments from Colombia or the Caribbean or wherever."

"We'll need to do that quickly, before the supplier finds another outlet."

"True. And our first question is, exactly how do you hide cocaine in a load of furniture? If you put a bag of coke inside a drawer or a cupboard it's hardly well hidden, is it?"

Jack took a sip from his teacup.

"I managed to get him to talk about that side of things once he'd calmed down a bit. He said there were a few different ways to hide the stuff, such as false bottoms in chests, hollowed out woodwork. Stuff like that. The favourite is inside the stuffing in upholstery. You can get a lot in there."

"Sounds a little too obvious. Almost amateurish."

"But it works. Most of the furniture comes in clean in any one load. And most of the loads come in completely clean. And the people who check all this stuff at the ports are a bit stretched at best, so that stacks the odds on our side from the outset."

Hamish, sitting holding his steaming pot of noodles, looked thoughtful. "And what about the smell? Sniffer dogs? Isn't that a problem?"

"I did ask him about that. He said they had one or two guys at the docks on the payroll. They did what they could to keep the shipments in the clear. And they once had to bribe some official. God knows if they ever threatened anyone, but I certainly wouldn't put that past them."

"But the dogs?"

"Yeah, the sniffers could be a problem, I imagine. Anyhow, he said the guys at the other end, the ones who put the shipments together, are expert at dealing with that. There's vacuum packing, washing, spraying with other scents and so on. Quite a few options to use against the dogs."

He could feel things beginning to move. Hamish was listening intently to what he had to say. Soon it would be too late to change course, if it wasn't already. But he wasn't sure he wanted to. He wasn't sure of anything.

"But I'm glad to see you have a few reservations here, Hamish. If we get caught drug smuggling, we'll do years inside. And I'm not sure you could cope."

"The best answer to that is not to get caught. We keep our distance. Get some third party to run the operation on the ground. Anything happens, they take the hit."

"But what if they talk?"

"We make sure they don't."

"How?"

"Bribes. Threats. Use your imagination."

"Aren't the Border Force guys and the NCA going to be watching out for these furniture shipments now? After the performance with the Smiths?"

"Watching out for what furniture shipments, exactly? For starters, after the fire there was no actual evidence that the shipments were directly involved in the drug wholesaling. As far as the investigators were concerned, the furniture could've been nothing more than a simple front."

"Maybe."

"And any future shipments will be directed to our new antique salesroom operation. Not to the Smiths. And there are scores or even hundreds of furniture shipments coming in all around the country, all the time."

"Maybe."

"Have you seen the size of some of those container ships? They're huge. All kinds of stuff comes in. And most of ours will be clean, don't forget. We're talking needles and haystacks. And we'll make sure the suppliers change the name of the shipper. There'll be nothing to link our imports with the Smiths' operation. It'll be fine."

"More whisky?" He asked. "I might need a few more shots to help me get my head around this."

22

The Makarov

"You need to remember," said Jack, as he and Hamish stood inside their newly acquired Baltic property, "that the police were looking for you not too long ago."

"No one's challenged me yet. And I doubt they're going to. People seem happy enough to accept me as Gunter. But what do you think of this place? Good or what?"

"Good," he said. Hamish's choice impressed him. The old warehouse looked as though it would suit their purpose well.

"Excellent location. Sizeable. Seems like this could be just what we need. So far, at least."

"Glad you approve," said Hamish, ushering him farther into the building.

"Especially since I've already taken it on a ten-year lease, with an option to purchase. Not huge, but big enough. And it's got character, so it looks the part. The kind of place where people would love to spend an hour or two checking out distressed antique furnishings for their Edwardian terraced refurb. And slap in the middle of the trendy Baltic Triangle."

"So what's the next step?"

"The next step is for you to agree to oversee the project."

"You want me to be the one to be standing here to take the hit if everything goes tits up? I thought we were buddies."

Hamish grinned. "And so we are. Bosom. No, we'll have people here on the ground, day to day. With a manager to run the place. You'll be in control, but you can stay safely out of sight. I'm aiming to go places, and I don't have time to mess about. I need someone I can trust. What do you say?"

He gave the matter all of fifteen seconds thought. Despite the risks, it appeared to him that Hamish's offer was manna from heaven. The alternative of a future spent alternating between sitting in the pub and sleeping off the effects on his sofa seemed not much better than a prison sentence. And now that Hamish seemed to have persuaded Freddy to hold off on his idea of moving banknotes across Europe, he could see that even his days playing second fiddle to Junior could be coming to an end.

"Count me in, boy," he said grinning. "When do I start?"

"You start right away. I'll need you to rustle up some bodies to go on the payroll here. Along with a manager to report to you. Goes without saying that you'll need to choose your people carefully. You should be able to identify a few suitable prospects, given what you've been doing for the past couple of decades. You'll want them to be the kind you can trust with your wellbeing. Which they should be if you're clear enough about the fact that they'll suffer serious consequences otherwise."

"We'll have to pay them well."

"And we will. Put them on a percentage if you like. I don't mind. Whatever works best. They'll have to be ready to move furniture, deal with customers, and then double up downstairs, dealing with the coke. You can spec it all out for them."

"Downstairs?"

"Follow me," said Hamish and led the way into a small back room. "This will be the office."

He walked over to a huge, overstuffed and ancient armchair standing in the corner.

"Left behind by the previous tenants," he said. He pushed the chair, with a tremendous squealing and screeching of ageing castors, across the floor, revealing a wooden trapdoor.

"This is good. Come and take a look at the basement."

Jack followed him down a creaking, wooden staircase into a large windowless room, flicking on a light as he went.

"There's another room below this," he said, indicating a further trapdoor. "But I doubt we'll have any reason to go down there very often."

"I'm guessing this is where you intend to process the stuff?"

"Precisely. There's a goods hoist, as you can see. Big enough to move the furniture between floors. All the items of interest in any one load will be marked somehow. Your guys will bring them down here and put in an hour or so, as and when, taking the stuff apart and retrieving the coke. They can then cut it, or not, as required. Then weigh it out and do the packaging. We'll have a machine to vacuum-seal the packages in plastic."

"I know zero about dealing with, or in, illegal drugs. I mean, you do know that, right?"

"No worries, buddy. I have a contact called John I can call on to come and show you the ropes. Check him out first, but sign him up if you like him. It's up to you."

"You'll want to equip the place properly. Needs a bit of fixing up too."

"Find some decent tradesmen. Use reliable individuals rather than a firm and pay them in cash. Tell them it's a workroom or something. Whatever you want. You'll need new electrics and plumbing. Put in a changing area with a shower and seal the sensitive area off with plastic."

"Right," said Jack, pursing his lips and looking thoughtful. It all felt slightly unreal. But he knew it wasn't.

Okay. If that's the way of it. Time to step up.

"Anyone coming in here to work will strip off before going into the coke room. There'll be overalls and a washing machine inside. On the way out they'll strip off again and shower, before getting back into their street clothes. And you'll need to install a state-of-the-art air filtration system. Something along those lines, anyway. Give it some thought."

"This will take some time. And some dosh."

"We have the cash to fund it. So, if you can find the right guys quickly enough, two months or thereabouts should see you up and running.

"I've scheduled the first shipment of furniture to arrive around then. If you aren't ready down here, leave it upstairs untouched until you are. And make sure no one gets to buy it.

"You'll know where to get the right people, and I have every confidence in your capabilities.

"And I've bought you a present," said Hamish, handing him a brown paper bag. It was heavy. He unwrapped the gift. It was a handgun, a semi-automatic.

"Oh," he said. "You shouldn't have. And it's not even my birthday."

"I'm assuming, I'm hoping, that you'll never need to use it. But it's loaded, just in case. It's Russian. Powerful, but stubby enough to fit into your pocket. I suggest you let anyone who knows what this room is actually being used for see that you have it. I'm told it's a Makarov. It's got a full clip of 9mm ammo. Like I said, I hope you'll never have to, but would you be able to use the thing if need be?"

"Are you joking? My years in the army taught me something. Where on earth did you get it?"

"A pub near the docks. Easy enough."

He took some time to examine the weapon, making sure everything was in full working order. He explained each step of what he was doing to an amused looking Hamish in the process.

"As I said, I doubt you'll ever have to fire it," said Hamish. "At most, I reckon you might need to wave it about a bit. That should be enough to put the wind up anyone who might consider giving you a problem."

"So, why the ammo?"

"That's just in case. I wouldn't lose any sleep over that."

They spent the rest of the afternoon drinking in a succession of trendy, and not so trendy, bars as they made their way across town to the railway station at Moorfields. They managed to appear sober enough to be allowed through the barrier.

Back in the semi, they continued to drink until well past nightfall.

The following morning found them propped unglamorously at the kitchen table.

"I feel like shit," groaned Hamish. "Why, in the name of all that's holy, did you encourage me to drink like that? You know I can't stop."

"Welcome to my world," said Jack, trying but failing to muster a smile.

"I'll do us some coffee," said Hamish. "Where'd you put the Makarov, by the way? Somewhere safe, I hope?"

"Makarov?"

"The semi-automatic. The pistol."

He was silent for a long moment. Thinking hard.

"Oh fuck. Don't you have it?"

"Don't tell me you..."

"It was digging into my waist. Me not being exactly sylphlike and all. I took it out for a minute and put it on the table. Still in the paper bag, natch."

"And?"

"And, God forgive me, I think I must have left it in that last bar. Forgot it."

"You what?" Hamish almost screamed. "You lost the fucking gun? With our prints all over the fucking thing!"

"S'all right," he said. "Just teasing. It's in the laundry bin in the bathroom."

23

Stirring the Pot

Hamish's phone was ringing. Unknown number. He answered anyway. Claude.

"The thing is, Hamish," said Claude, "that you'll have to be a lot more ruthless. Even more than you've been so far. If you're serious about making a go of all this."

"Dad? You're phoning me? You can do that?"

"I can, as you can witness. I have a fresh perspective on everything now. I'm beginning to see that many things are possible. It would surprise you. But we should talk."

"What about?"

"About this big-time, criminal tendency you seem to be developing. Drug dealing, money-laundering, killing folk. All that."

"But you were a criminal yourself, Dad. You of all people should recognise that I'm trying to carve out a career for myself, in the best family tradition. I would have thought you'd be pleased."

"Did I say I was here to judge you? I simply want to make sure you understand where you might be headed. I was a criminal. If you want to be pedantic about it. But in the same way some city bankers are. Low profile. No blood on my hands. Who cares if I moved on a few bits of dirty money for the big boys? I kept my head down and left the rough stuff to the likes of Gus."

"And?"

"And you're moving along a very different path. Higher profile. More noticeable. Not just a little money-laundering on the quiet. You're involving others. And drug dealing? Scary. Especially at that level. I mean, importing cocaine? Good God, boy. That's serious. And you seem to leave a bit of carnage in your wake, don't you? You okay with all that?"

"I can handle the scary stuff. People change and I've been changing ever since I took on my new identity. I'm enjoying all this. For once, I'm in control of my life. Or I soon will be. But the carnage? It was you wanted me to kill Gus, remember? Revenge?"

"True enough. I'll give you that. But I wanted you to murder your uncle for sound, family based reasons. And I do happen to think revenge is very much underrated. But the other deaths? Percy? Lily? Harry Love? And what happened to young Lawrence?"

"I admit I shot Percy. But only by accident. You know that. Lily was an unexpected, tragic suicide I had no way of preventing. I don't know for sure who killed Harry. Do you? It certainly wasn't me. And Lawrence was trying to kill me. You needn't put all that to my account."

"Maybe not directly, Hamish. But you can't deny that a certain pattern is emerging here. And now it's guns again. Just reflect on it. That's all I'm saying."

His phone made a sound like someone crushing a sheet of gift wrapping into a ball and then went dead. Strange, to say the least. Had he spent the last few minutes in conversation with his father's ghost, or had he been talking to himself? And which was the better option?

More to the point, was he okay with his current direction? Well, that was a no-brainer. From being a nobody, doing odd jobs at the Blue Warehouse and living like a parasite on his family, he was on his way to becoming a big-time player on his own account. If there was a price to pay down the line, then he was ready to deal with that. Not that he expected to need to. All that was needed to stay safe was to take a few simple precautions.

He checked the calls on his phone. The most recent had been a day ago.

*

"What are your feelings about the Davidsons?" asked Hamish, right out of the blue.

"They've been okay, so far as I can see. What do you mean?"

"They've been okay so far, Jack, because we've been of use to them. And they'll continue to be okay for so long as they find it expedient. But they're an old family firm and their loyalty is to themselves. Remember the arrangement we had? They were supposed to be putting some business our way after that deal we all did. How's that been working out with Freddy Davidson since you got back from the Canaries?"

"Well, there've been the two money mule jobs, right?"

"Chicken feed. He strings you along, playing second fiddle to Junior. I'm pretty sure he doesn't actually want you there. Eventually they'll dump you. Perhaps they have already."

"So you want to do what, then? We have the drug wholesaling in development, don't we? So why would I worry about Freddy's money-laundering?"

"I just wonder whether we should consider our position, that's all. I can be as loyal as the next man. More than most. But not when I'm being played. I got Davidson into the money-laundering business. And it was me, and you, who brought Giuseppe back from his hideout in Naples. Along with two million in offshore funds. Half a million of which Freddy now has. Meanwhile, he and Junior are calling the shots."

"Never realised you felt so strongly about all this. But what's your point?"

"I want us to be the ones running things. Not Freddy. And certainly not Junior."

Later, Hamish went back to the Blue Warehouse and settled into his old room. It felt reassuring to be home, lying on his own bed, staring at the ceiling. He even thought he saw Claude, once or twice, wandering the corridors.

24

The Statement

Over a leisurely morning coffee at his kitchen table, Jack mentioned that DI Slaughter was becoming annoying.

"Obviously he's under pressure to come up with something, and he's still floundering. I could be his only lead. So now he's started phoning me, asking questions and hinting about problems I might soon find myself having."

"Has he had anyone tailing you or watching the house?"

"There was the Sergeant Styles farce, not too long ago. You know that."

"You told me about Styles. But has there been anyone else since then?"

"I haven't spotted anyone, but they're being very cautious. I think they're using a concealed video link in a car parked across the road to watch the house. It's not too hard to spot if you know what you're looking for."

"So they've seen me visiting?"

"It'd be surprising if they hadn't. Doesn't mean that they'd twig who you were. Not for sure. But if they've managed to track you back to the nightclub on your visits to Stella, they'll put two and two together soon enough. Even Slaughter and Styles couldn't be so dumb as to miss that."

"You think?"

"My guess would be they most likely have you tagged by now. It's not like you've been too careful about covering your tracks lately and you've spent more than

251

one drunken night here. You'd better steer clear of my place for the foreseeable, just in case."

"So you think they might be following me rather than you?"

"I'd guess they must be keeping tabs on some of your movements, at least. I'm surprised they haven't pulled you in for questioning before now."

"So why not pre-empt them?"

"Pre-empt them how?"

"I reckon I should talk to Slaughter. Try to get him off our case."

*

The next day Hamish took the train into town. Over lunch at the Blue Warehouse, he explained his plan to Stella.

"The thing is that the cops are already interested in me. And I have certain activities in progress that I can't risk them finding out about."

"So why not simply stay out of their way? It would seem safer."

"If I do that, they're going to carry on digging. And eventually they'll stumble across something unhelpful. They might already be aware that Gunter is actually Hamish."

"They might know all kinds of things. And then they might not know very much at all."

"But if I go to them, and present myself as a victim rather than an actual criminal, I could throw them off the scent. You see? All I need you to do is to be prepared, if it comes to it, to back up my claim that it was you who put Jack on my case. Out of concern for my safety. That's all."

"I should come with you. Do you want me to?"

"You needn't. I don't expect it'll take long, and I doubt they'd be too keen to let you sit and hold my hand. And if you're there, they might even decide to grab the opportunity to ask you a few questions.

"I'm going to go over there right now and get it done. The sooner it's out of the way, the better."

It was a sunny afternoon as Hamish Beard walked through the eclectic conglomeration of businesses that made up the centre of the Baltic Quarter. He was headed for the police headquarters down by the dockside, where he imagined Slaughter's Special Investigations Unit would be based. Best to get this situation with the law sorted as quickly as he could.

He turned off Jamaica Street onto Blundell and then swung right, along Wapping. He took out his phone and used the number Jack had given him. The call was answered at once.

"Slaughter."

"Inspector Slaughter. I'm Hamish Beard. I need to speak to you."

"Mr Beard? Good. I've been intending to interview you for some time. Where are you right now, Hamish?"

"I'm on Wapping, across from the dock."

"That's good. Please stay where you are. I'll come to you. Okay?"

"If you like," he said, puzzled. "I don't mind walking over there. You're in the building down at Canning Place, right? It's not far."

"Please do as I ask and enjoy the sunshine. I'm already on my way to the car. I'll be there before you know it."

Slaughter rang off. A very few minutes later, an unmarked car pulled up beside Hamish. Slaughter and Styles climbed out.

"Hamish Beard?"

"Yes."

"I am Detective Inspector Slaughter of the SIU. I need to question you in connection with the deaths of

Claude and Gus Beard of the Blue Warehouse. You can talk to us voluntarily, or I can arrest you if you'd prefer. You choose."

*

"The cops won't let me see him, Stella," said Jack with a shrug. "I've been down there. I can't even speak to him on the phone."

"Perhaps they'll let me? I mean, I am his stepmum after all, and he's practically a child."

"He's twenty-three. And they won't let you in there, Stell. Forget it. I've sent him the best lawyer I could get at short notice. He'll pull him out of there soon enough."

"But why have they got him, anyway? What's he supposed to have done?"

"To be honest? There's a fair range of options. Depends on what evidence they've picked up. If they have any at all. They could simply be trying it on. Fishing. His best course is to keep schtum and let the brief deal with it."

*

But Hamish had already said more than he'd intended to say, while waiting for the lawyer to arrive.

"So," said Slaughter, shuffling his notes on the desk in front of him, "you've now gone on record, in the presence of myself and Detective Sergeant Styles here, as alleging that your father's death, Claude Beard's death, was not an accident. You've claimed that the fall which killed him was set up by his brother, your uncle, Gus Beard. You've suggested that he did this in order to gain control of some business operation, possibly illegal, that your father was involved in. Possibly against his will. You've also suggested that the attempt

254

to murder Gus Beard by means of an explosive device was carried out by others involved in this unspecified business operation. And that his gassing was not suicide but a second, and this time successful, murder attempt. Right so far?"

"Yep," said Hamish. "That's it. Can I go now?"

"Your lawyer'll be here soon, and you wouldn't want the poor man to have a wasted trip, would you? And anyway, I haven't finished."

He had long since grown tired of this. He glanced at the window behind Slaughter. They were high up in the police building. High enough for seagulls to use the broad window ledge as a perch. There was one out there now, sitting in the sun, enjoying a peaceful afternoon.

"You have further proposed that the disappearance of Percy and Lawrence White might also be the doing of these mysterious 'others'. Correct?"

"That's absolutely right, Inspector. So, can I go?"

"I think you'd better stay here until I say we're done. Unless you want me to arrest you after all. I might just do that anyway. I'm still considering that one."

He sighed. He had already been sitting in Slaughter's office for over two hours. This whole police thing was becoming tedious.

"And that you yourself had nothing whatever to do with any of it," continued Slaughter.

"That you changed your name and appearance. And went trailing off to the Canary Islands, of all places, to avoid falling victim to these 'others'. Leaving your mother, Stella Beard, to face any consequences. Right?"

"Kind of. But it's not as though I abandoned her. You're making it seem like I did. I tried to make her understand the situation, but she wouldn't believe me. And I had no way of proving anything. Anyway, she wasn't involved, so the chances were she'd be safe. Just as she has been."

"So why didn't you come to us in the first place and ask for help?"

"Because, as I told you at the start, I had no evidence and I was afraid the bad guys would find out and get me too."

"And yet you claim that you were on your way here to request our protection when I met you earlier."

"I was."

"So what made you change your mind?"

He wished he hadn't been so naïve as to believe that he'd be able to bamboozle the police. Slaughter didn't seem to be anything like as slow-witted as he'd hoped and had got him to say much more than he'd meant to. And where was that lawyer? Wasn't there supposed to be a lawyer? Jack was arranging that. What was taking so long?

"I'm just trying to put this entire business behind me. Rule a line. Fresh start. All that. I decided I might rely on you lot to protect me, after all. So isn't that what happens next? Police protection?"

"What happens next," said Slaughter, leaning forward in his chair, facing Hamish, "is that we get all this into our system and print it out in the form of a statement. Which you will sign. After that, I'll think about whether it would be a good idea for you to go or not. Sergeant Styles is pretty efficient at typing stuff into the computer. In fact, she's got most of what you said in there already, so it won't take long."

"Good. Can I get a coffee or something? I'm feeling parched."

"In a minute. Only a few more questions."

"Yes?"

"Are you sure you don't know who these 'others' are? The ones who've been causing all these problems? You see, my problem about letting you go right now is that you're the only suspect. And that makes you the prime suspect. See? Awkward."

He was feeling uncertain about how to proceed. He tried to work out his best way forward.

On the far side of the office, Amanda Styles thudded away at her keyboard.

"There might have been one name mentioned. If I tell you, can I be sure he won't find out it was me put you onto him?"

"I give you my word."

"Smith."

"That all? Just Smith?"

"That's it."

"There's a world full of Smiths out there, Hamish. Try a bit harder. You're almost there."

"Longridge. It's a place somewhere out in the sticks. North. Near Blackburn. Or Preston. Maybe both."

"Well done," said Slaughter. "See what you can do when you try? Didn't hurt, did it? And don't worry yourself, I think I know where Longridge is. Your Longridge Smiths have been in the news lately, have they not? Some of my colleagues have already been in conversation with them. In fact, most of them are sitting quietly on remand, as we speak. Or is your Smith a different Smith altogether?"

"I've no idea. None at all."

There was more thudding from Amanda and then the sound of a printer. Slaughter strode over to the output tray and collected the single sheet of A4 on which Hamish's statement had been printed. He glanced through it as he wandered back to the table where Hamish was waiting.

"Seems fine, Amanda," he called across the office. Then he pushed the sheet along to Hamish and handed him a pen. He picked up his phone to examine an incoming text.

"Sign that, Mr Beard, and then you can piss off if you want. Your lawyer's just arrived."

The seagull opened its huge yellow beak and screamed. At nothing, so far as Hamish could make out. Then it spread wide its wings and glided off into the blue.

"And don't try to leave the country without telling me first. In fact, you'd best bring in your passport and surrender it to the sergeant in reception."

25

A Surprise Visit

Jack was about to finish for the day when Hamish called into the antique furniture and drug lab project. He knew that he'd see much evidence of progress. Walls had been patched and painted, floors scrubbed, windows cleaned, and where necessary, re-glazed. New wiring had been installed, plumbing refurbed and renewed, and a ventilation and air filtration system fitted. The storerooms, the salesroom and the office were close to being ready to open for business.

"Looking good, Jack. Seems as though you'll be on time for our first shipment."

"We'll be on time. They're coming to put in the security systems early next week. Want to have a gander down below?"

He took Hamish into the office and pushed aside the old armchair from over the trapdoor. He pulled it open and led the way down the staircase.

At the bottom of the stairs, he flicked a switch on the wall, flooding the area with light.

"All done," he said. "Exactly as you wanted it, barring a few odds and ends. The men I've found to run the operation are both onboard and ready to go. The older one's acting as manager for the present. We'll see how he does.

"And I'm thinking we should bring a couple of the cats from home. Make sure the place is rodent free. They can live here."

"And John? You used the number I gave you?"

"I did. Your man John's been here already. He's going to be extremely useful. He'll be here to help with the shipments."

After Hamish had made a show of carefully inspecting all the arrangements in the cellar, they climbed back upstairs.

"This is great. And I mean totally. We're on our way up, for sure."

"Oh, yes. I meant to ask if anything came of that interview you had with DI Slaughter. Did you ever hand over your passport?"

"I gave them my Hamish Beard. The one they would be expecting. I've still got the Gunter Roth."

"So is that it? They've moved their spy-car from opposite my house."

"Well, I did point him at Craig, didn't I? That could work to our advantage. If he goes inside, it should make things simpler and even more lucrative for us."

"Could do, but I don't rate your chances if Craig comes to believe you've dropped him in it. But we'll have to see how that works out, won't we?"

"I think for now, though, we should assume that the police could decide to take some further action in our direction," said Hamish. "It's not likely, but they might search your place as a next step... so... where's the gun?"

"Here," said Jack, pulling the Makarov from his jacket pocket and putting it on the desk. "I'm getting tired of carrying this about, and it's making holes in my lining."

"You should get yourself a shoulder holster, I suppose. Maybe you'd best leave it with me for the time being. Just in case the cops get to be too nosey. I'll take it to Stella's and hide it in the false wall until we need it. No one'll find it there."

"Be my guest. I'm off. I haven't eaten since lunchtime. You coming?"

"Maybe I'll stay here for an hour and think things through. It's quiet here, and no one's going to bother me."

*

It was around sixty minutes later when he got up to leave. He smiled to himself as he lifted the latch on the heavy wooden door leading out of the building. Overall, he was pleased with his scheme and with the way everything was working out.

In addition to the drug wholesaling enterprise he was now creating, he felt he might soon find a way to gain complete control of Freddy's money-laundering operation. He simply needed to avoid pointless sentiment and plan a step ahead of everyone else. Like when he'd pointed DI Slaughter at Craig. A nice touch. He was proud of that.

On the money-laundering side of things, he needed to find a way to prise Giuseppe and Freddy apart. Careful preparation and a bit of judicious tweaking, that was the key.

But nothing could have prepared him for what happened next. The door was flung open suddenly, with considerable force, striking him hard in the face and chest. Instead of stepping outside into the evening shade, he found himself propelled backwards into the room.

He fell back heavily onto the floor and saw the silhouette of a man standing in the doorway. Then the man was inside and kicking the door closed behind him.

As Hamish struggled to stand, wiping what he knew must be blood from his face, his assailant turned on the lights. He recognised the intruder at once. Lawrence White. The very Lawrence White he'd lost all trace of on that wintery night when they had fallen into the

261

dark and chilly waters of the Albert Dock together, locked in drunken conflict.

"Lawrence," he gasped. "You fucker! I hoped you were dead."

"I almost was, thanks to you. But you certainly would have been if I'd managed to climb out of that dock any quicker. You'd disappeared by the time I did."

Lawrence, who was bigger, heavier and stronger than Hamish could ever hope to be, grabbed him firmly by the neck and pushed him backwards, his feet scuttering for purchase, through the gallery and into the office.

"Nice and private in here. And we have business to finish."

"Always happy to help a friend, Lawrence. What seems to be the problem?" asked Hamish between gasps, spitting blood, as he spoke, onto the newly cleaned floorboards.

His enquiry was answered with an agonising knee to his groin, and he dropped once more to the floor, doubled up with pain. Lawrence sat down in a swivel chair beside the desk, facing his victim.

"I'll save you the trouble of asking the obvious questions, Hamish, or what the hell ever it is you call yourself these days.

"After I'd climbed out of the dock, where you left me to drown, I told myself that, whatever it took, I'd make you pay for what you did to my family. You killed my dad, and you caused my sister's suicide. You almost killed me. You're a murdering bastard, and I'm going to make you pay for everything you've done."

Hamish gave a strangled gasp in reply as he struggled against the pain. He wanted to keep Lawrence talking while he recovered his senses. He would need to act quickly.

"Where'd you go?" he asked, gasping for air as he used the edge of the desk to pull himself upright. "Even the police couldn't find you."

262

"They didn't look too hard. I went over to Paris and rented a garret in the Latin Quarter. I'd been a student at the Sorbonne, so I knew my way around. Wasn't too bad, actually. And at least I ate well.

"I figured if I stayed here I could have your Uncle Gus on my case, backed up by those thugs of his. He might not have wanted to risk me deciding to spill the beans about what had happened to Dad and all the rest of it."

"So why show up now? What is it you want?"

"Gus is dead. I found that out online. So I thought it would be safe enough to come home and check things out for myself. I stayed out of sight and kept my eyes open. And there you were, poncing about the place, pretending that you were somebody else.

"You even had me fooled for a while, but something made me take a closer look. And when I did? Well, it just had to be my old mate Hamish, didn't it? Underneath all that suntan, hair and beard and that fancy suit and all."

"So here we are," said Hamish, leaning forward onto the desktop for support, certain that Lawrence was here to kill him, "having a lovely chat. But you still haven't told me what you want. Money?"

"No, it's not money."

"What then?" he asked, playing for time.

"You know what. Remember that old phrase the highwaymen were supposed to use when they had some poor bastard at pistol point? 'Your money or your life'? Well, in your case, as I said, it's not your money I'm after."

He knew he had only one chance. The Makarov was in his jacket pocket. He had his phone in the right-hand pocket, so he'd put the Makarov in the left. He sensed the weight of it and the hard bulk against his hip. He would have to use his left hand. Lawrence was too close to give him time to switch it to his right.

Lawrence was on his feet now. In his fist, a baseball bat that Hamish had somehow overlooked before. He yanked the gun from his jacket and pointed it at Lawrence as he stood up.

"Stay where you are," he ordered, surprised to find his voice steady. "Or I..."

He got no chance to finish the sentence as Lawrence came bounding at him, straight over the desktop with the baseball bat swinging. Instinctively, he pulled the trigger. 'Nothing. Fuck it! It's the safety. The fucking safety's on!'

He fumbled frantically with the pistol, but his thumb found only bare metal. The safety catch was on the left-hand side of the gun, positioned for a right-handed operation. Then he ran out of options as Lawrence's club connected with his gun hand and sent the Makarov clattering across the floorboards. Crouching on the desktop, Lawrence took a second swing, aiming for his head.

He ducked the blow, causing Lawrence to pitch forwards off the desk. He scrambled out of reach, trying to get up before his attacker was able to come at him again. But he was still on his knees when Lawrence came to stand over him, already raising his bat, ready to strike.

'Shit,' he thought. 'It's not supposed to end this way.'

The shot seemed deafening in the small room, and everything was still for a long moment before Lawrence fell backwards to land, with a dull thud, on the floorboards.

"Christ," said Jack as he pulled Hamish up off the floor. "What the fuck did he do to you? You look like you've been hit by a truck."

"Lucky for me it wasn't worse," said Hamish. He staggered out of the office and through the showroom to push the street door closed before locking it. "It seems that Lawrence believed he owed me."

"The guy you thought you'd left for dead in the dock?"

264

"The very same. He came close to killing me. Thank God you came back. If not for that, I'd have been a goner."

He was starting to shake and seemed unsteady as the reality of what had just happened began to kick in. Jack stepped forward and took his arm in support.

"You're in no condition to go walking about at the moment, buddy. You need to sit down. Let me help."

He led Hamish through to the office and placed him in the armchair.

"You're looking pale. You'll have to rest for a while. It's shock. It'll pass if you're lucky."

"If I'm not?"

"Best not worry yourself about that. But if you don't improve soon, I'll have to get you into the car and up to A and E, pronto."

He removed his coat and laid it over the still trembling Hamish before dragging a chair from under the desk and putting Hamish's feet up on it.

"Stay there and keep warm. You're looking a bit pale under that tan, and it's not as though I can call an ambulance right now, is it?

"I came back to help you hide the gun here, in the lower basement somewhere. I was worried you might decide to hang onto the thing. There'd be a risk the cops would pick you up and find it."

There was a silence as they both turned to look at the body lying on the floor.

"Is he dead?" asked Jack. "I fucking hope so. I don't want to have to shoot him again."

He bent over the fallen Lawrence and checked his pulse, holding his fingers close to Lawrence's nostrils, checking for signs of breathing.

"He's dead for sure. As a doornail."

"So now what?"

"Well, we'll have to pray you make a speedy and complete recovery, so you can help me haul him down to the lab. We'll seal the fucker up inside some of the plastic film we got to package the coke. We can vacuum pack him. Should help a little with the forensics until we can get rid of him. We'll take his wallet and any other obvious i.d.."

"Good idea. It'll give us a chance to try out the new equipment," said Hamish, getting to his feet and handing Jack his coat. "And don't worry about me. I'm feeling well enough. I was a little shaken there for a few minutes, that's all. Unexpected brush with death and all that."

In Jack's experience, people tended to need much longer to recover from shock. But then Hamish was like a one-man death cult. Obviously, he was well able to take the odd killing or two in his stride. But this particular death was down to him, not Hamish. It tied him in with his young partner for the foreseeable future, for better or worse.

Fuck it. At least I'm not bored anymore.

"Now we know that the vacuum packing equipment does its job," said Jack an hour later. "So at least we got something positive out of the experience."

"Exactly. And next, we need to shift our friend well away from here."

"Where to?"

He was surprised at how lightly he was taking this. But it wasn't only him. He noticed that Hamish was smiling. He seemed to be enjoying himself.

"How about somewhere on the Smiths' turf? We could drop him behind a wall on one of those lanes going up into the fells. One with thick trees and undergrowth at the back of it. Lots of places like that up there."

"Might be good," mused Jack. "Could be decades before anyone came across him, and there'd be nothing to link the body to us even if they did.

"I'm using the old hatchback today. Helps keep it in running order. I'll reverse it into the bay, so we can load him up and cover him with some packaging."

Hamish washed the blood off the floor and flushed away all the little bits of Lawrence he could find lying around the place. There wasn't much. Jack wiped the gun clean of prints and wrapped it in plastic sheeting in the lab. Then he took it down into the lower basement and hid it carefully behind some loose brickwork.

"And the bullet and the cartridge?"

"The bullet passed right through his chest and finished up in the office wall. I dug it out. I have it in my pocket along with the cartridge. I'll lose them on the way over to Stella's."

"Thorough. I'm impressed. I'll take the car home with me tonight and collect you from the Warehouse tomorrow. We'll have a ride out into the country."

*

In the early morning, they drove up to the Longridge fells to deposit Lawrence's vacuum-packed corpse.

They made their way along a narrow, deserted lane, a mile or so from Heaven's Gate, until they found a small copse, standing behind a dry stone wall bordering the roadway.

It was a struggle to reach the wall with the body. They had to negotiate a drainage ditch and the tangled remains of last summer's plant life. But they managed it well enough.

It wasn't yet twenty-four hours since Lawrence had met his fate, and the corpse was in the grip of rigor mortis, in the foetal position necessary to fit it into the luggage area of Jack's old hatchback. Even so, they managed to balance it along the top of the stonework.

Jack took out the box cutter he had brought with him for the purpose and quickly sliced through the layers wrapped around the body. Then it needed only a push to topple the remains of Lawrence White off the stones and down into the edge of the copse.

They burned the wrapping in the ditch a hundred yards away.

"Better without all the plastic. He'll rot all the quicker. Or be eaten by foxes. Should be pretty much unrecognisable before you know it. Should anyone ever even find the fucker."

"Nice," said Hamish. "How about I buy us a steak lunch and a pint at a country pub? If we can find something with a beer garden, we can enjoy some sun and fresh air before we drive back to town."

Steak and chips and a pint led quickly to several more pints as the pair celebrated their successful disposal of Lawrence's corpse.

The result was upsetting for them both. Rounding a tight bend at some speed, soon after pulling away from the pub carpark, they found their way blocked by a farm tractor exiting a field onto the lane. Jack tried to brake and swerve. But they hit the tractor at an angle. It was a small tractor, suited to use on a steep fell-side, and the collision sent it and its driver sideways into the ditch.

The little hatchback fared even worse, leaving the ground altogether before executing a series of spectacular cartwheeling flips along the tarmac. It showered the road surface with sparks and flames as it went.

Then the driver's door flew open, sending Jack, who hadn't troubled to fasten his seatbelt, on an impressive flight above the roadway.

As the car turned through the air alongside, he caught sight of Hamish sitting in the passenger seat and being shaken around like a rag doll amongst the inflated airbags. After that, he saw nothing at all. Only blackness.

Epilogue

Lying in the white room with black curtains, Jack drifted in and out of consciousness. For most of the time, he found it hard to tell whether he was dreaming or hallucinating. Or whether he was asleep or awake.

He didn't know how long he had been there or why.

People dressed as medical staff came in and out to attend to his needs. They often spoke to him in encouraging tones, but it was difficult to follow much of what they said. His neck and jaw hurt so badly that he never felt inclined to speak. He doubted that he would be able to.

Once, Stella seemed to come to sit by his bed. It might have been a dream, or she could really have been there. He had no way of knowing.

After that, he didn't notice any more visitors. Apart from Wendy. She was as young as she'd been when he last saw her. Sitting silently at his bedside, smiling.

Before You Go

It looks as though you've reached the end of this book. If, as I so desperately hope, you've enjoyed it, would you consider leaving a review on Amazon? It would help a lot, and I would very much appreciate your input.

Thank you.

If you would like information about future books in this series, please 'follow' me on:

amazon.com

or

amazon.co.uk

Printed in Great Britain
by Amazon

61589019R00166